OTTO PENZLE
AMERICAN MYST

THE RED W MURDERS

John Dickson Carr (1906-1977) was one of the greatest writers of the American Golden Age mystery, and the only American author to be included in England's legendary Detection Club during his lifetime. Though he was born and died in the United States, Carr began his writing career while living in England, where he remained for nearly twenty years. Under his own name and various pseudonyms, he wrote more than seventy novels and numerous short stories, and is best known today for his locked-room mysteries.

Tom Mead is a UK-based author specializing in crime fiction. His stories have appeared in *Ellery Queen's Mystery Magazine*, *Alfred Hitchcock Mystery Magazine*, *The Strand Magazine*, *Mystery Scene* and *Mystery Weekly* (among others). His debut novel, *Death and the Conjuror*, was released in 2022.

THE RED WIDOW MURDERS

JOHN DICKSON CARR

writing as
Carter Dickson

Introduction by
TOM MEAD

AMERICAN MYSTERY CLASSICS

Penzler Publishers
New York

This is a work of fiction. Names, characters, places, and incidents either are the product of the author's imagination or are used fictitiously. Any resemblance to actual persons, living or dead, businesses, companies, events, or locales is entirely coincidental.

Published in 2023 by Penzler Publishers
58 Warren Street, New York, NY 10007
penzlerpublishers.com

Distributed by W. W. Norton

Cover image: Andy Ross
Cover design: Mauricio Diaz

Paperback ISBN 978-1-61316-395-5
Hardcover ISBN 978-1-61316-390-0
eBook ISBN 978-1-61316-396-2

Library of Congress Control Number: 2022917497

Printed in the United States of America

9 8 7 6 5 4 3 2 1

THE RED WIDOW MURDERS

INTRODUCTION

John Dickson Carr was round about my age (twenty-nine) when he wrote *The Red Widow Murders*. This fact astonishes me, as it's a book written with such a mastery of form, not to mention inventiveness and verve, that it's difficult to read it as anything other than the mature work of a genius at the peak of his powers. And "genius" is not too strong a word to describe John Dickson Carr. Along with Agatha Christie, Ellery Queen, Christianna Brand and perhaps a very select few others, he was in the uppermost tier of golden age mystery writers. In my opinion, he was the greatest of them all.

Born in Uniontown, Pennsylvania in 1906, his early fascination with the work of authors such as Arthur Conan Doyle, Gaston Leroux, Thomas and Mary Hanshew, and Jacques Futrelle commingled with his love of gimmickry and illusion as practiced by the likes of Harry Houdini. This proved a fertile cocktail of influences which guided the young Carr toward one of the most rarefied, difficult, and ultimately satisfying subgenres of detective fiction: the locked-room mystery. Under his own name and the pseudonym "Carter Dickson" he proved himself the maestro of the impossible crime and one of the leading lights of mystery fiction's golden age.

Carr adopted the "Carter Dickson" pseudonym by necessity, as his publishers feared saturating the market due to his astronomical creative output. But there is virtually no difference in style between the Carr books and those published under the Dickson by-line. His two long-running series detectives, Dr. Gideon Fell and Sir Henry Merrivale, may be ranked equally alongside Hercule Poirot, Ellery Queen, Nero Wolfe, and just about every other luminary of the era.

By the time he wrote *The Red Widow Murders*, Carr's authorial style was well-established, although his own literary tastes remain discernible to the keen-eyed reader. For instance, his first few books were heavily influenced by Edgar Allan Poe, who was himself a progenitor of the locked-room mystery in "The Murders in the Rue Morgue." And, like Poe, Carr was fascinated with certain morbid facets of French history.

While Carr's veneration of Poe diminished as his own nascent genius developed, echoes remain throughout his later work. Case in point: the fabled "red widow" herself is a reference to the guillotine. This recalls the Poe-inspired gothic that characterised the first phase of the maestro's career, the most effective example of which is probably Carr's very first (and highly francocentric) novel, *It Walks by Night*. *The Red Widow Murders* showcases its author's trademark innovation alongside the morbid, folkloric tendencies he derived from Poe. Carr manages to create a fresh and imaginative mystery tale, infused with the eerie fireside atmosphere of an oft-recounted horror story.

The Red Widow Murders was published in 1935, a year in which Carr also produced not one but *three* other novel-length works. It was an almost embarrassingly prolific period for him, when he seemed to be conjuring up dazzling mysteries as though his life depended on them. That same year he published *Death-Watch* and *The Hollow Man* (US title: *The Three Coffins*), two magnificent Dr. Fell mysteries written under his own name, as well as another Dickson title, *The Unicorn Murders*. It's fair to say that he was at his creative peak, producing a string of absolute gems. 1938 was another such year, with *To Wake the Dead*, *The Crooked Hinge*, *The Judas Window* and *Death in Five Boxes* all appearing in a short space of time. That's the kind of prolificacy mere mortals can only dream of.

And these are not "one-note" books; they are crammed with ideas, teeming with atmosphere, elaborate and multi-stranded puzzle plots, and effortlessly readable prose.

Carr's unique gift was a combination of style and structure. He was not merely a great mystery writer, but a great *constructor* of mysteries. Each chapter in *The Red Widow Murders* is a work of art in itself; a miniature masterpiece of rising tension, culminating in a dramatic crescendo.

Dr. Michael Tairlaine, the protagonist, is a young adventurer in the classic Carr mold, making a return appearance following his introduction in an unsung gem among Carr's admittedly crowded catalogue, *The Bowstring Murders*. Like Carr himself, Tairlaine is a young expat living in London. He also serves as our window into the nightmarish world of *The Red Widow Murders* when he is roped into an evening of horrors that begins with the irresistible question: "Do you believe in a room of such deadly qualities that anybody who goes into that room alone, and stays there alone for more than two hours, will die?"

The "deadly room" is an excellent device, one which can be found in plenty of thrillers and murder mysteries from before Carr's time. Wilkie Collins's "A Terribly Strange Bed" is an early example, and one which sets the benchmark for quality very high indeed. But in *The Red Widow Murders* Carr is more than able to match it.

The problem posed is unique in the maestro's oeuvre: The victim has been poisoned, that much we know for sure. But the question is *how* the poison was introduced into his system. If it were cyanide or strychnine, suspicion would naturally lean towards the food or drink taken by the victim prior to his decease. But our man was killed with curare, a lethal toxin famous for its usage on poisoned arrows, which must be administered *through the skin*. Since the victim has not even the tiniest blemish on his body, the corpse itself becomes a kind of "locked room" within a locked room: how was the poison administered? It is a puzzle which only one man can solve: the boisterous amateur sleuth, Sir Henry Merrivale (H.M.).

It's well known that Carr's *other* great detective, Dr. Gideon Fell, was based on G.K. Chesterton, creator of Father Brown and author of such superb short stories as "The Oracle of the Dog" and "The Secret Garden." There are no such obvious models for Henry Merrivale. However, it has been noted as highly significant that the year Carr ceased writing about Henry Merrivale—1953—was also the year that his beloved father died. Whether or not Carr Senior was the model for H.M., there's no denying that the great detective swoops into the narrative bringing with him an avuncular, fatherly air. He is a necessary counterpoint to the sinister impossibilities which surround him. A decidedly more comic figure than Gideon Fell and the austere Henri Bencolin, he is "appallingly devoid of dignity" (to quote chapter 3). His appearances are punctuated by periodic slapstick interludes not present in the Fell books, but he is no less skilled a detective.

The character of Sir Henry Merrivale is an interesting paradox. He is a barrister who also holds a medical doctorate. He is a high-minded speaker of Latin with a penchant for pranks, practical jokes, and low humour. He is a baronet (and thus an embodiment of the Establishment), and yet he is a Socialist. These contradictions inform his style of detection. Who else but a walking blend of inconsistencies could unravel a problem as startling as this one?

Carr had been living in England since the beginning of the 1930s and, by the time he wrote *The Red Widow Murders*, he was a firm fixture of the country's mystery fiction scene. Famously, he was one of only two Americans to be admitted to the prestigious Detection Club. His initiation took place in 1936, the year after he published *The Hollow Man* and *The Red Widow Murders*, and while *The Hollow Man* is frequently (and rightly) cited as the apogee of the locked-room mystery subgenre, *The Red Widow Murders* is in its own way no less impressive.

Although the abiding reputation of the H.M. books tends to focus on their comedic aspects, the fact remains that the early works to feature the illustrious detective are also heavily steeped in the macabre. Indeed, some of the crimes tackled by H.M. (those in his first outing, *The Plague Court Murders*, for instance) are decidedly gruesome. So in several ways, *The Red Widow Murders* offers the best and most comprehensive introduction to John Dickson Carr for lucky readers who have not yet sampled the many delights he has to offer. It is a gothic work dappled with humor and it features a larger-than-life burlesque of a detective who just happens to tackle some of the most sinister, wicked, and dazzlingly ingenious crimes ever to grace the pages of a murder mystery.

—Tom Mead

THE RED WIDOW MURDERS

CHAPTER ONE

Invitation in the Fog

When Dr. Michael Tairlaine boarded the bus that evening in March, it must be confessed that his somewhat elderly pulse was not so quiet as usual. The distinguished holder of the Lyman Mannot chair in English at Harvard was, to be exact, as hopeful as a boy playing pirate.

Hopeful—it might be well to ask himself—of what? Of adventure tapping his arm in a London mist, a shadow on a blind, a voice, a veiled woman? They did not, he thought in his muddled, kindly way, wear veils nowadays. And he was aware that in any adventurous situation outside a book, because of this muddled, kindly way, he would be lost. Yet he reflected he had not done so badly during that business at Bowstring Castle last September. It was the Bowstring affair which had convinced him that the prosaic world had queer, terrifying holes in it; that he, at fifty, had met danger and found it exhilarating. That was why he had left a warm flat at Kensington tonight. He did not object to a fool's errand, provided it was the errand that was foolish and not himself. Since George knew his weakness, it might be an elaborate practical joke. But George's intuition had been right about the terror at Bowstring.

Undeniably Sir George Anstruther had seemed serious when he came into Tairlaine's flat that afternoon. Again Tairlaine could see him scowling in the firelight, holding out his hands to the blaze; his rough coat damp from the mist, a shapeless hat jammed on his head. George, short and burly, with his big bald head and his red country squire's face. George, Director of the British Museum, given to scholarship, devious thoughts, and explosive speech.

"Do you believe," he said without preamble, "that a room can kill?"

Tairlaine gave him a whisky and soda. Tairlaine supposed, in comfortable anticipation, that this was merely an ingenious beginning to some sort of philosophical argument, which George had been turning over in his mind as he stumped past the park. Sitting back expansively, the tall frail man half-shut his eyes and prepared to weigh words in luxurious controversy. George eyed him in some malevolence.

"Stop a bit," he added explosively. "I know what you're going to say. You'll say, 'Let us define our terms and endeavor to discover—' Bah! That's the academic mind. I mean exactly and literally what I say. Do you believe that a room can kill?"

"A room," said Tairlaine, "or an agency in the room?"

"Your mind," the other grunted, "goes instantly to ghost stories. I'm not speaking of ghost stories. There's not a single ghost, or suggestion of one, in connection with what I have in mind. Nor, on the other hand, any human agency like a murderer. . . . To be more definite, do you believe in a room of such deadly qualities that anybody who goes into that room alone, and stays there alone for more than two hours, will die?"

Something stirred at the back of Tairlaine's dry, curious, insatiable brain. Intent on his pipe, he glanced sideways at his companion, who had sat down in the firelight with pudgy hands clasped round the glass and a deeper scowl on the bulging red forehead.

"A year ago," he answered slowly, "I should have said no. Now I prefer to be agnostic. Go on. Of what will this man die?"

"Well—of poison, presumably."

"Presumably?"

"I say that," returned the baronet, hunching his neck back into his coat as though he were trying to burrow into it, "because nobody knows, and it seems the most feasible explanation. The last man that room killed died nearly eighty years ago, and in those days post-mortems weren't especially thorough or medical knowledge of poisons much advanced. 'Death in syncope, the face of blackish color,' might mean anything. They all went west in the same way. The whole point is——"

"Yes?"

"There was absolutely no poison of any kind in the room."

"Don't be so damned mysterious," said Tairlaine, and knocked out his pipe in some irritation. "If you have a story to tell, tell it."

Sir George studied him.

"I'll do better than that," he suggested, beginning to grin. "I'll let you see for yourself. Look here, old boy. Do you remember a certain conversation you and I had in a railway carriage over six months ago, when you'd first come to England on your sabbatical? You were complaining of the lack of adventures and rowdyism in your prim, buttoned-up life. And I said, 'What do you mean by adventures anyway? Do you mean in the grand manner?' I said, 'Do you mean a slant-eyed adventuress, sables and all, who suddenly slips into this compartment, whispers, "Six of diamonds—north tower at midnight—" or some such rubbish. And you answered, with the utmost seriousness. . ."

"That I supposed I meant just that," agreed Tairlaine blankly. "Well?"

Sir George stood up.

"Then I'll give you your instructions," he said, with the air of one coming to a decision. "Take 'em or leave 'em as you like. I'll make only the customary condition: you are not to ask questions. Is that clear?" The small sharp eyes blinked at him. "Very well. This evening, as near eight o'clock as you can manage, you will take a bus down Piccadilly, and get off at Clarges Street. You will be wearing evening kit; don't forget that. You will walk up Clarges Street to Curzon Street. At exactly eight o'clock you will be walking along the north side of Curzon Street in the short block between Clarges and Bolton Streets. . . ."

Tairlaine took the pipe out of his mouth. He did not ask the obvious question, but the other anticipated him.

"You know I'm serious," said Sir George, very quietly. "It may not work. But I'm bargaining on there being very few people thereabouts at that hour, and also on your—well, patriarchal appearance. . . ."

"Look here!——"

"To continue. If it does work, however, and at any subsequent time you see me, you are not to drop any hint that I put you up to this. You were merely strolling casually along; got it? Very well. You will continue to patrol that street until ten minutes past eight. If nothing has happened by then, it won't happen at all. But you are to be looking for a queer thing, and, if somebody approaches you with no matter what sort of odd remark, you are to agree with it. Oh, and be sure not to have dinner before you come out. Is that clear?"

"Admirably. What sort of queer thing am I to be on the look-out for?"

"Any sort of queer thing," replied Sir George, staring blankly at his glass.

Those were the last pertinent words he could get out of his companion, who went stumping away with an un-lighted cigar between his teeth. They left Tairlaine doubtful, but they also left him chuckling. Consulting his watch when he climbed to the top deck of the bus, he found it was twenty minutes to eight.

London looked unreal. It was not fog as the town knows fog, but a smoky white mist that distorted every lamp and made sleek the crawling lines of cars. He had done well to allow a sufficient margin of time. The bus rocked amid honking uproar; jerked and started; jerked and stopped, until he began to drum on the smoked window in crazy impatience. Past Hyde Park Corner, when shop-fronts began to glow and faces swim past, all the town's traffic seemed to crush down Piccadilly. He hopped off after nearly missing Clarges Street, dodged a taxi, and arrived on the pavement in a ruffled state of mind. It was three minutes to eight, but he must get his brittle bones in order first.

After the hooting din, the dark little street which runs up into Mayfair was grateful. But he hurried at a rather unpatriarchal stride. He was hungry, and cursing George for this foolishness. Still—if anything happened, it must happen soon. Emerging into Curzon Street, he adjusted coat and top-hat, threw back his lean shoulders, and glanced about in some trepidation. He must not look as though he were out to chase and pounce on adventure like a wind-blown hat. A dignified saunter would be best, blast George Anstruther!

Then he chuckled, and felt better.

The street was very quiet and dim-lit, a backwater in itself, which curved round to the right towards the mysteriousness of Landsdowne Passage. And, towards Landsdowne Passage, the heavy house-fronts began to fall away in startling ruin. They were tearing down many of the stolid town-houses that had bulwarked Mayfair for two hundred years. A ragged side-wall or two still remained standing, still patched with the wall-paper of vanished rooms; a heap of stones, a gaping vastness of cellars in the open spaces, a street gutted to ruin. That was on the north side, where he had been told to walk. The "odd remark," the odd person to deliver that remark, might come from there—but it was too far along.

Crossing over, he inspected the houses as he walked very slowly past. They were uniformly tall, with heavy bay-windows, areaways, and high steps. Muffling curtains hung heavy as the stone at their windows. With one exception, they were dark save for a misty underground glow from their areaways, where caretakers sat to watch over hollow rooms and shrouded furniture. The one exception was a somewhat larger house, with a light from the vestibule shining down its steps. Tairlaine could see the link-brackets beside the door. And he could see something else. Just inside the vestibule someone was standing motionless, watching him.

The person did not move. Tairlaine walked even more slowly, affecting a casual air; but he felt his heart bumping against frail ribs. Goblin or Caliph—or what, in this muffled street where the faint hoot of a motor-horn, from the direction of Berkeley Square, came as a surprise?

Tairlaine came abreast of the light; and then the figure moved, looming big against it. It began to descend the steps.

Although Tairlaine had been preparing all evening for this, still he felt something like a shock when the figure spoke to him.

"Excuse me, sir—" it said, rather hesitantly.

Tairlaine stopped, and turned round slowly. He saw a butler even though he could not see a face. The other made a slight gesture.

"His Lordship will offer his excuses for troubling you, sir," the man went on. "But would you mind stepping inside for just a moment? His Lordship would like to speak to you."

Tairlaine pretended surprise, and spoke accordingly.

"No, sir, there is no mistake," the other assured him. "It is odd, I know, but there is no mistake. If you will——"

"You are thirteen at a table," said Tairlaine, suddenly conscious of irritated disappointment, "and you have been sent out to invite in the first passer-by. Not very original. My compliments to Haroun al Raschid, but——"

"No, sir," said the other in a curious voice. The night was chilly, and his bulk appeared to shake. "I assure you, you are mistaken about that. His Lordship will be glad of your company at dinner, of course. But I think he wants you present at—well, at a sort of experiment." He hesitated, and then added very gravely: "You needn't—er—have any fear, sir, if you know what I mean. This is Mantling House. Lord Mantling——"

"I'm not conscious of any fear," said Tairlaine curtly. "Very well, then."

He followed his guide up the steps and into a big white-paneled hall whose utter absence of any noise made him instinctively lower his voice. And he did not like the place. The patterned chilliness of the eighteenth century was encrusted with too much flamboyance of gilt and glass and mirrors. Glancing at the crystal chandelier in the roof, Tairlaine thought of the late Lord Mantling's slogan, "Buy the Best." It had been assumed that he would know the name. Anybody knew it. Half the woolen products of Manchester had been Mantling's. The old lord had splashed into the newspapers only when he died three or four months ago, with death-duties almost sufficient to balance Mr. C.'s budget; and, whatever may be the life-size of an angel, life-sized marble ones guarded his tomb. And the new Lord Mantling? Disposing of his hat and coat, Tairlaine saw at the rear of the hall the first of all the curious things.

He saw, in fact, a shower of playing-cards.

That is not a figure of speech. In the chandelier only a few globes were burning, and the over-dressed hall was dusky. But he could see the lacquer cabinet standing against the right-hand wall, near one of the doors at the rear. He saw somebody dodge back towards that door, somebody who had one hand on the cabinet. Either by accident or design, there was a white flutter in the air, and spilled cards flew wide. The door opened and shut; Tairlaine heard the lock click.

It was too absurd to take seriously, and he did not comment, although he looked at the butler. The latter, who had a round honest-shining face (as though he wore nothing but Mantling's woolens) did not appear to notice. But he seemed uneasy. He elicited Tairlaine's name, and led him to the back of the hall towards a door on the left-hand side. Still he made no move to pick up the cards, or even to notice them. With grotesque unconsciousness he walked straight across the litter and opened the door.

"Dr. Michael Tairlaine, your Lordship," he said, and stood aside.

The small room inside was fitted up as a study, half with books and half with what Tairlaine supposed to be South American blankets, drums, and war-trophies. The red-and-yellow colors of the blankets lent somber richness to dark oak; there was a tinted shade on the lamp, which stood in the middle of a big claw-footed desk. There were two men in the room. One of them—Sir George Anstruther—stood with his back to the fire, wriggling slightly as though with the heat or apprehension. The other was a massive red-haired man, who sat behind the massive desk and rose at Tairlaine's entrance.

"I must ask you to excuse me," he said, with a heartiness which indicated that he had given it no thought whatever, "for this little New Arabian Nights entertainment. Come in, sir, come in! My name is Mantling. I am your host; your Prince Florizel of Bohemia—hey, George?" His big laughter boomed. "You haven't dined? Good! Will you take a sherry, then? Cocktails if you prefer, though I don't hold with 'em personally. Sherry? Good! Now, then, sir, to be as blunt as business: if you've a few hours to spare, and are of a sporting turn of mind, I can promise you in recompense some devilish good sport. Hey, George?"

A striking figure, this host, his vast expanse of glazed shirtfront trembling with his mirth. He was two or three inches over six feet, with an expression of bellowing good-humor and a thick neck. Dull reddish hair was plastered in wiry rings against his big head; he had a heavy face faintly mottled with freckles, twinkling blue eyes under ragged red wisps of eyebrows, and a broad mouth that showed most of his teeth when he laughed. About Lord Mantling—as about all things in this house—there was that same sense of the solid overlaid by the flamboyant. He wore a massive opal ring on his little finger, his clothes had a distinctive cut of their own, he fitted into the room against the hues of both primitive blankets and English oak. With the air of a conjuror he flicked open the lid of a cigar-humidor, thrust it across the desk, poked it round at Sir George, and laughed again.

"Little idea appealed to me," he declared, squaring his shoulders aggressively, "though Guy doesn't like it and that fellow Bender didn't seem any too keen. *And* why we've got to keep it from Judith beats me. Anyhow, it's my show for to-night—as Prince of Bohemia. I know my Stevenson and my New Arabian Nights, though you wouldn't take me for a readin' man; would you? No! I like the title. It's a damned good title. Better than some we've had applied to us, anyhow." He reflected, heavily. Then he chuckled and rubbed his hands. "Well, time to break up that foolery anyhow. What d'ye say, sir? Ready for a bit of amusement?"

Tairlaine sat down.

"I am grateful," he said, "to Florizel of Bohemia. But I should like to know more about the sport. If I remember rightly, the first of your namesake's adventures was to get himself and his equerry into the Suicide Club, where they drew cards to see who should. . ."

He stopped. Lord Mantling suddenly closed the humidor with a sharp snap, as though he were catching something inside.

"I didn't bargain on a mind-reader," he said. "Hey, George?" Tairlaine discovered that the stare of the pale eyes could be rather disconcerting. "Or do you know something about this, by any chance? Didn't quite catch your name. 'Dr.' something . . . Medical fella?"

Now Tairlaine could have sworn there was something like suspicion in his look. But there was no time to speculate on it, for Sir George intervened. He fully introduced Tairlaine, and mentioned their previous acquaintanceship.

"Come to think of it," George went on, rubbing his head with that Pickwickian simplicity he affected at times, which could be very deceptive, "it's not very surprising that you should have caught him here after all, Mantling. Blast it, I remember now. You did say you might drop in on me to-night, Michael, and since I'm just up the street . . . Sorry; I completely forgot it . . ."

A clumsy speech, Tairlaine thought. George could do better, if he were not flustered; but he wondered why George felt it necessary to handle this man with such kid gloves, and why he was flustered anyhow. Mantling was all geniality again. The bass-drum heartiness had returned.

"Mustn't mind me," he urged, with a smile of very genuine charm. "Rotten manners. Been too long in the brush, I expect. Ha, *ha!* But I don't like doctors, you see, ever if Judith does happen to be engaged to one. Have a cigar. Ah, you've got one. But just between ourselves, now"—his tone changed to a bull-like confidential air as he leaned over the desk, and his eyes opened, "how *did* you come to mention drawing cards? Eh?"

"Well, it's the first adventure in the New Arabian Nights. And also——"

He paused, remembering.

"Also? Eh?"

Hesitantly, Tairlaine told about the spilled cards. Mantling strode over and yanked a bell-pull. Then he crossed to the hall door, opening it as though he were setting a trap for the butler. In the interval, Sir George took the opportunity to whisper to Tairlaine.

"For Lord's sake," he said, "don't mention doctors."

Nightmare fantasy had begun to take hold of Tairlaine, as well as a feeling that the whole affair might be a practical joke.

But Mantling's back gave no impression of a joke. When the butler appeared, he said:

"I say, Shorter, did you see those cards chucked about in the hall just now?"

"Yes, sir."

"Well? What's *your* version?"

The other hesitated. "It looked as though they had been lying on top of the cabinet, sir, and somebody had knocked them off in passing. The—the person went on into the dining-room, I thought. I picked up the cards."

"Who was the person?"

"I don't know, sir."

"And what were the cards doing loose on top of the cabinet?"

"They weren't, sir, the last time I saw them. I put a fresh pack, in its box, inside the cabinet; ready for this evening, sir, as you instructed me. Er—they must have been taken out."

"It'd seem so, wouldn't it?" asked Mantling, without reflection. He turned away, lumbered with his conquering stride to the desk, and tapped it with his knuckles. "H'm. Well. By the way, where are the others?"

"Mr. Carstairs and M. Ravelle are in the drawing-room, sir. Mr. Bender has not come down yet. Neither has Mr. Guy or Miss Isabel. Miss Judith had already gone out with Dr. Arnold . . ."

"Yes. One thing I want you to be certain of, though. See that we get a fresh pack to-night; new box, seal unbroken. That's all."

When the door closed he turned to Tairlaine, who was beginning to wonder uncomfortably whether he had strayed into some sort of gambling establishment. Mantling seemed to catch this thought. He smiled grimly, twisting the ring on his finger.

"You will wonder," he said, "at my taking such precautions.

But you needn't worry, sir. You were asked in only as a witness, and in a sense to see fair play. You will not be asked to take part in the game."

"The game?"

"Yes. And you can see why we must take precautions to make sure that the cards are not—stacked. A group of us to-night mean to play what may prove a very dangerous game. We are to draw cards to see which one of us is to die within two hours."

CHAPTER TWO

Headsman's House

Again Mantling's big laughter boomed. He eyed Tairlaine as though the latter were being subjected to an experiment. Tairlaine felt the scrutiny, detested it, and only blinked mildly at his cigar. But for the presence of Sir George, he would have thought he had strayed into a madhouse.

"I see," he remarked, with some little effort. "So it's another Suicide Club, after all?

Mantling's expression relaxed, and his teeth gleamed in an admiring grin.

"Good! I like that," he nodded. He sat down, wheezing. "Got to apologize again; bad manners. No, it's not a Suicide Club. It's tomfoolery, if you ask me, but I rather like it. Now—to business."

"About time," growled Sir George. "Look here . . ."

"Steady," interrupted the other curtly. "Tell it in my own way. My brother Guy is the antiquarian of the family, and has all the details. He can give you the lurid ones. But *I'm* head of the house, and I'll open the ball.

"This house was built six generations ago, in 1751, by my father's great-great-grandfather. That was before we'd a title or any money to speak of. The whole subject of this game to-night is a room in this house—a room at the end of a passage off the dining-room—a room whose door has been locked and sealed up with six-inch screws through the jamb since 1876, the year my grandfather died. Nobody's set foot in it since then. Nobody's wanted to. And, but for one thing, maybe nobody ever would.

"Bluebeard's chamber, hey? Personally, *I've* always wanted to have a go at it. When I was a kid I promised myself, I said, 'Alan, my boy, when the old man shuffles off and you inherit the lot, you'll pitch your kit in that room and make devilish certain you don't die in two hours.' But the old man forestalled that," nodded Mantling, bringing his hand down on the desk with a grunt of admiration. "And damn neat, too! Condition of the will—old man was a hide-bound sort; primogeniture every time; I inherited everything—condition of the will was that nobody should ever enter that room until the house was torn down.

"Hah! Naturally I wouldn't upset my own apple-cart. Eh? So I let it alone until now. But what's happened? Old Mayfair's going, and maybe a good thing. They're buying up all the good sites for big blocks of flats and cinemas; you noticed? Now, to me this place is a white elephant. Nobody likes it except Isabel and Guy, and I could buy an island in the trade routes with the ground-rates I pay. Well. The Crest Building Development crowd offered me a cool twenty thousand for the site alone. I took it. They're to begin demolishing week after next, so I can open up Bluebeard's room."

He leaned across the desk, taking hold of each end as though he were about to push it forward, and looked fixedly at Tairlaine.

"Now I'll ask you something. You've heard of my father. Do

you have any idea that old Buy-the-Best Mantling was a superstitious fella?"

"Not knowing him personally——"

"Then I'll tell you," said his son, with a short bark of mirth. "He wasn't. Hey, George?" He looked round briefly, and the baronet nodded. "He was about the least superstitious, rock-chinned lump of sense I ever knew. But he believed the story. And what about my grandfather? He laid the foundation of the fortune and squeezed the blood out of half the slums in Manchester in the what-d'ye-call-it?—Industrial Revolution. He not only believed it; he died in that room, in the same way as the others. That was why my father had it sealed up. I'm telling you this to show you that it's no question of any rubbish about a curse or a bogey. There's no bogey in that room. But there was—and may still be—death in it. Another glass of sherry?"

During the long silence, while he moved towards the decanter, Tairlaine exchanged a glance with Sir George. They heard Mantling's heavy breathing. Tairlaine asked quietly:

"What sort of death?"

Mantling grunted. "Poison, my boy. Not a doubt of it. Bah! One of the sawbones said fright, but that's rubbish. Poison in something or some article of furniture." He was speaking violently, as though to convince himself, and he forced drinks on them as he might have swung a whip. "It's no ghost-chase. Question of cold science, *I* say. Poison—like one of those rings you see in the Italian museums. You know. Chap had it on his finger; shook hands with you; fang jabbed your finger . . ."

He gestured.

"Yes. But I've been given to understand," Tairlaine said, "that most of those stories of Renaissance poisoning are either fables or exaggerations. I know the *anello della morte* exists, as you say, because I've seen several such rings at the museum in Florence. But——"

"They're not fables," interposed Sir George, "and they're not exaggerations. It's only the damned modern way to say that, without any proof whatever, and in spite of proof to the contrary. Nowadays our grave historians won't allow villainy to anybody except someone who was previously considered good, or goodness to anybody except someone who was previously considered villainous. And they won't allow any scientific knowledge that wasn't spawned out of our own greasy machines. . . . I remember one ass solemnly writing that the Borgias, for instance, used only white arsenic, and very little of that. But go and see a few of the exhibits which really exist. If only white arsenic was known and used, how did the poison rings work? Arsenic doesn't act on the blood-stream; a dab of it on the fang of a box or a ring would be no more dangerous than a grain of salt. And the *anello della morte* is older than Venice. As a matter of plain history, Hannibal killed himself with one, and so did Demosthenes."

"Well, then?" demanded Mantling.

Sir George rubbed his forehead with a sort of obstinacy.

"I'm not questioning the possibility of a powerful poison that acts on the blood-stream. I'm only saying there couldn't be one in that room. You told me your father——"

"I'm coming to that," said Mantling—obviously, he liked the center of the stage—"if you'll let me go on. Now, look here: let's look at the thing in a practical light.

"This house, as I told you, was built by my reverend ancestor Charles Brixham in 1751. For forty-odd years there was no trouble whatsoever with that room. They say the old boy used it as a study. Right! Then, in 1793, his son Charles returned from France with his French wife. She was followed by a wagon-load of fancy furniture. Bed-hangings, carved gilt stuff, cabinets, mirrors, enough to smother you. It was her room. But *he* died there, the first of them. They found him in the morning with his face black. I think that was in 1803."

"Forgive the interruption," said Tairlaine, studying his face. "It was a bedroom?"

He could not understand why Mantling slurred his words in this part of the story; why his face had grown heavy and ugly, with the freckles starting out on it; and why his breathing had become labored.

"It was a bedroom," Mantling answered, recovering himself as though he had forced a thought into the background. "There was—a big table there, and some chairs," he darted a sharp glance at his guest. "But it was a bedroom. Yes. Ha. Why do you ask?"

"Was his wife harmed?"

"No. She had died a year before. Some disease or other; but not poison. Well, there were three more deaths. The second Charles, the one who died, had two children; twins, a boy and a girl. The girl died in that room on her wedding-eve, in the eighteen-twenties. Same way. That was when the legend started."

"Stop a bit," interposed Sir George. "Had the room been used in the meantime?"

"No. It was a whim—damn it, I don't know! Ask Guy. She was the first person who had slept there since her father's death. A maid or somebody came in and found her less than two hours after she'd entered. Black talk started; curses and such rubbish. It was locked up, and wasn't used until a French business associate of my grandfather came here and insisted on sleeping there. Hah! Never even got to bed, *that* 'un didn't. They found him in front of the fireplace next morning. I remember the date of that, because it was the year of the Franco-Prussian war. 1870. My grandfather tried it six years later. He said he'd got a theory. But he died. They heard him calling, my father said. He was in convulsions, and trying to point to something when they found him. He never spoke."

Mantling, who had been pacing up and down, wheeled round.

"Now comes the damnable part of it. My father was twenty years old then. And he had sense. He did what people had been urging my grandfather to do: have every stick of furniture in that room, every fancy French gim-crack, examined by an expert on furniture and cabinet-making. Hey? He got Ravelle et Cie., the greatest of all authorities on that period. Old firm; been making the stuff themselves for God knows how many years. Old Ravelle himself came over from Paris, with two expert assistants. They practically took the place to pieces, looking for traps or needles. Not a stick got past 'em. Some of the stuff they took away and dissected. But——"

"Nothing?" said George, raising his eyebrows.

"Nothing. Then the old man had in architects and builders and whatnot. *They* had a cut at it. Though they had the carpets up and the chandelier down, still nothing that could harm a fly. But that nothing killed four healthy people. Live people, as healthy as—as I am." He drew back his shoulders, glaring. "Now, there's got to be an explanation. Maybe it's tomfoolery. I think so. Hoax or something. Hang it, men don't die like that! And we'll find it. To-night.

"You see what I've done, hey? I've assembled everybody who might be interested, and two outsiders. There's my younger brother Guy, and my aunt. There's George Anstruther, an old friend of mine. There's Bob Carstairs, an even older friend; been in the bush with me; coolest hand in an emergency, with or without express-rifle, I ever saw. Fact. There's young Ravelle on the technical side. Related to the old chap who was here once; not a bad feller for a Frenchman. A sane crowd, by God! Sane as—as I am!" He drew down his sandy brows, and puffed out thick lips. He began to pace up and down again, under the barbaric hues on the wall. "Finally, there's that chap Bender . . ."

"By the way," Sir George put in abstractedly, "just who is Bender?"

"Hey? Bender? You know. Little dark-faced feller with the soothin' manner. Bedside manner, I call it; gets on with the ladies; like a blasted sawbones." He chuckled heavily. "You met him, didn't you?"

"Yes, but I mean—what do you know about him?"

Mantling stopped. He peered round. "Know about him? Not much. He's another of Isabel's protégés; artist or something. In from the provinces or somewhere. Why?"

"Oh, I was only wondering. Get on with your plan."

"Right. To sew up the business, there are the two outsiders. One was to be chosen at random. I told Shorter to go to the door at precisely eight o'clock, to stop the first, harrumph, presentable person who went by, and invite him in to dinner." Mantling nodded. "Yourself. The second outsider was deliberately chosen—and ought to be here now, blast him. I'll give you only his initials; they ought to be enough. Ever heard of H.M.?"

George started.

"You don't mean Sir Henry Merrivale? The war-office chap? Man who——"

"Who nailed the White Priory murderer. The great bear. The grouser. Best poker-player I ever met," said Mantling with satisfaction. "I knew him at the Diogenes Club. He's coming along. And if there's anything rummy in this business, he'll spot it."

Tairlaine had heard the name from two sources. His friend John Gaunt had mentioned it—almost (for Gaunt) with admiration. The other person had been a former student of Tairlaine's, named Bennett, who spoke of Sir Henry Merrivale with roaring approval. Mantling went on grimly:

"When he arrives, the four of us will go back to the room I spoke of. The door will be unlocked and the screws taken out, and we shall have a first inspection. Place will be in a mess, after all those years shut up, but never mind . . . Then we all go in to dinner; I told you the room's at the end of a passage opening off the dining-room. After dinner we all draw cards to see who spends two hours there alone. That is, all but three of us. The two outsiders won't. Neither will Isabel."

Sir George wandered moodily over to a leather chair and sat down.

"I say—this drawing cards. Was it your own idea?" he demanded.

Mantling glanced at him with some sharpness. "Neat, hey? No, it wasn't my idea. Wish it had been. I wanted to be the one to sit in the room. But old Bob Carstairs said—and it was a damn neat idea—he said, 'Look here, old boy, why not give us all a sportin' chance? Leave out Judith,' he said (that's my young sister) . . ."

"Why leave out Judith? She's over twenty-one, anyhow."

Mantling rounded on him. Tairlaine felt that he had just prevented his voice from taking on a roar.

"It seems to me," he said, "that you're getting dashed finicky all of a sudden, aren't you? Why, why, *why!* All you say is, 'Why?' We'll do it because I say it's best. She's gone out to dinner with Arnold, and when she gets back it'll be all over. . ." He stopped suddenly at his own choice of words, plucked at the edges of his coat. "Anyhow, one of us will go in there. High card wins. The rest'll stay in the dining-room. We'll sing out to the other chap at fifteen-minute intervals, and make sure everything's all right. Now let's have an end of your confounded whys."

"Yes. All the same," replied the other, "they may be necessary. It's worth asking why somebody tried to hocus those cards."

"Rot! Somebody knocked 'em off the cabinet . . ."

"After taking them out of the box. No, no, my boy. It won't wash. Somebody wants to palm off a card on somebody else. Somebody wants somebody else to draw the high card. . . ."

Mantling breathed hard. "Then *you* think there's danger?"

"I should like Gaunt's opinion. Oh, don't worry!" said Sir George, with an irritable gesture. "I don't mean to back out. By the way, has that room got a name?"

"A name?"

"Big house," George said rather vaguely. "Rooms generally have names to distinguish them. And, when you know the traditional name of a room, you generally know what's associated with it and find some clew to what may be wrong with it, if you follow me. . . ."

"It's called the Widow's Room. Does that help you? Hanged if I know why, unless it's a reference to the homicidal effect of the place."

A quiet voice said:

"Why don't you tell the truth, Alan? You know perfectly well."

In this house of muffling carpets, people could come up behind you with unnerving effect. Mantling was apparently used to it, for he stood slackly, only blinking his reddish eyelids. But Tairlaine jumped.

A thin, high-shouldered woman stood in the doorway to the hall. Her age baffled Tairlaine, as it baffled nearly everybody. She might have been a dozen years older than she looked—which was about fifty—or she might have been a dozen years younger. Her long face was thin, but not angular or wasted; she had a high-bridged nose like her nephew, but humorous lips; and her bobbed hair, molded against her head, was clear silver. Tairlaine thought she might have been beautiful, or at least striking, but for one thing. She ought to have closed her eyes. The eyes were of a very pale blue, so pale that they seemed to mingle with the whites; and they had an unnervingly direct stare which was like that of a blind woman. Her voice was melodious. Far too noticeably melodious, like that of a woman announcer on a radio.

"Since we have invited our guests," she went on, and looked at Tairlaine with sudden charm, "we ought at least to be frank with them."

She moved over with extended hand, and he took it.

"Dr. Tairlaine, I think? Shorter told me your name. I am Isabel Brixham; my brother was the late Lord Mantling. It is a pleasure to welcome you to my—our house. Good evening, Sir George."

"Gracious hostess," said Mantling, with a bark of mirth. His big chest swelled. "Well? Anything you want, Isabel?"

She ignored him for the moment, and turned to the man who stood behind her in the doorway. "Let me present," she went on, "Mr. Bender, a very good friend of ours. . . ."

Afterwards (although this may have been merely an *arrière-*

pensée, and worth nothing) Tairlaine always maintained that it was his first sight of Bender which made him fully certain of terror knocking, and deadly movements to come. He does not know why. Certainly there was nothing to suggest it in the man's appearance. He was colorless, of an engaging personality rather than other-wise. He was small, neat, with thinning dark hair and a strong placid face which seemed trying to mask its own sharp intelligence. Yet he looked nervous—or say not so much nervousness as a kind of half-ludicrous unhappiness. And he was not at ease. He had a nervous trick of rolling his tongue in his cheek, his smile was forced, and his hand shook slightly. Perhaps Tairlaine's impression was suggested by the faint bulge in the inside pocket of the man's coat. The wild idea of a weapon occurred to him, until he saw that the bulge was too flat. A flask, then? Dutch courage? No. Too small for a flask. Besides, why bother? . . .

"I've met Mr. Bender," Tairlaine heard Sir George say. He was studying the newcomer. "I say, you look a bit done in. Been working hard to-day?"

Bender glanced at him.

"Expect so," he answered rather jumpily, and without point. His voice was pleasant and colorless. He tried to smile. "Grinding work sometimes, you know, but I like it. Miss Brixham has been good enough to encourage me."

Sir George's tone became cheerful, but his expression told of something else. He said slowly: "Yes, I dare say she has. Still, you mustn't overdo it. Going to exhibit soon?"

"Very soon, we hope," said Miss Brixham quietly. "But let's not talk of it now."

There was a strange and ugly silence; Mantling, it seemed, was the only one who did not notice. He prowled about the room in heavy impatience, his hands in his pockets, seeming to fill the room. He paused by one of the oak shelves, straightening the bronze figure of a horseman. He glanced up at two short broad-bladed spears, crossed behind an ox-hide shield. And, as he lifted a hand to straighten one, Isabel Brixham's too-melodious voice went on smoothly like the quiet continuing of a previous sentence:

"I have often expressed a wish, Alan, that you would refrain from handling those poisoned weapons. The servants have been warned not to touch them."

Mantling swung round, heavy with anger. The bellow rose.

"And *I've* expressed a wish," he said, "that you would refrain from talking nonsense." He had mimicked her tone. "And, if you've given any orders like that, *I'll* give orders to the contrary . . . Now may I ask, in all humility, what you want in here? My father didn't allow petticoats in his den. No more do I. Is that absolutely clear? . . . Besides, not that it matters, you don't need to shake in your petticoats. Those things don't happen to be poisoned. Arnold tested the whole batch of arrows."

"But not," said Miss Brixham coolly, "your other curios."

"These?" His knuckles rattled on the spear-blade.

"If you like. Since you ask me what I want here, I will tell you. First, I wish to know why you sit in this room and do not join your guests in the drawing-room. Second, I am afraid I must insist—as a member of the family older and possibly wiser than yourself—on taking a hand in this ridiculous game." While she spoke, Tairlaine thought, it was strangely as though she had two faces. One of these she turned towards Mantling, and they could only see a part of it; but, each time she looked at the others, the face wore a pleasant smile. "Yes, if you insist on drawing cards, I shall certainly be included. . . . Do sit down, gentlemen. I shall expect you in the drawing-room presently, you know. . . . Finally, Alan, why weren't you frank?"

"Frank?"

"Why not tell your guests the whole story? You denied, for instance, that you knew why that room was given its name. Why did you deny it?"

Mantling's big face and reddish contracted eyelids seemed to swim closer. The tight curls of hair gleamed in the lamplight.

"Maybe," he said heavily, "because I am not any prouder of my ancestors than I am of my living relatives."

She turned softly to the others. It was strange how she kept her pleasant smile, her poise; how the pale blue eyes remained on Tairlaine's face in their unnerving direct stare.

"Perhaps I should tell you, gentlemen," she continued, "that in the days of the Regency our home was known, facetiously—I believe it was a jest of the Prince Regent himself—as Headsman's House. As for the 'Widow's Roam,' Alan did not tell you everything." She played with a string of beads, turning it over round her wrist with a queerly fluid gesture. "It was first called *La Chambre de la Veuve Rouge.* I mean, of course—the red widow. That is—the guillotine."

She smiled again, giving the French syllables an unctuous melody of pronunciation. Tairlaine started as a knock at the door sounded sharply in the quiet.

"Sir Henry Merrivale, your Lordship," said Shorter.

CHAPTER THREE

At the Dark Door

So THIS, then, was the great H.M., about whom Tairlaine had heard so much from young James Bennett. H.M., the former head of the British Counter-Espionage Service. H.M., appallingly devoid of dignity, hating to show his own kindliness, and addicted to white socks. Two hundred pounds of him came waddling in the doorway, with his big bald head, his Buddha-face with the spectacles pushed down on the broad nose, and the corners of his mouth turned down as though he were smelling a bad breakfast egg. A rush of sanity seemed to come with him. H.M., who was a qualified barrister and physician, spoke with dour affability.

"Good evenin'," he said, making a vague gesture with one big flipper. He blinked. "Hope I ain't late. Burn me, but they're always delayin' me! Nobody thinks *I* got any affairs. Oh, no. It was at the Diogenes. Old Fenwick'd invented a Latin crossword puzzle, and Lendinn insisted on arguin' about it. The answer was *'Enchiridio.'* O' course it was. Six across, ten-letter word meanin' collection of magical prayers invented by Pope Leo III and given to Charles the Great in 800. . . . I told Lendinn so. But he would argue. Ha, harrumph. How are you, Mantling?"

Mantling greeted him jovially, and H.M. doddered about while introductions were performed. Something like a smile moved on H.M.'s wooden face as his big flipper gripped Tairlaine's hand.

"I know you. Burn me, I'm kinda glad to meet you. Jimmy Bennett—you know, the one who got into that mess last year, and the old man had to get him out—told me about you. I got a book of yours. Not bad. . . . By the way, Mantling, since you came up to my office the other day I read something about you in the paper. You didn't tell me. Paper said you'd been in Northern Rhodesia, and were wearin' the hair bracelet . . ."

Mantling came to life.

"I've bagged my elephant," he said complacently, "twice. But that was last year. I won't go again. What's South Africa? They've cleared the country right up to the edge of the Belgian Congo. Game-preserves, like a ruddy pheasant-shoot. Government park, where tame lions'll come up and sniff at your motor-car. *Pfaa!* Give me South America, that's what *I* say. Just give me South America . . ."

"And South American poisons," interposed Isabel, as though she were speaking of a rare dish. Her eyes grew hard. "Shall we keep to the subject, Alan?—You, Sir Henry, are the detective. I have heard of you."

H.M. blinked at her, moving round his lumbering bulk. His expression did not change.

"Now that's very interestin', ma'am. When I hear somebody speak like that, it generally means they want to ask questions. So soon?"

"I do want to ask questions. . . . You may give Sir Henry

a glass of sherry, Alan." Her hands tightened over her folded arms. "I have heard of you as a dangerous man, and I am a little afraid of you. So I wish to put some questions to you before you have the opportunity of asking any. . . . My nephew has told you the story of the Widow's Room?"

"Well . . . now. A little. A very little." H.M. seemed bothered by an invisible fly. "Just enough to tickle my curiosity, curse him. He interrupted me with this funny story in the middle of a lot of work. Bah. It was the Hartley case, that rummy business about the gun in the bowl of punch, but small thanks I'll ever get from Masters for discoverin' it. . . . Anyway, he told me the circumstances, so of course the old man hadda trot along to see what was what. But I don't know much. Not yet, ma'am."

Isabel brushed this aside.

"I wish to know whether you think there is danger here."

"Well . . . now," said H.M., rubbing his forehead. "From the past, you mean? From a bogey or a poisoned needle? No, ma'am, I don't."

There was a little grunt of satisfaction from Mantling. Tairlaine thought that there was also a pale satisfaction in the woman's face; but she kept on with a soft, eager persistence. Her neck came forward slightly.

"Yet you do not deny, surely," she asked, "that four people, alone in that room, died violent deaths from a cause we cannot understand?"

"Funny," said H.M. in a musing tone. Then his sharp little eyes wheeled towards her. "One word there interests me more than all the rest of the sentence. The word is 'alone.' It's the keyword. It's the puzzler; and, burn me, I'm curious about it.—Admittin' that they died, why was it necessary for them to be alone, hey? Was the room any the less dangerous if, say, three or four people sat there for over two hours?"

"I can tell you that," Mantling interposed. "With more than one person in that room, it was as harmless as a Sunday School. Fact! My grandfather tried it. My grandfather and that French chap—the one who came to see him on business and later died in the room—well, the two of them sat there for hours. Nothing happened. But the Frenchie remained there, and pegged out not very long after my grandfather'd left him."

"Did he, now?" said H.M. with dull curiosity. He glanced at Isabel. "By the way, ma'am, what was his name?"

"His—his name?"

"Sure. You know. The French feller who came to see that particular Lord Mantling on business?"

For the first time the pale eyes narrowed slightly; with a rather horrible contraction, as though they had no lids.

"I really don't know. Perhaps Guy can tell you. Is it important?"

"Well, he died here, d'ye see," explained H.M., rather vaguely. "Now lemme see. Oh, I know. Mantling, didn't you tell me that one of the guests here to-night would be another Frenchman—hey?"

"Oh, you mean Ravelle." The other stared at him. "Right. What about him? He's a pretty decent sort, Ravelle is. Funny to see a blond Frenchman, too. . . . Have a brandy?" He had drained a neat one, behind the cover of his broad back, and now he swung round with a curious expression, "What about Ravelle?"

"Well, I was only wonderin'. . . For instance, did he make you an offer for any of the furniture in that room?"

Mantling stared. "How'd you guess that?" He appeared impressed. "Damn neat, if you ask me! Neat—eh, George? I mean, guessing a thing like that right off. As a matter of fact, he did."

"Uh-huh. I was wonderin'. For any particular piece?"

"N-no, not exactly. He said he'd just look about, if I'd got a mind to sell. Stop a bit!—he mentioned a table, or some chairs, or something."

"It would be better," said Isabel crisply, "to sell them to Madame Tussaud's."

The words jarred. Only H.M. showed no surprise. He remained half sitting, half leaning against the desk; hands folded over his big stomach, blinking.

"Uh-huh. I was wonderin' about that too, ma'am. I believe they already got the original guillotine knife at Madame Tussaud's. But let's leave that for a second. . . . I want to know something about your niece, ma'am. You know—what's-her-name—Judith, ain't it? Pretty gal. I want to know why she wasn't allowed to be present at the show to-night?"

She nodded, a sort of fiercely repressed pleasure in her look.

"That's clever. I think you know why she isn't here. And I'll tell you what my nephew would never have had the courage to tell. . . . She was not allowed to be present because she would probably have informed her *fiancé,* Dr. Arnold."

"Heard the name," grunted H.M., with a dull nod. "That's the brain-specialist, hey? I thought so. Well? What of it?"

Mantling had gone muddy pale behind his spectacles. Suddenly and surprisingly, a mutter of protest came from the quiet Bender. He moved with a jerky hurry towards Isabel Brixham's side; and, in the same moment, H.M.'s big hand shot out and caught him easily by the left-hand lapel of the coat.

"Easy, son," said H.M. without flurry. "Watch where you're goin'. You'd have tripped over that lamp-cord and gone into the book-case. . . . All right, ma'am? What difference would it have made even if Dr. Arnold had been informed?"

"He would have prevented what the police themselves could not prevent. Possibly by drastic means. And we can't have scandal." She picked her words with the care of a woman seeking ripe fruit in a basket. She smiled. "You see, it happens that somebody in this house is mad."

What made it worse was that her voice never left off its pleasant tone. The sultry pause lengthened, and then thunder broke.

"That's a bloody *lie!*" Mantling suddenly roared.

"Hear me out, please," she went on with preciseness. "You will kindly not interfere in what I have to say, Alan. It would doubtless seem silly to make such a statement to the police, of course, on the basis of a parrot and a dog. They are such ordinary things, such placid domestic pets." She drew a long breath. "In this house, a week ago, my parrot was strangled and his neck broken. Poor Billy was strangled; and that sounds absurd, doesn't it? But you men like dogs. Judith owned a fox-terrier. I personally did not like it, but it was a—a quiet creature that did not get in my way. It disappeared. Judith thought that it had strayed away; she still does. *I* found it in the dust-bin. I need not describe its condition. Some sharp, heavy sort of instrument had been used."

The stiff figure began to waver, as at some uncontrollable jerking of the knee. Bender moved out (ostentatiously avoiding the wire of the lamp, with a sharp glance at H.M.) and got her a chair. She said, testily, "I am all right. I am quite—all right," but she coughed a little, and she was pale.

"You will kindly let me alone," she continued, jerking Bender's hand away from her wrist. "I am perfectly all right, and I mean to continue. If Alan had been frank with you, gentlemen, he would have told you it was an inherited taint. He would have told you that the Charles Brixham who brought his wife here, and died in that room in 1803, was mad long before he died. He was . . . what we should now call criminally insane. He was driven insane, for a very horrible reason. Alan should have told you what that reason was. Guy will."

She lifted her hands stiffly, and let them fall in her lap.

"I do not suggest: I flatly tell you that the disease has cropped out again. You may laugh at a strangled parrot. You may even laugh at a butchered dog. I do not. I say that to-night you are putting horrible opportunities in the way of a poor crackbrain, who may be after—bigger game."

"Putting opportunities," said H.M., "in *whose* way?"

"I do not know," she replied. "That is why I am in hell."

Nobody spoke. They heard Mantling's stertorous breathing, and the rattle of a bottle on the sideboard. Out of the corner of his eye Tairlaine could see a big freckled hand, dusted with reddish brown, grasping a bottle. The woman rose.

"Give me your arm, Ralph," she said to Bender. Then she spoke with a stiff graciousness, and that queer half-unpleasant charm. "I don't wish to be a croaking raven, Sir Henry. I can be content with one warning.—Shall I see you presently in the drawing-room?"

When the door had closed behind them, H.M. slid off the desk with an irritable wheezing; he lumbered over and yanked the bell-cord. After a moment he said to Shorter:

"Get Guy Brixham and a French feller named Ravelle. Tell 'em they're wanted here right away. Hop it." Then he turned and blinked at Mantling. "Rummy business, son. Very rummy business. Why didn't you tell me about the parrot and the dog?"

Mantling spoke in a voice that suggested a punctured drum.

"But I didn't *know* about Fitz, poor devil!" he rumbled, with a querulous blankness. He made gestures. "Good God, this is frightful! I mean the old girl. Isabel. I say, do you think she's quite? . . ."

"Well, she obviously thinks somebody ain't. Know anything about it?"

"No. It's rubbish, I tell you! This is the first I'd heard of the dog. But that parrot . . ." His chin came out. "All I've got to say is, it ought to have been scragged, anyhow. I hate parrots. Mean as sin, parrots are. Ever notice their eyes? Inhuman, like a snake's. Try to stroke 'em, and they'll take your finger off . . . Stop a bit! Don't misunderstand. Not that I'd have hurt the brute. *I* didn't do it."

"Uh-huh. Know who did?"

"No. Servants, maybe. *They* don't like Isabel, and they didn't like that parrot either. It had a scream that'd set your teeth on edge. Used to hang in a cage in the dining-room. It'd screech, 'So it's you, so it's you,' and laugh like a lunatic." He stopped, reddening a little, and went on hurriedly as the door opened. "Guy! I say, Guy! Did she tell you? Somebody killed Fitz, and hid him in the dust-bin. That's what Isabel says, anyway."

Two men had come into the room. The first of them, whom Mantling addressed, stopped short. He was a little, sharp-featured, pleasant-smiling man who wore—startlingly—a pair of dark glasses. He had a high bony forehead, and the same wiry reddish hair as his brother. Though he must have been half a dozen years younger than Mantling, his face was full of fine wrinkles under his hollow cheekbones, stretched round his smiling mouth. And, despite Alan's boom and swagger, Tairlaine inexplicably felt that the frail Guy had a harder core. It was an intelligent face, but . . . mirthful, or sly? That queer look, Tairlaine knew, might be merely the look of the dark glasses. He did not like those glasses. Behind them the man's eyes were dark daubs that moved about like rats behind a screen. They seemed always moving.

Guy hesitated—very slightly. He looked deprecating.

"Yes," he said. "I knew Fitz was dead. I say, old boy, why shout so?"

"You knew it?"

"Since yesterday." Another smile, a crisp, sharp fashioning of syllables. "I was afraid Isabel might find out, with her . . ."

"Snooping? Eh?"

"Tut, tut!" His eyes moved swiftly round. "We want no more trouble and screaming, do we?" With a gesture as though making an end to the matter he took out a silver case, extracted a cigarette, and gave it a sharp rap on the case. "Come in, Ravelle. They wish to see us."

"It is quite all right with me, old man," declared a hearty and unexpectedly English voice from behind him. "But what is this about 'Fitz'? Who is Fitz, may I ask?"

Strangely enough, it was Ravelle's exact and well-pronounced use of idiomatic phrases which most emphasized his foreignness. He used the right phrase as he might have played a golf-stroke, with emphasis and ostentatious form. He was tall, with crisp yellow hair and a ruddy face on which faint veins stood out at the temples. His eye was jovial, he was a little overdressed according to Anglo-Saxon standards, and he lounged in with his hands thrust into his pockets.

"We are getting jolly hungry," he added, fashioning the words with careful precision. "Ha ha ha."

"You know who Fitz was," said Guy, his dark glasses-fixed

on H.M. "Judith's little dog. You saw him when you came here; remember?"

"Ah, yes. Yes," Ravelle observed, with an obvious contraction of memory. He added perfunctorily: "Jolly little dog. What about him?"

"Somebody cut him up," replied Guy, and gave another rap of the cigarette. He nodded to H.M. "You will be Sir Henry Merrivale. I am delighted to see you here, sir." He did not look delighted; the wrinkled face had rather more of a smirk, but he extended his hand pleasantly enough.

"Forgot, dammit! Introductions!" boomed Mantling. "H.M., that's my brother. And you'll have spotted the other." He tried to be heavily jocose, and nearly caused trouble. "I say, H.M., you ask Guy about that dog. Guy's interested in magic or demonology or voodoo or some blasted thing. Never could keep 'em straight, except that in the stories the only one who ever gets it in the neck is the feller who tries to practice 'em. Maybe that dog's part of a spell. You know, Guy. Like when you kill a black cockerel and burn its feathers, and . . ."

There was an ugly pause; palpable as a fire in the atmosphere of the room. Guy's expression did not change. But his fingers closed round the cigarette-case, gripping it, and the cigarette slid to the floor.

"Nowadays," he said—the voice had become unpleasantly soft—"a man is forced to conceal even a belief in God. I will keep my beliefs to myself, if you please. Therefore I shall get on tolerably enough in this world without challenging it. . . . Shall I tell you what you are thinking about, Sir Henry?" he demanded, with a swift turn of the subject. He touched his glasses. "You were wondering, as everybody does, why I go about with tinted glasses in a London fog. I do it because a naked light on my eyes would be a little more pain than I could bear."

Mantling seemed uneasy.

"Look here, Guy; I mean to say, can't you take a *joke?*" He appealed to H.M. "Poor beggar seems to blame it on me, but how the devil could I help it? Eyesight's been wonky ever since I persuaded him to go with me on my last trip. Thought it'd do him good——"

Guy retrieved the cigarette. His hand shook when he snapped on a pocket lighter. For the first time Tairlaine noticed how high and lean and bony his forehead was; with an unpleasant illusion as though his glasses were in the middle of his face. But he spoke pleasantly, with gentle sarcasm.

"Surely someone hooted at the idea of sun-glasses. . . . It was a very satisfactory expedition, Sir Henry. Of course, I wasn't interested in any romantic ideas of Green Mansions or the Amazon; or of being done good. I went with Alan and Carstairs on the understanding that I could drop off at Haiti to investigate . . . tribal customs. But Alan decided that there would be no time. I stayed at Macapa. I stewed there for three months in a floodlight glare, until they triumphantly returned with a couple of stuffed snakes and a handful of arrows they hoped were poisoned. But I knew you were wondering about the glasses——"

H.M. wheezed.

"Point o' fact," he said, "I was wonderin' why everybody in the house seems so intent on talkin' about poisoned weapons. Never mind, though. What I wanted to ask was this: You're the expert on family history here, hey? The guardian of documents and skeletons and curses?"

"If you want to call it that, yes."

"Got a lot of family documents, I suppose?"

"Yes."

"Open to inspection?"

"No." Guy's expression had become—there is no other word for it—very cool. He hesitated. "Come, sir! I hadn't meant to sound, er, brusque. I'll be glad to give you the gist of them, or tell you anything you care to know."

"Uh-huh. I see," nodded H.M., studying him. "How do these documents descend, hey? I mean, father to eldest son; anything like that?"

Guy nearly laughed outright. "You wouldn't interest Alan in *that*," he pointed out. "They are given to the person most interested."

"Good. Later on I'll get at the howlin' legend and the bogey behind it. For the moment, I'll pass over the Charles Brixham who's supposed to have died there first in,"—puffing, H.M. reached into his inside pocket and produced a sheet of notes. His black tie was skewered half-way under one ear; it impeded his neck as he peered at the sheet,—"in 1803. Humph. Well, this feller had two children. Son and daughter. Know anything about the son?"

Guy shrugged. "He was slightly feeble-minded, I believe. Not insane, you understand, *but* . . . His sister took care of him."

"Uh-huh. And she died in this Widow's Room, on the eve of her wedding. Exact date?"

"December 14, 1825."

H.M. cocked a dull eye at the ceiling. He moved his glasses up and down his nose. "Eighteen twenty-five, hey. Now lemme see. What happened in eighteen twenty-five? Lot of treaties. Independence of Brazil recognized. Nicholas I Emperor of Russia. Drummond invented the limelight. First voyage by steam from England to India. Pepys' Diary deciphered for the first time . . ."

"You seem remarkably well informed," Guy said sharply. There was a contraction in the wrinkles of his forehead.

"Oh, that? I'm encyclopedic, son. I got to be." H.M. rubbed his forehead. "Lemme think. Year of the great commercial and financial panic . . . H'm! How were the family fortunes in that year?"

"Excellent, I am glad to say. I can show you proof of that."

"So-ho. Means you got somethin' else to hide, then? Well, this daughter Marie died in that room, *on her wedding-eve.* That's what puzzles me. All of a sudden she took a fancy to spend a night in that room. Why? What made her sleep in an unused room, in that room especially, at that time?"

Guy shrugged again. "I don't know. Some sentimental whim——"

"Tender sentimental whim," grunted H.M., "of spendin' her wedding eve in the room where her father died mad. Very rummy. Who was she goin' to marry?"

"A man named Gordon Bettison. I know nothing about him."

Across H.M.'s broad face went a gentle expression which said, "You are lying." He made a note, stolidly, and only blinked. "Well . . . now. Let's come to the next victim, the Frenchman who died in, hum, 1870. Who was he?"

There was a chuckle from behind Guy.

"It was my own great-uncle, old man," said Ravelle, with unexpected affability. He frowned. "I think that is what you call him, is it not, when it is the uncle of a father? Ah, yes. Yes. Thank you. My great-uncle. That was something sinister, what?"

Jingling coins in his pockets, teetering on his heels, he regarded them with one eye shut up and an expression of disinterested pleasure beaming in his face. That reddish face, with its protruding veins at the temples, gave him a somewhat intoxicated look.

"So. That's interestin'. Was he a member of your furniture firm?"

"*Ah?* Ah, no. Not exactly. He was the head of our branch at Tours. He was old Martin Longueval, after whom they have named me, and I have seen his picture with all the whiskers. That, old man, is why I am so interested in laying this ghost, you understand."

"Got any other reason? Any business reason?"

"Well . . . my old papa, who has once examined the furniture for my friend Alan's papa, has once told me that if ever I have the opportunity I shall find much that is worth-while. Mostly I am a friend of the family. *Hein?*"

"Martin Longueval," growled H.M., musingly. "What business did he have with Mantling, then?"

Ravelle reflected, his head on one side as though he were sighting down the barrel of a gun.

"That, by God, I do not know. But I do not think he had any business. Perhaps he liked England; *hein?* Big spoons," said Ravelle, puffing with glee, "whisky-soda. Ha ha ha."

H.M. put the paper back in his pocket. He craned round.

"All right," he said drowsily. "I'm ready, if you are. Didn't you tell me we were goin' to form a party to go out and open your sealed room? We'd better be gettin' on, then, if we're to do it before dinner."

Mantling woke up with enthusiasm. In the screech of the desk-drawer as he pulled it open, Tairlaine found himself waking out of a sort of hypnosis to the business that was before them. Mantling took out a chisel, a hammer, and a heavy screw-driver. Last of all he unlocked a lower drawer and produced a large key with elaborate flanges and traces of rust.

"This'll unlock the rubbish," he growled rather malevolently, "and kill the bogeys. Good thing this hasn't a poison fang on it, or I'd be dead already from cleanin' it. Right! Come on, you chaps."

To Tairlaine's surprise, Guy offered no objection whatever when his brother announced that he would not be included in the ceremony. Only Mantling, H.M., Tairlaine, and Sir George were to be present. Guy bowed them out. He was smirking again, one finger tapping his upper lip.

The dim lights and quiet in the house struck Tairlaine after the warmth of the study. It could have stood a good deal more light. Shorter was in attendance with a box of candles and a tin of machine-oil for the lock. With some uneasiness Tairlaine began to think about what they were doing, and despite himself to create pictures of that dusty, ruined room. It would be ordinary enough, no doubt. But he was not going to touch anything there.

They went into a cold music-room, through double-doors and into a long white dining-room. H.M., stumping beside Tairlaine, growled under his breath as he peered about. Covers were set for nine on the long table, amid too great a profusion of flowers. The dinner-candles had not been lighted, and only firelight glowed on the walls. When Mantling rather hastily snapped out an order, Shorter switched the crystal chandelier into full blaze. Then Mantling, a broad bulk with the hammer in one hand like a weapon, stood and stared at the double-doors opposite across the room. He hesitated. His gaze traveled over to a bay-window; then—curiously enough—to the ceiling over it. There was a brass hook in that ceiling, Tairlaine noticed. Well? Still before going on, Mantling mumbled to himself while he inspected the table with dull care. He moved up and down, hesitantly, the freckles beginning to stand out on his face again . . . because he was suddenly afraid.

"Come along," said Sir George brusquely. He nodded towards the doors at the other end. "That's it, I suppose?"

"Those doors—they go to the passage. *Our* room's at the end of the passage. Right! Light the candles. . . . Got the key to the double-doors, Shorter?"

"Yes, sir."

"Right. Go on! Open up, then. . ."

Even that lock was stiff, and they had to use machine-oil freely before Mantling could wrench it open. Beyond stretched a narrow passage between black paneled walls. It was musty-smelling enough, and tattered with cobwebs. When five candles were raised high, they could see at the far end of the passage a heavy door. Then with a start Tairlaine noticed something else. Mantling's nervousness exploded.

"Shorter!" he said. His candle-holder rattled against the white door. "What the devil have you been up to? Who's been *sweeping* this place?"

The voice behind said, steadily enough: "Nobody, sir. That is, since last year. His—the late Lord Mantling told us to sweep the passage once a year; only the passage, of course. It hasn't been touched."

"The hell it hasn't! There's a space cleaned . . ." Mantling's hand holding the candle was yanked away by H.M. Tairlaine smelt burning wood, and saw a thin brown gouge in the white door. Mantling thrust the candle forward and got Shorter by the collar. "Not cleaned, hey? Take a look at that. See it? There's a space cleared straight down to the door."

He pushed the butler aside and strode down heavily towards it. At the door he handed his candle to Shorter and took the screw-driver.

"I'll have those screws out in a jiffy." He paused in bending down, and glanced up with a heavy, somnolent, rather terrible face. He said: "People really have died here, you know."

Tairlaine looked round at H.M. After the first ripping twist of the screw-driver, the only noise was a steady creaking. Five candles burned clearly, although they should have been half smothered by dead air. This air was comparatively fresh. Looking at the crooked path swept back to the glow of the dining-room, Tairlaine remembered that hook in the ceiling of the dining-room. Mantling had mentioned it: the parrot's cage had hung in the dining-room. He thought of the parrot flapping on the bars, screeching, "So it's you. . . ." Then something rattled on the floor at Tairlaine's feet, and Mantling cursed.

"Screw broke off in the middle!" snapped their host. "I thought it came out too easily. Hope it broke on the other side of the frame. If not——"

H.M. said, very quietly: "Y' know, son, if I were you I shouldn't bother with the screws. Fact is, I'd take a bet that they're all dummies, and you pulled one out. Try that key and see if the door'll open. If that lock's oiled. . ."

"It's not only oiled," grunted Sir George, "but it's still damp. I've got a smear on my cuff. See? Get the key!"

Mantling fumbled like a drunken man. But the door opened.

The lock turned with a faint gritty sound, and the door seemed almost to open of its own accord. They lifted their lights across the threshold, on a gleam of gilt furniture and smothering hangings . . .

Then Tairlaine found himself staring, and the candle shook in his hand.

CHAPTER FOUR

The Death-Card

THE CANDLE-FLAMES at the dinner-table had sunk in broad sheets of grease, and the cloth had that rumpled look of many courses having passed over it, when Mantling rose at the head of the table.

"Shall we get down to it?" he said. "Shorter! We're not goin' to adjourn. You can bring the coffee here. *And* the cards. Mind it's a new pack."

Quiet settled round the table as at the shutting of a lid, so that they could almost hear the echo of their own talk a moment before. Even Ravelle, in the midst of a boisterous anecdote, stopped dead. Tairlaine glanced round the table. He himself sat at the top of the table, on Mantling's right. Just opposite him, H.M. sat at Mantling's left. Next to H.M. was Mr. Ralph Bender: silent, still more uneasy, having eaten nothing since the soup and drunk very little wine. But his silence was more than obscured by the exuberance of Martin Longueval Ravelle, who sat next to him. Although Ravelle had not been drinking with any great freedom, it either affected him strongly or else his naturally rather intoxicated expression had been heightened to glowing color. Next to him sat Sir George Anstruther, trying to keep pace with Ravelle's anecdotes while he frequently glanced down at Tairlaine and H.M. Isabel Brixham was at the foot of the table, facing Mantling. Then, on her left, sat Guy. He was on Tairlaine's side of the table, and the latter could not see him for the intervening presence of Mr. Robert Carstairs.

Tairlaine could not help liking Carstairs. From Mantling's description he had imagined somebody of at least Mantling's own age, if not older. Carstairs was a lank young fellow with a ruddy face, a brown toothbrush mustache, and a genial manner, whose hobby seemed to be any sport which entailed the more spectacular ways of breaking your neck. As an example of the Silent English Sportsman, he was a surprise. Not only did he impart most of his life history in the first fifteen minutes, but he illustrated each adventure with a powerful piece of acting and a wealth of gesticulation. He used everything on the table to plot out the course for a motor-race, making frantic *brr-r-ing* noises as the salt-cellar which represented his car went plunging round the track. In the stealth of a hunting expedition, he leered behind imaginary rifle-sights and expelled his breath triumphantly as the express bullet went home. And, oddly enough as Tairlaine found, he was not a liar.

But he confessed himself a failure. After Eton and Sandhurst he described how his old man had got him into the air-force, but they politely ordered him to resign his commission after half a dozen premature descents at the government's expense; especially because in his last chance to make good he smacked into an officers' mess with a bomber costing six thousand pounds, and emerged with only a sprained ankle. Also he confessed to Tairlaine (in strictest secrecy) an undying passion for Judith, Mantling's sister. He said he had declared his love, but she was interested only in men who Made Something of Themselves. This Mr. Carstairs described as unmitigated bilge, and sneered heavily. He described Dr. Eugene Arnold as the oldest-looking white man he had ever seen, although the doctor's age was only thirty-six, and gave a libelous imitation of the latter's facial expression. Finally, he had a theory about the Widow's Room. It was, he said, either gases or spiders.

"You take my word for it," Mr. Carstairs had declared after the third cocktail, when Tairlaine met him in the drawing-room, "it's either gases or spiders. It always is. You sit down in a chair, or lie down on a bed, and the heat of your body releases the deadly gas. *I* know. Believe me, sir, if I draw that card I'm going to open the window and keep my head stuck out most of the time. Or else," said Mr. Carstairs, tapping his finger excitedly into his palm, "it's a deadly spider, one of those tarantulas as big as your fist, that's kept in a chest. In an unguarded moment you open the chest—whoof!—cheerio. Eh? I read about that somewhere."

Tairlaine had objected mildly that it would be rather a venerable spider that could live a hundred and twenty-five years without anything to eat. Carstairs said he had read somewhere about spiders being walled up in stonework for longer periods than this; but Ravelle, who had joined the discussion, insisted that he meant toads.

"Speedairs," Ravelle declared oracularly, his English not being so correct as at first, "speedairs enjoy lifetimes of a comparative shortness, old man." He seemed uneasy. "But myself I hope it is not speedairs. I tell you frankly I am scared of them. Blimey! If I am seeing any speedairs, then I run like hell, you can believe me."

In this heated discussion Tairlaine had tried to distract

his mind from what he had seen in that room when the door opened so easily. He could not do it, despite what H.M. had said. And, throughout the long dinner, he knew Mantling could not. It was with a sense of relief that he saw Mantling rise at the head of the table.

"Shall we get down to it now?" their host repeated.

Mantling stood up behind silver holders full of crooked candles, his back to the white double-doors. The dining-room was full of shadows, for the fire had sunk. In the uncertain candle-glow, Mantling's face showed flushed and shining; his coarse curls were damp and his eyes had a round, pale-blue prominence. But he was smiling as he knocked his knuckles on the table.

"I've ordered a fresh pack of cards," he went on, leering out, "because there was something wrong with the other one. Something very wrong. Come now! Own up, and no hard feelings." He bent still further forward. "Which of you tried to doctor that other pack. Eh?"

Isabel Brixham, at the foot of the table, spoke calmly. "I dare say you realize, Alan, that you have been drinking?"

He ignored that, studying her with a dull, thoughtful air.

"It wouldn't be *you*, auntie," he roared, and then laughed, "because you're not goin' to draw a card. But I ask the rest of you, because I've got information. Some one of you wants another to go in there—why? We've already unsealed that room; if it needed unsealing. And we saw something there."

"Did it scare you?" asked Guy's voice, very clearly. Then Guy laughed.

Mantling craned down at him: "Have *you* been in there?"

"Been in there? No," said Guy. Dark glasses and a wrinkled

forehead appeared round the edge of Carstairs' shoulder. "But you needn't keep us in suspense. What did you see?"

"Here you are, Shorter," said his brother, breaking off. "That the fresh pack? Good. Let me see it. You know what to do. When you pass round the coffee, each person with the exceptions I've told you takes a card. . . . Now, gentlemen! When you get your cards, look at 'em if you like. Then put 'em face down. Don't announce what you've got—yet! Before you do, I'm goin' to tell you what we saw in there. Then any of you can back out if he likes. . . . All right, Shorter; we'll keep our hands off. Break open that pack. Spread it out on the tray—right. I'll draw the first one. . . ."

Still keeping his rather protruding eyes on his guests, without glancing at the fan of cards held out on the tray, he fished one from the pack. He barely looked at it, kept a surprising poker-face, and put it face down beside him. Shorter moved past Tairlaine, who was conscious of a tightening tension—and also a jerk of relief that he was not required to draw. The tray was extended to Carstairs. Tairlaine saw the blue backs of the cards, worked out in a colored shield which he supposed to be the Mantling arms, and Carstairs' muscular hand hovering over them. Carstairs hesitated, rubbed his hands together, moved his shoulders, and then dived. His ruddy face was shining.

"Gimme a middle one," he said. "Wish me luck, sir. Ho ho ho. Here we go. I pray to have . . . *Hell!*"

He slammed down the card, and then tried to adjust a poker-face. Shorter moved on to Guy, who casually flicked up a card and placed it down without even glancing at it.

"I've changed my mind," Mantling announced suddenly. "Don't go on, Shorter. Give Miss Isabel a shot at it, if she likes."

"Thanks so much," she acknowledged calmly. She lifted her light-colored eyes without surprise as she stretched out her hand. "I had already determined to take a choice, you know. I believe there was no question as to my not doing so."

She took a card, glanced at it briefly, and was expressionless. Shorter moved on to Sir George, who wrinkled his forehead over his choice, but said nothing. Ravelle, very flushed, studied a long time with many mumblings and loud whispers for silence while he concentrated. Descending on one, he altered his intention and snatched up another.

"I have never had the luck at the cards," he announced. "And in this case, blimey, I do not expect . . . Hein? Oh, Lord hooray! Ha ha ha."

He beamed, writhing in his seat, and chuckling over the card. He was evidently as pleased as Bender was sullen. When the tray was offered, Bender turned sharply to Mantling.

"I suppose I must take one, sir?"

Mantling's lip lifted . . .

"Or be called—" said Bender. "Very well." He drew one out carefully; but his hands were shaking when he guarded it so that the others could not see. He put it down in his lap to look at it under cover of the cloth, and the dark face did not move when he lifted it again. H.M. glanced at him curiously; but throughout the meal H.M. had not spoken. "The game's made," said Mantling, nodding. He wheezed a little. "And now I'll tell you about the room.

"Isabel," he continued abruptly, "says there's a crazy person in the house. If you don't know that already, she can't be kept from tellin' you. I've begun to believe her.

"That room's open, my lads. Somebody took the screws out of the door and substituted dummies that go half way through the frame. Somebody got an impression of the lock and had a key made; somebody oiled the lock and hinges, and swept the passage to leave no footprints. But that's not all. If you expect to find a wreck of a room, with two inches of dust and cobwebs—don't. That room's as clean as the day it was locked up nearly sixty years ago. There's a big gilded bedstead, and the wood's polished even though the hangings have rotted. My grandfather had gaslight put in that place before he died; the gas-jets have been cleaned out, and they'll light. Somebody, d'ye see—somebody has been spending nights there while the rest of us were in bed."

He paused, breathing hard. Again Tairlaine saw the big square room, with the chandelier of open gas-jets burning in yellow-blue flames and throwing harsh, dusky light on decayed finery. The walls had once been dark purple and gilt; they could not be cleaned. He saw a white marble mantelpiece, a full-length mirror in gold leaf on each wall, a heavily gilded dressing-table and bed with half-tester in the fashion of the late eighteenth century. But the outstanding thing—the inexplicable and unreasonably grotesque thing—Mantling went on to describe.

"Somebody's greatest care," Mantling said, "was for a big round table in the middle of the place, with a lot of chairs set round it. The chairs are pretty-lookin' things, I'll admit, in a kind of light yellowish wood with brass fastenings . . ."

"Ciseleurs!" exclaimed Ravelle, and slapped the table. He quieted himself as Mantling's heavy gaze turned towards him. "No, no, old man, I will not interrupt. That is only a type of furniture-making, you see. That I will tell presently. You shall go on, *hein?*"

Guy reached out to light a cigarette at one of the candles. He said:

"You noticed, did you, Alan, that there is a name carved on the inside of the back of each chair? That each chair belonged to a special person? One chair is engraved 'Mon-sieur de Paris,' another, 'Monsieur de Tours,' another, 'Monsieur de Rheims,' another . . . Ah! I see my honest friend Sir George Anstruther scowling at me in dire suspicion. I know that, my friend, because it is a part of family history. Like Ravelle, I'll tell it presently. The point is——"

"But hang it all," interrupted Carstairs, pushing away his cup as though he would clear the table for fair play, "it don't make sense! I mean to say, Alan, why should anybody go mucking about with a lot of furniture in the middle of the night?"

He looked at Mantling, who was staring down at Isabel, and Carstairs followed his glance. Isabel's eyes had a pale blaze like her silver hair.

"Shall I tell you," she said pleasantly, "what the more intelligent members of this group will already know as the answer to that question? Thank you. You are occupied with a poison-trap which killed people in the past. Granted that there was such a thing; it would long ago have lost its power. That is—unless it were reset. There may not have been one there two weeks ago. *But there may be one now.*"

After a rather terrible pause she went on:

"I will take a cigarette, if you please, Guy . . . I have already said, gentlemen, that I would not repeat my warning. *Soit!* If you care to gamble with your lives in this card-drawing, I can only evince my submission by drawing a card as well. In my way, I dare say I am a fatalist. But I know it would be better if we were to lock up that room again, and find the person whose brain has cracked . . . What does Sir Henry Merrivale say?"

H.M. stirred. His breath whistled, and the corners of his

broad mouth were still turned down. He had been sub-dued; he had been not at all like the person Tairlaine had heard described, whose roars and grumblings and loquacious wanderings upset half the War Office. But that, Tairlaine learned, was because H.M. was worried—as worried as he had ever been in his life. He ruffled a hand slowly across his big bald head.

"Ma'am," he said, clearing his throat after a silence, "ma'am, I say you're right."

Mantling whirled to stare at him. "But you told me——!"

"Hold on, now. Wait a bit, dammit!" growled H.M., with a querulous gesture. "Lemme make my position clear." He glared. "I told you over an hour ago, when I shooed you and the doctor and George Anstruther out so I could give that place a thorough goin' over alone . . . well, I told you I could swear there was no funny business in that room. I know a good deal about poison-traps, for my sins. There was that Turret Room case, with the arsenic in the wall-paper; there was that Cagliostro's Box affair in Rome last year, where the cyanide needle jabbed the feller just under the finger-nail and no post-mortem could ever discover the puncture where the poison'd been introduced. Son, I overhauled that room. Old man Ravelle, sixty years ago, said that room was all right and it *is* all right. But——"

"Well, then?" demanded Mantling.

"I smell the blood of an Englishman, that's all," said H.M. with great seriousness, and sniffed like an ogre in a pantomime. He made gestures. "Dammit, that's the most I can tell you. Somethin's wrong, son. There's blood somewhere, and maybe death. I'm not star-gazin'; it's fact. My brain can't tell me anything, my brain tells me that nothing's wrong and I'm a wool-gatherin' ass. And maybe right down in here," he pointed to somewhere in his stomach which evidently represented his heart, "I *want* you to play out this tomfool game . . . just because it's a problem I can't work out, and I'd feel better if my brain was right. I'm not goin' to interfere with you. I advise you to let it alone. But if you won't——"

Mantling turned back to the table.

"Fair enough," he agreed, with a grimly triumphant look round the group. "Anybody want to back out, hey? Look deuced queer, you know, if you do, but . . . anybody want to back out?"

There was a barely perceptible stir round the table, but nobody spoke. Some saucers clinked, and chairs creaked as though with an indrawing of breath. Tairlaine felt his own heart knocking. His coffee was cold when he lifted the demi-tasse; a little of it spilled over his hand, and he set it down. He wished, now, that he had offered to take a card. He wished——

"We'll begin with me," said Mantling, "and go round to the right of the table in order; Bob Carstairs, Guy, Isabel, and so one. Right. Then I drew,"—he held up his hand, exhibiting the card in the light,—"I drew the nine of clubs. Who beats it? Follow on."

The shuffling at the table increased. Carstairs cursed, trying to pull at his toothbrush mustache, and flipped over his card.

"Three of hearts," he said, pointing. "That's luck: I don't think. I could have won if we'd been playing for money. Well, Guy?"

Guy carefully balanced his cigarette on the edge of the saucer. His face was wooden, rather contemptuous as he lifted the outer edge of the card, glanced briefly, and picked up his cigarette again. He said:

"Fortunately or unfortunately, Alan, you are still high man." (Tarlaine, with a sharp side-glance, saw that Mantling was wiping his forehead. The stir at the table had grown to slight movements of the cloth as though somebody were pulling it.) "I hold the seven of spades. Your luck may still be in, unless Aunt Isabel . . ."

"My luck *is* in," interposed Isabel, with a heavy ring in her voice, "according to one of you."

Without removing her pale eyes from Mantling's face, but with the thin fingers of her left hand gripping the cloth so that dishes moved, she held up the queen of clubs.

"But, blast it," Mantling shouted, "*You* can't——!"

"Continue," said Guy coolly. "The queen. Continue."

"I can't beat it, I'm afraid," Sir George announced. Tairlaine felt a sense of relief, and caught a humorous gleam in the little baronet's eye as he glanced down. "Ten of diamonds is the best I can do. But I agree with Mantling. We can't let Miss Brixham . . ."

"Ha ha ha," said Ravelle with chortling glee. He lifted his finger and tapped it impressively against his nose. "She will not have to, old man. No, no. Regard the old man. I have the poppa. I have the king of diamonds, you see? Now then. Where do I go? Where——?"

"There's just one more," Mantling said heavily . . .

The silence lengthened. Bender sat very straight, one hand shading his eyes.

"Well?" demanded Carstairs. "I say, get on with it!"

Bender reached out slowly, turned up his card, and exposed the ace of spades.

There was more noise at the table in the releasing of the tension. Bender took away the hand that shaded his eyes; the expression of the shrewd, swarthy face was baffling, but for a flash Tairlaine could have sworn he saw there something like a look of fierce mirth.

"You know, young man," Guy said abruptly, "some people would call that the death-card."

Carstairs hooted. Bender got up, carefully dusting away crumbs with his napkin. "I doubt it, sir," he answered with great composure. (Now why did he "sir" Guy and not Alan? He seemed almost obsequious.) "I think I can take care of myself. What do I do now?"

"We install you," returned Mantling, with a return to his jovial manner. "At least, Tairlaine, and George, and our friend H.M. and I do. The rest of you may go or stay if you like. We'll sit out here afterwards and wait. Hah! You'll have to keep the door to the Widow's Room shut, to keep to the letter of being alone. But we'll have these double-doors open, and sit near 'em. Got a watch? Good! We'll sing out every fifteen minutes, and you'll answer. It's now three minutes past ten. Vigil ends at three minutes past twelve. Right! We'll do this up in good style. You take one arm, Tairlaine, and I'll take the other . . ."

Bender turned sharply. An unhealthy tinge showed in his face.

"You needn't treat this like a procession to the gallows," he said. "I'll walk alone, thanks."

Yet there was a rather unpleasant suggestion of just that; a constraint and a dragging of steps, as though nobody wanted to go through with this now. When the ceiling lights of the dining-room were on, the passage was fairly well illuminated. They went down to the Widow's Room, and again Tairlaine saw the big square room with the now black-and-gilt paper peeling off the wall. Bluish yellow gas flames burnt low in the chandelier. In the wall opposite the door was a long window after the French style; it was secured by rusty steel shutters with narrow horizontal slits for ventilation, the shutters still fastened with bolts so corroded that no amount of wrenching had been able to move them earlier in the evening. But one or two of the panes in the old window must have been broken, for a small draught blew through the room.

Bender looked round curiously. He looked at the massive bed, shaped like a gilt swan with its crooked half-tester and rotted pink hangings, cater-cornered on the right of the window. He caught his reflection in the gilt-leaf mirrors, twisted round to see all of them. But he always looked back at the polished satinwood table, a full ten feet in diameter, and the chairs grouped about it. . . .

It was not a pleasant business, because they could hear the voices of Carstairs and Ravelle shouting out facetious warnings from the dining-room, and laughing. Ravelle uttered one rather ill-timed pleasantry about speedairs which made Tairlaine jump.

Mantling said gruffly: "I don't suppose you'll want a fire? Right. Anything you want? Er—cigarettes? Bottle of whisky? Something to read, maybe?"

"Thank you, no," said Bender. He pulled down his coat, and seemed to have trouble with his cuffs. "I don't smoke, and I am not in the mood for drinking. I—I may employ my time in writing."

With a somewhat defiant air he pulled out one of the satinwood chairs and sat down. Mantling looked at him doubtfully, lifted his shoulders, and motioned the others out with him. They left Bender sitting bolt upright amid the greasy finery, with the gas singing thinly and a scuttling of rats in the wainscot. The door closed.

"I don't like it," growled H.M. suddenly. "I don't *like* it." He glared a moment, and then stumped down ahead of them to the dining-room.

Carstairs and Ravelle alone remained in the dining-room. Shorter had put several decanters on the table; the facetious ones were clinking glasses across the table, and uniting on a toast of the lurid variety.

"Guy and Aunt Isabel?" repeated Carstairs, falling back into his chair. "Gone, my boy. Couldn't persuade 'em to stop. Isabel didn't look pleased, and Guy—I can never tell what Guy is thinking."

Mantling put his watch on the table just as a clock in the hall struck the quarter hour. They sat down at the end of the table, everybody keeping a wary eye on the open double-doors to the passage. Fresh coffee was called for, and many cups poured out; but Tairlaine's always seemed to get cold before he tasted it.

It was the longest two hours he could ever remember. Conversation was brisk at first. As though deliberately to shut out the subject at hand, Mantling and Carstairs indulged in the do-you-remember-when pastime through three continents and every rifle caliber; Carstairs was slightly drunk, slightly noisy, and sometimes possessed of a surprising wit. Tairlaine and Sir George spoke in low tones, with Ravelle addressing anecdotes to both. Only H.M. was dull and somber. He sat ruffling the tufts of hair at each side of his bald head, growling to himself and drawing at a dead pipe. When Ravelle tried to lead round to the subject of the Widow's Room he spoke for the first time.

"No!" said H.M. explosively. "Not yet. Not now. Lemme think. Don't confuse me. I'd looked forward to this two hours. I wanted to get the *story* from Guy. What curse, blast it? What about those chairs; those harmless chairs? I want the story—and I don't dare leave here." He looked speculatively at Mantling. "You can't or won't tell it; hey?"

"Quite right," nodded the other, looking straight at him. He returned to the design that was being built up before him with table implements. "Now look here, Bob my lad. Here's the Zambesi. All this up here is spear grass and wait-a-bit thorn; no beaters are goin' through there. Out in a circle—this is veldt—you got the shield-beaters . . ."

The clock struck the half-hour. Mantling stopped, hesitated, and then turned to boom out a hail towards the room at the end of the passage. Bender's voice answered: not cheerfully, but it answered. The first onrush of fear had gone. . . .

Fear kept on dwindling. The clock chimed the quarter again, and then the hour, in liquid notes that grew louder as the mutter of London died away outside. White fog masked the windows in a muffled world. They could hear hootings when an occasional taxi crept along the curb outside. A quarter past eleven chimed and rang; each time, while the cigar-stumps accumulated, and each time the hail was reassuringly answered from the Widow's Room.

As fear went from them, they left off talking. Mantling leaned back in the blue haze of smoke, grinning. At half-past eleven, when they received the customary muffled cry that all was well, Ravelle got up with an oddly disappointed air. He said he had some notes and a telegram to get off, and would return at midnight. His effervescence seemed to have gone when he left them. At a quarter to twelve Mantling woke up, boomed jocosely, and poured out a final drink when they received a reply. "He's done it," chortled Carstairs. His lean face shone. "He's done it, by God! Good for old parson-face! The bogey's busted and sanity's itself again. He's only got fifteen minutes to go now. If the goblins haven't snaffled him by this time, they never will."

Sir George drew a deep breath. "I'm more glad," he observed, "than I'm willing to say. *And* I'm beginning to feel a fool . . . I suffered from premonitions, like our silent friend here. There seemed to be something wrong about that fellow Bender, something out of place and misfit, but I couldn't spot it; and it worried me."

Mantling snorted tolerantly. "Well, he's an artist, old son. Maybe that's what——"

"Artist," said H.M., "my eye."

Somebody's cup rattled. Mantling jerked up his head.

"Artist my eye," growled H.M., blinking at his pipe. "Where's your eyes?"

"But if he's not an artist," said Sir George, in the midst of a silence, "what the devil is he?"

"Well, I may be wrong, son. But I got a strong suspicion he's either a young doctor or a medical student. . . . Didn't you see what he did in the other room, when the old lady showed signs of a faintin' fit or a hysterical outburst? His fingers went straight off—automatic—for her pulse, and she had to yank her wrist away. Notice? That ain't a layman's gesture. H'm. And then I was a bit curious about that bulge in the breast pocket of his coat. I nearly tripped him up so I could grab his coat and feel what it was. It was a notebook; big notebook. There was somethin' else there, but a notebook on the outside. Rummy sort of chap who carries a notebook in dinner-kit. He said he meant to do some writin' . . ."

Mantling was on his feet in a fury.

"You may be satisfied, son," H.M. added. "I'm not. Even yet."

An outer door in the hall closed, and Mantling stopped

as he was about to speak. They heard voices approaching the dining-room, and the door opened. A man and a woman, cheerful of face despite the dampness of their clothes, stamped in.

"You're sitting late, Alan," the woman called. "We should have been here earlier, but the cab had to go sl . . ." Her eyes moved to the open double-doors, and she stared.

Alan rubbed his hands. "It's all right, Judith. The bogey's gone, and you can know now. We tested it out. No more scares, old girl. There's a chap in there now; testing it, you see; in fact, his time's just about up. We'll let him out as soon as——"

The clock chimes rang smoothly, and it began to strike. Mantling drew a deep breath.

"And there it is. *All right, Bender!*" he shouted. "Time's up now. Come out and have a drink."

The man in the doorway, who had been taking off his sodden coat, turned round. "Who did you say is in there, Mantling?" he demanded suddenly.

"Chap named Bender; you know . . . I say, excuse me! This is my sister Judith—Dr. Arnold, let me present . . . Come on, Bender! Time's up, I tell you!"

"Who told him to go in there?" asked Arnold. His full voice was very steady, but there was a queer look about his face.

"Well, we drew cards, and he got the ace of spades. Dash it, Gene," cried Mantling with a sort of pettish querulousness, "don't look at me like that! It was fair play. We've lifted the curse. He's all right. He went in there two hours ago, and he's still all right . . ."

"Is he?" said the woman. Tairlaine was conscious of dark eyes and a white face. "Then why doesn't he come out? *Ralph!*"

It was H.M. who moved first. Tairlaine saw his lips moving as though he were cursing; he heard his wheezing breaths and the creak of his big shoes in the silence as he lumbered towards the double-doors. Arnold was after him, then ahead of him; Tairlaine and Sir George just behind. Never in his life would Tairlaine forget the sight of that bulky figure in the creaking shoes lumbering, with a beaten droop of his shoulders, ahead of them down the passage . . . Then Arnold threw open the door.

The room was unchanged, nothing out of place, and for a second it looked empty. Sir George began, "Where is——" and then stopped, for they all saw it. In the left-hand corner of the room was the elaborate dressing-table with its Cupids and roses, set cater-cornered; its gilt-leaf mirror was tilted slightly inwards, and reflected a part of the floor across the room. They saw a reflection of the decaying carpet. They also saw the reflection of a face.

The man was lying on his back, nearly hidden by the great gilded bed across the room, so that they could only see his face reflected. It was swollen, of a blackish color, and they saw the white slits of eyeballs.

"Stand back," said Arnold quietly. "Stand back, I tell you!"

He moved across creaking boards, round the bed, and bent down. H.M., still with those inaudible curses, stared blindly at it.

"But it couldn't—!" Mantling began, and his own roar seemed to scare him. He began, with a weirdly childish gesture, to bite his fingernails. "He's alive! He was alive fifteen minutes ago . . ."

Arnold straightened up.

"Think so?" he said. "Shut that door, somebody! Keep out, Judith! This man has been dead for over an hour."

CHAPTER FIVE

Too Many Alibis

It was plain that nobody wished to touch anything or sit down anywhere, except H.M. H.M. sat on the edge of the bed, his hands folded. Sir George stood over by the window, and Tairlaine with his back to the fireplace. Tairlaine looked across at the vacant space on the other side of the bed, from which they had just removed Ralph Bender's body. The photographs had been taken, the place was streakily dusted with the white powder of the fingerprint men, and there was trampled disarray like the aftermath of a party. Two constables had carried out Bender's body on a stretcher: not a pleasant sight. Although the man's clothing was scarcely disarranged, he had died in convulsions. The right leg was drawn up to the abdomen, the head hunched down into back-thrown shoulders, the lips sealed back across the teeth. And there were other details which will read better in the technicalities of the postmortem report.

They had carried him out to a room with a better light, so that the police surgeon could make a preliminary examination. Of his presence there remained only the two odd things they had found near his body. On the floor close to his right-hand side had lain a crumpled playing-card—easily identifiable, by the shield on the back, as one from the special packs used in this house—and the card was the nine of spades. The other object had been found lying *on Bender's shirt-front.* It was a long but very narrow strip of stiffish paper, rolled up so tightly that it would fit into a thimble. There were some curious words upon it.

These articles lay now on the table. And staring down at them, stood Chief Inspector Humphrey Masters.

Chief Inspector Masters, exactly as Tairlaine had heard him described by James Bennett. Masters, portly and sedate of dress, with his bland shrewd face, his genial manner and heavy jaw, his grizzled hair carefully brushed to hide the bald spot. He stood pinching his underlip between thumb and forefinger, craning his neck to look at the articles from every side. If they told him nothing, he did not show it. He pushed his bowler hat to the back of his head and turned towards H.M. with a faint grin.

"Well, sir," said Masters, in that deprecating tone of his, "so this time you were actually on the spot, eh? Just so. You know, I'm getting used to this. I'm getting used to being dragged out in the middle of the night to be told some outlandish thing has happened, and that Sir Henry Merrivale is grousing in the background. Lummy, I am! Before long I'll be considering myself above an ordinary little matter of a knifing in Poplar or a smash-and-grab raid in the West End. Eh, sir?"

H.M. lifted a heavy fist and shook it. He regarded Masters' beaming placidness with an eye of malevolence.

"Son," said H.M., "I was on the spot in more senses than one. Burn me, what could I *do?* They say they're goin' to have this little game. All right. What tangible reason could I give for stopping 'em, when I combed this room through and was willing to swear there was no hocus-pocus about it? And even if I had a mind to stop it, how would you suggest I went about it? Rush out and collar a policeman, hey? 'For God's sake, constable, come quick! One of Lord Mantling's guests is in horrible danger. He's going to go into a room and sit down.' Bah. 'Now, sir, you take my advice and go along home quietly,' says Robert. And there we are. . . . Oh, *you* can look chirpy enough at the start," grunted H.M., stirring restlessly. "That's because I'm at your elbow to give advice, and I can't wriggle away even if I wanted to; I'm a witness. I'm a hell of a witness, if you ask me. I'm a pompous ass, if you want the bitter truth of it—and it hurts, Masters; it hurts a good deal. It's no real good sayin', 'What could I do?' The fact remains that I didn't."

"Now, now," said Masters soothingly. "We must remember——"

"We must remember," interrupted H.M., pointing a finger at him, "that I didn't see how that poor devil could come to harm. And I still don't. I tell you frankly, son, for the moment at least the old man's licked."

Masters pinched at his underlip. He seemed uneasy.

"Well, sir, there's no denying it's a queer case," he admitted. His eyes wandered round the room. "I mean, in the sense that the circumstances are queer, and the clews queerer still. But at least it's something we can handle and prove. To begin with, it's a clear case of poison . . . Harrum! I suppose there's no doubt of that?"

"Oh, no. It's poison right enough. I hope that helps you."

"Doesn't it? Come, now!" urged Masters persuasively. "Let's see what we've got. It's just possible, you know, that the room may be flummoxed after all. Nobody's infallible, you know. And if—hem!—by any chance we do find a poison-trap here, and the mark of it on the poor chap's body . . ."

H.M. subsided into dull quiet. He blinked over his spectacles.

"Uh-huh. All right. If you do, then you'll have the pleasure of crowin' more than you are now. I think I can tell you what poison the poor devil died of, and I'll jolly well insist on standin' by at the official p.m. to make sure. But until Doc Blaine gives us a little hint, let's play a game of supposing. Let's suppose—hey?—that you don't find any poison-trap here, or any means of administering a dose subcutaneously. What then?"

Masters looked at him. "Excuse me, Sir Henry," he volunteered, with a sort of restlessness, "but aren't you . . . yes, and everybody else as well . . . aren't you taking a bit of a short-sighted view of this business? Eh? Come, now! It seems to me you've got poisoned needles on the brain. It's hypnotized you, in a way. You can't see anything but a poison with a local action, through the tissues of the body.

"But look at the facts. I'm no medical man, I admit, but I do know a bit about poisons. Got to. Right, then: look at the symptoms! Tetanic condition; mouth drawn back, head and shoulders back. The back a little arched: what they call opisthanatos. One leg drawn up instead of both straight out, but that's not——un——"

"Inconsistent?"

Masters nodded somewhat doggedly. "If you like. I'm saying that those are more or less the symptoms of a dose of strychnine poisoning, which Mr. Bender *swallowed.* Swallowed, sir, and no hanky-panky. You'll say that there's no receptacle in this room, nothing from which he could've swallowed it. Of course not! It was given him, somehow, before he came into the room at all. Strychnine takes some little time to act; according to the dose, of course, or the—um—toleratory condition of the person.

But," insisted Masters, tapping a finger into his palm, "there are symptoms. For instance." He turned to Tairlaine. "You, sir, gave me a description of Mr. Bender. Now I'll quote you a sentence I remember out of my manual: 'The victim of strychnine first assumes a slight stiffness about the neck, and his aspect exhibits signs of uneasiness or terror.' I put it to you that it describes Mr. Bender? Ah! Thank you. Just so."

"We'd better dispose of this fancy theorizin'," said H.M. "That's what you think, is it? All right. What about the cyanosis of the face?"

Masters hesitated.

"Yes, I admit that's a bit queer——"

"Queer?" roared H.M. "It'd be a bloody miracle if it happened like that. Hang it, son, you know better! To put it flat, whenever you get a swelled and congested face you have somethin' working on the respiratory system. The victim can't speak . . . But strychnine acts on the spinal column. If Bender had been given a dose of pure strychnine, as we know it, why didn't he yell for help when he felt it overcoming him? But there wasn't the mildest kind of peep out of him. He didn't even complain of indigestion, although you say he'd swallowed the most painful poison on the register. He didn't—because he couldn't. Something paralyzed his muscles. He was a corpse even before he was dead.

"What I want to impress on you, son, is this. That was a devilish swift-working poison. It was administered in this room. Above all things, it could not have been swallowed."

"But why not?"

"Because it was curare," said H.M.

After a pause, while Masters carefully took off his hat, laid it on the table, and produced a notebook, H.M. went on dully:

"Any other toxic agent, and I'd have agreed with you. But not curare. That's the exception. Swallowed, it's absolutely harmless. We could eat it on our bread-and-butter, or drink it in our beer, and never notice anything; a tenth of that amount, injected under the skin, would kill us in ten minutes. Sure it has some of the same symptoms as strychnine! They're derived from the same plant: *Stranchnos Ignatii*, if you wanta get technical about it. But this is a little weed-killer of uncommon potency. It's the South American arrow-poison. And, somehow, Bender got a dose of it jabbed into him."

Masters said thoughtfully: "Arrow-poison. Yes, I'd heard of that." He grinned. "Now, now, sir, no reason to get upset! Bit of a surprise, seeing you upset. And I'm bound to admit I'd like to get a bit of my own back. But—theory! All this is theory. We simply come back to the fact that the room must be flummoxed somehow. Just so. And if it's *search* that's required," Masters announced with grim satisfaction, "I don't mind saying I'm the man for your money."

Sir George Anstruther stirred. He stood by the window like a rather sinister-looking Pickwick, his head lowered and his hands folded under his coat-tails. He said sharply:

"I don't want to butt in, Mr. Masters. And naturally I'm grateful for being allowed at the—council. But the fishiest part of this business doesn't seem to have struck you yet. If Bender got himself jabbed by a poison-trap, then who was the other person in this room?"

"*Other* person, sir?"

"The other person who was singing out Bender's replies to us after Bender was dead. Didn't you hear what Dr. Arnold said? Bender died at somewhere around eleven o'clock. In that case, who obligingly answered us three times afterwards?"

"Ah," said Masters. He looked less bland now. His head was a little on one side, and his eyes had narrowed. "As to that, you see—the only people from whom I've had any information are you gentlemen. I haven't interviewed the household yet. I *did* hear something of the sort. But a mistake in diagnosis, made in a hurry . . . ?"

"It wasn't a mistake in diagnosis," grunted H.M., "unless you want to write me down an even bigger fathead than I am. I examined him, too, you know. Humph." He had got out his black pipe and stuck it in a corner of his mouth, but he was too lazy to light it. "I put the time of death at about eleven-fifteen. Definitely there was somebody imitating Bender. 'Tisn't hard to fake a shout, you know; the door's thick, the distances are long—any kind of muffled wail would do, provided we heard it. But *why*, Masters? Why did somebody do that? Somebody was here, right enough. The person also pinched Bender's notebook . . ."

Masters sat down at the table and opened his own notebook.

"Oh, I know what you're goin' to say," protested H.M. "I admit I've given you a pretty sketchy outline so far. But I'll let you have hard facts.

"I looked for Bender's notebook straightaway. It was gone—as I knew it would be. There might be dangerous things in that notebook for somebody here. Finally, somebody put that little roll of paper on his shirt."

"*And* the playing-card," said Masters, craning his neck round. He scowled. "As for that bit of paper——"

"Parchment," corrected Sir George. "Mind if I see that, Inspector?"

Masters handed it over, and Tairlaine looked across George's shoulder as he opened the crackling little strip and flattened it out against the wall. It was about eight inches long and half an inch wide. The small, clear words were printed in ink:

'Struggole faiusque lecutate, te decutinem dolorum persona.'

"What about it, gents?" inquired H.M., blinking owlishly. "Let's have the resources of the British Museum and Cambridge. What d'you make of it?"

Sir George let the roll snap together. He looked worried. "If the thing weren't absurd, I'd say it was intended for an amulet or a talisman. Of course, it's a joke." He looked at H.M. sharply. "It's apparently a spell or a prayer of some sort, to 'cast out the pain from this person.' Or '*dolor*' might mean sorrow. The thing's muddled. It's medieval Latin; the bastard sort where they distort some words and clip off others, and are just as apt to use the infinitive to express purpose. The use of '*faius*' I don't see offhand. As I say, it's a joke . . ."

"Uh-huh. You're a good friend of this family, aren't you? That's what I made of it, I admit. But ain't it rather an ugly joke to put on a dead man's chest a pious prayer to cast out the pain from him?—Do you begin to see, Masters, that this is a very rummy household indeed?"

"Granted," agreed Masters, and swore under his breath. "But . . ."

"And yet, though you don't see your whole problem yet, there are compensations, Masters. I'll give you the compensations before I give you the hard kick in the eye. If you want to find the person who was in this room, you have a narrow field. Because why? Because, with the exception of two persons, everybody in this house or connected with this house has a cast-iron alibi that the Recordin' Angel himself couldn't smash.

"Listen, son. While they were screamin' and phonin' the police, I did a little soft-shoe work. The people connected with this case are as follows." He lifted his hand and checked off the list on his fingers. "First, there's the party that sat down at table: Alan, Guy, Isabel, Carstairs, Ravelle, Tairlaine, George Anstruther, and myself. Second, there are the two absentees, Judith and Arnold. Third, there are the servants: butler, housekeeper, cook, two housemaids, and chauffeur. Get that?"

"Yes, sir. This," declared Masters, "is the sort of thing I like to hear. Well?"

"Take it backwards, then. Humph. From a quarter past ten o'clock until half-past eleven or later, all the servants were at table havin' a bite of supper belowstairs. Judith and her *fiancé* were at the theater with a whole party of their friends, three of whom brought 'em home in a cab and dropped 'em off at the door here at five minutes before midnight. Finally, every one of the others was under my own eye durin' the whole crucial time . . . with two exceptions. Looks easy, don't it? Burn me, Masters, it looks too easy! I don't like it."

"And the two exceptions," said Masters, making a decisive note, "were Mr. Guy Brixham and Miss Isabel Brixham. Eh? Just so. Stop a bit, though! Didn't somebody tell me that this chap Ravelle also left the table?"

"Uh-huh. 'These foreigners,' says Masters darkly, 'are apt to be a murderous lot.' But Ravelle didn't leave the table, y'see, until a minute after half-past eleven. In other words, Bender was dead before Ravelle left the table, and the unseen voice had sung out twice in Ravelle's presence. He's got as good an alibi as any of us."

"And the others give me enough to work on for tonight. I'm not going to trouble 'em overmuch this time," the Chief Inspector asserted. "The first thing, then . . . Come in, doctor! We'd been having a bit of an argument in your field. Have you——?"

The police surgeon, a brisk-looking official who resembled a prosperous business-man, had already put on his hat and overcoat.

"I want a removal order for him, Masters. Can't say absolutely without a full post-mortem, but it looks like a hundred-to-one shot on Sir Henry's suggestion." He dusted his coat. "It's curare. I've seen it used in tetanus cases at Guy's, or it wouldn't be much in my line."

"Go on, Masters," prompted H.M., as the other hesitated. His moon face was split with fantastic jollity. "Masters ain't sure but what the old man's a charlatan. What he wants to ask you is whether curare is deadly if it's swallowed. Ho ho ho. What do you say, Blaine?"

"No, it's not. And I can tell you this much," said the doctor, "that it damn well wasn't swallowed in this case. I took a blood-test, and you could almost see the result without a glass."

"Uh-huh. How long do you think it took to act?"

"Well—I could make a guess. Muscular paralysis in about three minutes. Death in ten."

Masters swore. "What about the puncture, then? How was it done?"

"Can't tell you absolutely—yet. Look here, I didn't go over his whole body. There's a scratch on the under-side of his jaw that looks as though he'd cut himself shaving. But, unless he'd brought along his tackle and had a shave in here, it didn't happen any earlier so far as the poison's concerned. He was a dead 'un within fifteen minutes at the outside. Anything else? If not, write me out that order and I'll get along. Oh, there are a couple of people out there who want to see you. Dr. Arnold and the old lady."

Masters, after a glance at H.M., gave instructions to send

them in. For the first time Tairlaine had a good look at Dr. Eugene Arnold. He remembered Carstairs' description; which, although slanderous, made him understand why Carstairs had never liked the man. There was assured success and poise about him. He was one of those people who are notorious for speaking straight out, and for whom you somehow do favors merely because you do not like them. He had a hard, handsome face which could become kindly like the turning on of an electric light; a portentously grave manner in the penetration of his light brown eyes, and thick dark hair with those grayish temples romantically favored by women. There was no nonsense about Eugene Arnold. Carstairs looked like a shabby child beside him. Seeing him guide in Miss Isabel Brixham, his head inclined at just the proper angle, towering over her in thin alertness, Tairlaine thought of those portraits of the first Duke of Marlborough. There stepped Arnold—conquering, logical, humorless, probably as fond of money as Marlborough and as mean about it.

"I wished to speak to you," said Isabel in a low voice, looking hesitantly from Masters to H.M. The rims of her pale eyes were red, and she looked shrunken. Her age was sixty now. "I must, because . . . in a way, you see, I am responsible for that poor boy's death. But must we stay here? Please! Can't we—go somewhere else?"

Arnold switched on one or two of his lights. They did not seem to impress H.M.

"I am afraid, gentlemen, that I must insist on that," the doctor said sharply. "Miss Brixham is in my care, and it will be obvious that she has suffered a severe nervous shock."

"Uh-huh," said H.M., who was trying to light his pipe. He cocked an eye round. "Then why'd you bring her here, son?"

Arnold glanced at him swiftly—appraising. He could not seem to make up his mind how he should treat H.M.

"Unfortunately, we have something rather important. I should imagine that you of the police"—a slight pause, wherein H.M. did not rise to the interrogatory bait—"that you of the police will be interested. It is about poor Ralph Bender."

"I see. So he was a doctor after all?"

"And *I* brought him here," said Isabel. "Oh, my God, I *let* him——"

"You are certainly not to blame, Aunt Isabel," Arnold interposed. Aunt already? He consciously interposed himself as a buckler. "In a sense, gentlemen, this is a breach of professional ethics. But since it has ended in murder, the facts must come out, and I have no intention of withholding them. Very well. Ralph Bender was the most brilliant student of his year at the Royal. After his clinical study at St. Thomas's, he wished to confine himself to psychological medicine, but he had no funds to rent a consulting room: especially in Wigmore Street. Consequently——"

"You took him in as a sort of dispensary-clerk, to handle your minor cases without fee?"

"I thought it was only a charitable action.—Look here, I do not possess a dispensary, my friend. Perhaps you are not acquainted with the nature of my work?"

"Oh, I dunno. Psychiatry, ain't it?"

"Only in some—" He broke off, his face hardening. "Excuse me, my friend, but would you mind telling me to whom I have the honor of speaking?"

"Now, now," said H.M. soothingly. There was a wheezy noise as he sucked at the empty pipe stuck in one corner of his mouth.

"Don't get your back up, son. Let no gleam of wrath darken that magnetic eye. Carry on about Bender."

"He worked for me, along with another young man who shows great promise." Dr. Arnold kept his temper, with an urbane smile, and considered. "A short time ago Miss Isabel Brixham came to me with—certain matters I think you know. I was in a difficult position. I also had thought—that is, I gave it consideration. Aside from the obvious matter of policy, I myself could not have intervened—investigated—questioned, even in the most discreet and carefully veiled way. You understand me?"

"I know Mantling hates doctors, yes. Especially loony-doctors."

Arnold chose to be amused. He was humoring H.M.

"Especially loony-doctors, as you put it. I myself am on sufferance. I am permitted to speak only of sport. Since I—happened to be a cricket blue of some small distinction in the past," said Arnold, flicking an imaginary speck of dust from his lapel, and smiling with deprecating charm, "I, of course, thoroughly enjoyed the company of that hearty sportsman. Ha ha ha. But that did not happen to influence me. If there were, to put it briefly, a madman in this house, that person must be placed under the proper restraint. If possible, without scandal. If not, with it. At Miss Brixham's suggestion, Bender was introduced here as one of her art protégés. This was easy. M. Ravelle was being entertained at the time, and that in itself was a distraction. Bender was to discover——"

"And did he?"

"Undoubtedly," said Arnold calmly. "You see, he was murdered."

CHAPTER SIX

The Box Without a Needle

"UNDERSTAND ME, please," pursued Arnold in his sharp, common-sense voice. "If I pretended to be deeply grieved at Bender's death, I should be talking rot. I think he was a fool to allow himself to be drawn into this trap to-night. But I regret his death. He was useful to me. And I should certainly have forbidden this insane performance to-night. Miss Brixham"—a momentary switching on of the kindly, pitying light as he glanced at Isabel—"Miss Brixham agrees with me that it was insane; and, I hear, did everything possible to prevent it. I do not blame her excessively, but I wish she had been more frank."

Having delivered himself of this stricture, Dr. Arnold straightened the wings of his tie, adjusted his coat, and smiled at last on Isabel to indicate that all was forgiven. It was remarkable how that calm woman had been snapped like a brittle stick in the past few hours; she was almost whimpering now. H.M. stirred restlessly.

"Well, now," he suggested, "you might do your duty, mightn't you, since the cards are on the table? What are you goin' to do?"

Arnold shrugged. "Fortunately or unfortunately, the matter

is in your hands now; not mine. All I can do is prevent your hanging the murderer after you have caught him. It is in your hands."

"And good riddance?"

"And good riddance," the other agreed coolly.

"Still, I don't see how you can duck out of responsibility as easily as all that, son," said H.M., examining the inside of his pipe-bowl. "I say, don't the thing give you any qualms at all? With somebody's brain cracked in the family— No, I see it don't. You've plotted your life like a garden suburb; you know who'll grace your dinner-table and who won't; and no mere matter of a crazy brother-in-law can make you forget that after all his strait-jacket will be stamped with a coronet. Hey?"

"I admire your frankness, my friend," said Arnold, who obviously detested frankness in anyone but himself. He kept cool. "You forget that I happen to be in love with Miss Judith Brixham."

"Yes, I know. That's why I'm bein' so insulting. You see, something will have to be done. You don't have any suspicions of Miss Judith's sanity, do you? No. Or Miss Isabel's——?"

"You never *thought!* . . ." cried Isabel.

"Now, now, ma'am! Or Miss Isabel's? No. Well, that leaves two and only two. If you can't help us in that direction, we shall have to take steps ourselves."

Arnold studied him. "For the moment, I must refuse to answer that hint. I have no data. I can form none without proper, and direct, questioning. But, without speaking of anyone else, I should always be willing to regard Lord Mantling as an exceedingly sane man."

"So-ho," muttered H.M., lifting his eyebrows. "I'm flat. I'm by. I want to sit and think. Carry on, Masters."

Masters came into action with his persuasive affability, his knack of making everybody believe he was only a young man seeking information from wiser heads—until he pounced. He urged Isabel to sit down, which she refused to do until he went and brought a chair from the dining-room. The room seemed to hypnotize her. Her pale eyes wandered round it, darting towards one article of furniture, moving away again; but for some reason Masters refused to permit the questioning in any other place.

"Now, you understand," he began, in a confidential tone, "that just as a matter of form we shall have to have a statement from each of you for our records? Exactly. So if you don't mind, Doctor, we'll take you first——"

"So that you may have Miss Brixham alone?" Arnold asked sharply.

"Well, we won't hurt her, sir. And after all, you know, you're a doctor; not a solicitor. Eh? If you'll just give me a rough idea of your movements to-night . . ."

For the first time a genuine smile began to creep across Arnold's face.

"God bless you, Inspector," he said. "I didn't kill the poor devil, if that's what you mean. Neither did Judith: I try to be as little of a fool as I can, and I do not think I am stupid enough to run the risk of being hanged." He seemed a trifle surprised. But Masters, who was humbled, he treated with great civility.

He went through his tale with the curtness of a dictation. Catching sight of his reflection in a mirror, he straightened his tie and adjusted his white waistcoat with supreme unconsciousness while he spoke. After dinner he and Judith Brixham had fallen in with a theater-party that was going to see *Ten-Minute Alibi* at the Haymarket. They left the theater shortly after eleven, drove with three others to a supper-club in Regent Street, had a dance and a drink, left the club at twenty minutes to twelve, and due to the slowness of the cab in the fog did not arrive home until nearly midnight. After this recital, Masters humbly forced Arnold from the room. The doctor's desire to stay and protect Isabel, Tairlaine saw, was more for effect than use. He went out in his conquering way, and Masters turned to the woman.

"Now, ma'am," he said kindly, "you mustn't be upset either by this room or what I'm going to ask you. There's absolutely nothing can hurt you—you see."

"I know I'm being a fool. I don't know what can be wrong with me. It's only that for some reason everything seems changed." She opened and shut her hands on her pearls, and there were hollow spaces between the ligaments of those hands. "Yesterday, two hours ago, I should not have believed I could feel like this. This—this is the first time I have seen this room. That is, to my recollection. I was three years old when my father died here; in '76, that was. But I can't remember what it looked like." Her dull eyes, which had been wandering round in a puzzled fashion, flashed back. "What did you wish to ask me?"

"You decided not to stay in the dining-room, ma'am, after Mr. Bender had come in here?"

"Yes. I felt I couldn't face it. Guy went, too. He said he was bored. Bored! Fancy that!"

"Where did you go when you left the dining-room, ma'am?"

"Upstairs, to my sitting-room. It's on the floor above. Why?"

"Matter of routine, ma'am," said Masters, smiling heartily. Tairlaine saw that H.M. was trying to catch Masters' eye, and H.M. was attempting to make a face like the Big Bad Wolf in disguise. "We have to ask these things, you know. How long did you stay there?"

"Until I heard Judith screaming down here. That was when—" she pointed suddenly at the bed, "that boy *I* brought here . . ."

"Of course, ma'am, and we all sympathize. Now was there by any chance anybody with you? A maid, someone like that?"

"Well . . . Guy was with me."

Masters' pencil, which had been starting to make a note, slipped on the paper and nearly got out of his hand.

"Hurrum!" growled Masters, clearing his throat. "Er—just so. Yes. But not all the time, of course, ma'am? I mean, young men—wandering about the house—that is . . ."

She looked at him. "I don't know exactly what you mean, Inspector, 'young men wandering about the house.' He was—yes, he was horribly restless when he came into my sitting-room."

"When?"

"About half an hour after they'd started the game. About half-past ten. I know, because, God, in heaven, how I was watching that clock! It's one of those clocks, you see,"—her finger made hesitant motions in the air—"where the minute hand doesn't move until the minute's up, and then it jumps. It was horrible, watching that. You think it will never move, and it startles you when it does. Then Guy came in, and said he was restless, too. We tried playing chess . . . we often play chess in the evenings . . . and then cards, and then reading. But none of it would do, so finally we openly *talked* about what was going on."

"And Mr. Guy Brixham was with you the whole time, from half-past ten until midnight?"

"Yes."

Tairlaine looked at Sir George, who was still scowling over

the strip of parchment. The little baronet had stuck a pince-nez on his nose; he lifted burly shoulders, but he seemed pleased. Excellent! Everybody in the house now had an alibi. Masters was not pleased. His scowl deepened when from H.M.'s direction emanated an absent humming in which could be discerned the mumbled words, "Ta-ta-big bad wolf; who's afraid of—" Masters peered round.

"Just so. Now, Sir Henry, perhaps you have some questions you'd like to ask this lady?"

The humming stopped. H.M. rubbed his chin. "Well, yes, I have. You say you and your nephew, ma'am, had a talk about this room. What did he say about it?"

"He reassured me. He said the place was absolutely harmless, and laughed at the idea."

"You mean, about a possible poison-trap?"

"Yes." There was a faded eagerness in her manner. "First he said, 'Do you think, even if there originally had been such a thing there, the poison would have kept its power through all these years?' "

H.M. frowned. "Well, I dunno about that. If it killed its first victim in 1803 and its last in 1876, it had rather a hearty period of virulence. Besides . . . I say, Masters, not to interrupt, but that reminds me of what I was speakin' of at the dinner-table to-night. You remember when I got invited to Rome a couple of months ago over that Cagliostro's Box case? Old Briocci, the collector, tumbled over dead in his private museum, poisoned, but not a mark on him. Remind me to bring that up later. Point is, the trick box that caused his death was proved to have been made in either 1791 or 1792. It killed a man this year because the sheathing for the stuff had kept it from disintegratin'. Remember that. . . . Go on, please, Miss Brixham."

She was staring at him.

"Then— Never mind." Again she peered round uneasily. "No, I didn't think of that. What I did say to Guy was, 'Yes, that may be true; but somebody,'" here she peered with furtive quickness at H.M., "'somebody has been in that room—cleaned it—restored it. And suppose that person has re-set the trap with arrow poison for just this opportunity?'"

Masters was himself again.

"Arrow poison, ma'am," he said, "happens to have been what was used. It's rare stuff, they tell me, very rare. Where would anybody hereabouts get anything of that sort?"

"Oh, I tried to warn you!" She clenched her hands. "Get it, you say? From the primitive weapons in my nephew's study. Not the spears and arrows he has on the wall. But from the two or three darts he keeps in a box in his desk drawer."

Masters whistled involuntarily. He was about to go after this in full cry when H.M. intervened.

"Yes, yes! Steady, son. We can go back to that. What I'm interested in now is that conversation you had with your other nephew. What did he say to the re-setting of the trap?"

"That's what reassured me. I—I almost believed him." She shuddered. "He said, 'Do you think that anybody who wanted to catch a victim like that would be such a fool as to clean up the room, put dummy screws in the door, and sweep the passage? He'd have left the room as though it had never been tampered with. Otherwise you'd have been suspicious—and you were, straight *off*.' And that's *true*, isn't it?"

She stared at him eagerly, and H.M. grunted in approval.

"Good for Guy. Uh-huh. That had occurred to me. And, unfortunately for my reputation, it reassured me, too. . . . Did he make any other remarks?"

"Well." She hesitated, as though she were in an agony of not knowing what to say. "He did make one rather odd remark, I remember. After he'd said the room was absolutely harmless, he said, 'And it's uninteresting, too, unless they guess about the putty.'"

"Putty?" repeated Masters, rather wildly. "Putty? You mean the sort of stuff you put in window-frames?" At this juncture Tairlaine thought that the woman gave a slight start, but she was strung on thin wires of hysteria already, and it may have been the chief inspector's tone. "Is that it? Just so. What did he mean by that?"

"He wouldn't tell me. I don't know! Don't you see," she cried, "I'm asking you for help? I'm throwing out all these things in the hope that you'll pick them up, and explain—somehow. That's all I can say."

"What I want to know, ma'am," returned Masters, tapping the table, "is how Mr. Guy Brixham happens to know so much about a room he's never seen."

She smiled a little. "He's the family historian, you know. He's the only one who ever grubs through *all* the records. Of course, I know the story of the room . . ." Here she glanced at the big round table at which Masters sat, with the polished yellow satinwood top in which was worked a *fleur-de-lis* pattern of darker design. There seemed no reason why it should affect her with repulsion, like the six chairs with their brass edgings and red satin seats. But her gaze was fixed on them for so long that they seemed to grow eerie under the fluttering gaslight. Their golden pallor stood out against the dark colors of the room.

"There they all sat," she added, pointing suddenly to the chairs. "Monsieur de Paris. Monsieur de Tours. Monsieur de

Blois. Monsieur de Rheims . . . Six of them altogether. You see——"

"Never mind that for a moment," interposed H.M. "Be quiet, Masters. You're gettin' purple with curiosity. I'm beginning to have a pretty horrible idea about the legend of this room. But I want it from Guy. I insist on hearin' it from Guy, because . . . Now, ma'am, there are just two more questions I want to ask.

"You say you know about this room, and the four deaths here. One of those four deaths I'm more curious about than the others. Marie Brixham, who died here in December, 1825, just before her wedding-day. Know anything about her? I asked Guy, but he wouldn't answer."

"What do you wish to know about her?"

"Not about her. About her intended husband. His name was George Bettison. Who was he?"

This obviously puzzled her. She dragged her pale eyes away from the hypnosis of the table. "Why . . . yes, I know. He was a very fashionable jeweler. There was quite a tragic tale made of that romance. After her death, he and his business went to ruin, and he disappeared. Why?"

"Now, now!—Pass that little parchment-roll over, will you? And Masters, give me the playing-card. Thanks. Now." He lumbered up from the bed, stumped across, and suddenly flattened the parchment-slip out on the table. "Ever see this before?"

Her body grew stiff, and for a moment she looked up at H.M. with a face of something like despair. Yet when she spoke her voice was calm.

"No. It's Latin, isn't it? I've forgotten whatever Latin I knew. What does it mean? Where did you find it?"

"No need to get alarmed. Somebody put it on Bender's shirtfront, y'see." H.M. was very easy, but his sharp little eyes never left her face. He thrust out the playing card. "Ever see *this?*"

"But it's only a . . . What card is it? Let me see it, quick! Surely somebody drew that card in the game tonight! I remember! Yes, nine of spades! Somebody drew it. Did you find that on him, too?"

"Steady, Miss Brixham. No, it'd be too easy if anybody had drawn it. You're mixin' things up. Your nephew Alan drew the nine of clubs; that's probably what you're thinking about. Thanks, ma'am. That's all."

"You mean I may go?"

"Yes. And would you mind sending Guy in here? We got some pretty important questions to ask him."

Wheezing, H.M. lumbered back to his seat on the bed. She rose, but still she seemed torn by indecision like a physical hurt. Moistening her lips, she made several efforts to speak before she blurted out a question as though it were a confession.

"Listen to me, please. You've got to tell me! I've answered your questions, and I have a right to know." She nodded, surprisingly enough, towards the rusty steel shutters that sealed the window. "Alan said they were, but I must know. Are those shutters really and truly bolted on the inside?"

"They are. And the bolts are so rusted that it'll take an acetylene blow-torch to open 'em.—Never mind why she wants to know, Masters! That's all, ma'am."

When she had gone H.M. produced a tobacco pouch and began to fill his pipe at last, while he looked satirically upon the chief inspector.

"They're very solid shutters, Masters. Think that over while you see your old *bete noire*, your old fancy hobgoblin with the thirteen tails, come creepin' up after you again. Ho ho ho. Ever have nightmares about impossible situations, son?—But that's not what I want to talk about just now. You remember I mentioned Cagliostro's Box a little while ago?"

"Yes, sir. What about it? I still think—"

"Well, there's a box very much like it in this room," said H.M. "Dammit, Masters, don't jump like that! You make me nervous . . . Uh-huh. A box so very like it that the two might 'a' been designed by the same person. Maybe they were."

"But you said there was nothing wrong here!" roared Masters.

Sighing, H.M. got up again and stumped over to the ornate dressing-table in the left-hand corner of the room. He inspected the fly-blown mirror, the marble top, and the two gilded lines of drawers. Under his tug the upper right-hand drawer squeaked open with a rattle through the whole frame. . . .

It was a heavy silver casket, tarnished to blackness; nine or ten inches long by half as wide, and set up on short bandy legs to a height of four inches. When he put it down on the center table, they saw that the bulging sides were embossed with simpering Arcadian figures dancing to pan-pipes; a fringe of carven rosettes ran round the edge of the box where it met the lid, except for an inch or so on either side of the keyhole. The lid was constructed in a peak like a shallow roof, with sides that sloped down level with the rosettes and had an open projection only over the keyhole. A small blackened key was still in the lock.

"There we are," said H.M., removing the key. "Now! It's unlocked. Go ahead, Masters—open it."

Masters rubbed his chin. "Well, now, sir . . ."

"Anybody got the nerve? *You* try it, Tairlaine. You can take the old man's word that it's harmless. Want to have a shot?"

Tairlaine found his wintry pulse stirring again. He felt as he once had when somebody in the zoölogical laboratory invited him to run a stick through the wire meshes and prod a somnolent rattlesnake in a box. The rustle and flash had been as startling as an explosion. But he could not help himself, then or now. Reaching out his forefinger, he gingerly touched the projection over the keyhole, edged under, and raised. Nothing happened. He lifted harder, and succeeded only in raising the box without lifting the lid. George said, "Damn it, be careful!" Taking the box in both hands, with his right across the lid and thumb under the projection, he pulled again. The lid gave a little. When that narrow line appeared, he got his thumb fully under and his thumbnail in the crack for purchase . . .

Something wrenched and snapped, and the box flew open.

Tairlaine felt himself go hot with fear, and his breath coming short. Still nothing happened, except a puff of dust from the box.

"Understand the trick now?" inquired H.M. "You did exactly what the victim would have done if that box had been hocussed. The lid sticks—it's meant to stick. It's built so that the only way you can get a grip on it is by puttin' your thumb under that projection. When it gives a little, you wedge in your thumb so that the nail is on a line with that tiny openin'. Resistance cracks; lid rises. When it rises, little steel point about an eighth of an inch long jumps out of the upper catch on the lid—catches you deep just under the thumb-nail—and disappears when the lid's fully raised. Neat, hey?"

Masters expelled his breath hard. Tairlaine, still unsteady, found himself staring at the inside of the box. It was lined with what might once have been plush. Something like a large discolored locket lay inside; nothing else. He set the box down with a thump.

"Neat enough," he said, trying to keep his voice level. "Needle catches you, and no trace is left. But there's no fancy apparatus in *this.* That is, unless I didn't feel——"

"Now, now! Don't get the wind up! The box is quite all right; I tested it myself. There's no hanky-panky, and never has been. But this box has its maker's initials worked into the lid. Look close, and you can make out the initials. M.L.

"Now I know something of the artisans of that period. Had to go into all that with that other box affair. One of 'em who made boxes like that was a French artisan *and furniture-maker,* mind, that nobody knew anything about except the name he gave."

"Well, sir?" prompted Masters.

"The name, son," said H.M., "was 'Martin Longueval.' Yes, you can think of somebody here who has those two first names. Well, d'ye think this feller was any relation to our friend Ravelle?"

Nobody had time to answer. They heard the door slam. The voice that spoke to them was alive with such fury that even H.M. whirled round.

"What the devil," said Guy Brixham, "are you doing with that box?"

CHAPTER SEVEN

Again the Ace of Spades

GUY, THEY realized later, was shrewd enough to see by the startled expression on at least two faces that they were not up to any dangerous mischief, whatever Guy's conception of dangerous mischief might be. But, though he had himself under control, he was still shaking and pale as though from a paroxysm. As he came stepping softly across the room, smiling, he took out a handkerchief and dabbed beads of sweat from his upper lip.

Tairlaine moved back, with an unpleasant sense of shock. If the man had offered to shake hands at that moment, he could not have done it. There was something reptilian about Guy; accentuated by his narrow head with its too-high forehead, hollowed out at the temples; by the slow way he turned that head; by his shifting wrinkles—even by his smile.

"You must excuse my outburst, gentlemen," he said, putting away his handkerchief. "I have strange ideas about some matters. Among them is a feeling that outsiders handling things that have belonged to my ancestors amounts almost to blasphemy. Ha ha ha." All the while, his eyes were roving behind the dark glasses. "So this is the famous room at last? Interesting! Er—come in, Judith."

They had not noticed her behind him in the doorway. She hesitated, staring round the room, and then seemed to nerve herself. It was as though she were trying to imitate Arnold's assurance and poise, without quite being able to manage it. Tairlaine's ancient soul had already admired her heartily. Judith Brixham was brown-haired, with a very clear face in which you noticed the whimsical thoughtfulness almost as much as the good looks. Also she had a trick of wrinkling one eyebrow, looking very thoughtful, and then smiling as though she were remembering some excellent and not very reputable joke. Her configuration, as Tairlaine would have put it, was admirable.

"Yes, I want to come in," she admitted. "I want to *see* it, anyhow." Blue eyes regarded H.M. doubtfully. "It doesn't seem to have bothered you people, does it?"

"They are unquestionably making very free with it," said Guy. "Tut, gentlemen, I have not the slightest objection! But look here!—just as a matter of curiosity, what interest have you in the miniature-box?"

H.M. blinked.

"The miniature-box?" he repeated. "That's a very rummy description of it, seems to me. Just as a matter of curiosity, how do you happen to know anything about it?"

"I could tell you more about this room than the people who have seen it. That box ought to contain, if nobody has stolen it, two portraits in miniature of certain—ancestors. I don't mind telling you, also, that the box itself was made by a member of one branch of our family."

Masters puffed out his cheeks and stared.

"Do you mean to tell us, sir," he said, "that Martin Longueval was a relation of yours, too?"

This was palpably a shock for Guy. He stood motionless, the wrinkles curling round his mouth, and the set of the jaw grew ugly.

"Astonishing," he murmured at length. "Scotland Yard knows a great deal more than we laymen ever suspect. You have heard of Martin Longueval, then. I suppose, Sir Henry, this is your doing?—Yes, a distant relation."

"And also related," Masters persisted, "to Mr. Ravelle's family?"

Guy shrugged. "Remotely, I believe. Have you examined that box?"

The question was just a shade too careless, so careless that Guy's voice quavered with the effort. Why? Tairlaine stared at the box. There was no death-trap in it. Well, then? He glanced up at H.M., whose face was wooden again.

"Very interestin'," replied H.M. with a peculiar inflection. "I can't see anything wrong with it, but then I'm not an expert. Maybe an expert can tell me. Never mind that, though. Did Longueval make any of the furniture in this room?"

Guy hesitated, and evidently came to a decision.

"Yes, I believe he did. I have certain letters which seem to indicate it. But I can't tell you what."

For some purpose of his own, H.M. deliberately turned his attention from Guy to the girl in the doorway.

"Come in, miss," he invited affably. "Come in and sit down and make yourself comfortable. If you're afraid of the other fixings, there's a dining-room chair that's guaranteed harmless. H'm. You're the gal who's engaged to Hippocrates Erectus, ain't you?"

"To? . . . Oh!" She looked at him as though scenting an attack on her *fiancé*, and became defiant. "If you mean Dr. Arnold; yes, I am. And you needn't be rude to me, too. I know you don't like him. Oh, he told me about you! He said the police didn't know their place, and he was going to report you to the Chief Commissioner."

"To old Boko? . . . Come to think of it," said H.M., with an angry start of recollection, "that so-and-so still owes me thirty quid he lost shootin' dice that time the House sat all night on the Milk Bill or some tomfool thing, curse him. Thanks for the reminder, my dear. You're a nice gal."

"Oh, I know." Wrinkling one eyebrow, she spoke with her own candor. "Alan told him who you were, and then Eugene admitted he must have been mistaken. Eugene knows your wife and your daughter and ever so many people you know. Eugene says that in your own time, before you were old, you know, your work was handled quite creditably." She smiled a little, meditatively, and then burst out: "But I say, you *do* take things easily, all of you! All this place has been a bogey to me, ever since I can remember. And now a man's killed in some horrible way we don't know, and you sit about in here as comfortably as though you were in a club!"

"It's one way of exorcisin' the devils, you'll admit, hey? But I did want to ask you: Just what do you think of the whole mess?"

She shifted. "Well . . . I didn't have much sympathy to waste on that nasty little Bender while he was alive. Oh, I'm sorry he's dead, and he was very conscientious, and he's a martyr, and all that! But I didn't like the way he went snooping about, and asking you funny questions you couldn't understand, and looking at you in a funny way. . . . Brr!"

"I know. Did you spot him as a loony-doctor?"

"Good Lord, *no,*" she said quickly. She was flushed. "If I had—well, I could almost hate Gene for hiding his little watchdog in the house. It seems to me there ought to be moderation in all things, especially in virtue. I like a man to be a human being, and get drunk and play the fool and lose his opportunities if he must do it, but at least not go mucking about with people's minds."

"Uh-huh. Like young Carstairs?"

"Bah," said Judith.

"I was only wondering." H.M. looked at Guy. "Did you spot Bender?"

"Eh?—Oh! No, I confess I didn't. I didn't pay much attention to him. I noticed his behavior, of course, but I thought he was only one of those amateur psychologists who pester you with their hobby. Besides," added Guy, with a wicked gleam of shrewdness behind his glasses, "he was such a solemn-minded young ass that I couldn't help anticipating his questions with answers that must have puzzled him considerably. Let's get down to it, Sir Henry? Exactly what do you wish to ask me?"

"Oh, I'm not unduly worried, son. I hear you got a good sound alibi. . . . Don't bow. So has everybody else in the whole place, which is worrying our friend Masters a good deal."

"Tut, tut," said Guy maliciously. "Sorry, Inspector."

"I also hear that you didn't believe in any poison-trick planted in this room," pursued H.M. "In fact, that you tut-tutted the whole idea."

"So she told you that. H'm! Frankly, I don't know. I scouted the whole idea because I thought it might make Isabel feel better. But I don't deny there might be such a thing. If everybody has an alibi, then a death-trap prepared beforehand would eliminate your difficulties, wouldn't it?"

"Ho ho! Unfortunately, it wouldn't. Somebody was in this room imitating Bender's voice; somebody pinched his notebook, put a little roll of parchment on his chest——"

"What?" Again Guy was caught off guard. It was a jump of genuine surprise; that Tairlaine could have sworn; and for a second it unnerved him. He opened and shut his mouth. Also, for the first time he began to look afraid. "You—er—parchment, you say? Yes. Excuse me, but you have a happy knack of taking me off balance. I congratulate you. May I see this—whatever-it-is?"

H.M. held it out. The other's hands were unsteady when he fumbled at it, and he had to flatten it on the table. After a pause he raised his head.

"Know what it is?" inquired H.M.

"Yes, I know what it is," he said quietly. Then his voice grew shrill. "It's an attempt to implicate *me*, that's what it is. Look here, Judith. Recognize that?"

She came swishing over in one of those ruffle-skirted evening-gowns which seemed to fit into the antiquity of the room, and her shoulders gleamed under the gaslight. But she would not come close to the table.

"It looks," she said, "like some of your——"

"It is. I bought half a dozen sheets of this stuff, gentlemen, as anybody in the house can tell you. This has been snipped off one of them. It's not the common vegetable parchment they use for maps and charts; it's made of goatskin, and damned expensive."

"You admit it's yours?" demanded Masters.

"I tell you," Guy cried, beginning to drop his elaborate affectations and act for the first time like an ordinary human being, "I had absolutely nothing to do with it! You're not lying to me, are you? You're not trying to trap me? You really did find it——?"

"Funny thing, now," said H.M., "but I believe you're tellin' the truth. What did you happen to want with parchment, anyhow?"

Guy groped after a chair and sat down.

"You may as well hear about it from me. I don't know whether I can make it clear to you, if you happen to be endowed with too much common sense. But I'll try. My hobby, one of my hobbies, is investigating ancient superstitions. High and low magic; occultism, necromancy, divinations, all the mumbo-jumbo of literally raising the devil. It fascinates me, like a toy. It——"

"I say, why apologize?" interposed Judith with some impatience. She faced the others composedly. "I love all that sort of thing, because I think what fun it would be if it really *could* happen. I like stuffed crocodiles, and magicians burning herbs—not that Guy does anything like that. But he has a thumping big library."

"It's something to do, anyhow," said Guy, "when you happen to be bored. As I am." He stirred. "I have the usual lot, like Horst and Ennemoser and Sibley; and a truck-load of odd stuff I've picked up, even what purports to be a translation of the *Great Grimoire.* I keep on with it, in spite of being so much irritated by Alan. He chooses to be amused. *I* choose to pull his leg as much as I can, and, by God, I'll give him a real scare one of these days! You heard what he said to-night? So, if I care to buy parchment and amuse myself by sketching a Pentacle of Solomon . . ." He shrugged, drearily.

H.M. studied him. "What about the inscription, then?"

This time Guy took longer to answer. He looked as though

something hitherto unsuspected had occurred to him, and a sudden triumphant malevolence began to creep round his mouth.

"Inscription? Oh, that? I don't know what it is. That is to say, it's clearly a talisman to banish an evil of some sort. Probably one of Albertus Magnus's recipes. I'll have a look for it, if you like, but Albertus wrote twenty thick folio volumes." He peered round softly towards Sir George. "*You* don't recognize it?"

"No," said Sir George curtly. "But I shouldn't be at all surprised if you did, Guy. Steady!—I don't mean you wrote it or put it where we found it. I only say you recognize it."

"Do I? Well, you may think what you like about that. Ha ha ha. I tell you this: we shan't be any wiser if we do spot the quotation. Some fool—" his fist clenched—"some fool copied out a talisman at random, and put it down there because it would lead straight to me. I'm the only one it could lead to."

"Got any idea who it might be?"

"Perhaps."

"Then, sir," Masters interposed heavily, "if you'll be so good as to give us a tip, I'm sure we should appreciate it. After all, you know, the burden of proof lies with you. We've only your word for it that you didn't——"

"Would I be such an ass? . . . No, Inspector; I don't mean to point out anybody to you. That would be slander, wouldn't it? And I am only a younger son, without patrimony. I couldn't stand being sued." He showed his teeth. "Perhaps I shall work on a theory of my own. You say someone stole Bender's notebook. Any other clews on which you want my opinion?"

H.M. laid the nine of spades on the table.

"Found beside his body, this little feller. I say, does it mean anything? Either practically or in cartomancy?"

"Beside his body, eh? Interesting! Now, I wonder—You flatter me, Sir Henry. Any gypsy fortune-teller can inform you that spades always mean trouble. The nine, I believe, is especially bad. This is a very pretty little problem. But I am beginning to wonder whether this card was put there as an omen after all."

H.M. leaned across the table. "You're in a bleedin' good humor all of a sudden," he said sharply. "What's on your mind?"

"I am in such a good humor," Guy acknowledged, "that I will give you a hint. That card unquestionably gives *me* a hint. By Gad, I never before fancied myself as a criminologist! It's a line I must take up. Remind me of that, Judith. Now, in trying to reason out this problem logically, if I may say so, you are committing one fatal blunder. You are not starting at the beginning. What is the beginning?"

H.M. swept his arm about the room.

"This is the beginning," he growled. "This is the beginning of the whole hocus-pocus that had its last performance to-night. The clew, the big thunderin' clew, is somewhere in the history of this room! And that's what we want to hear from you. Not any fancy theories——"

"Delighted to oblige. But listen to me one moment," urged the other. His finger-nail made a small ticking noise on the table as he tapped it. "I meant the beginning of Bender's murder. What is the beginning of that? Bender comes to this house. He comes as a physician to discover which of us is the crackbrained sadist who strangled that parrot and cut the dog's throat." Guy's sudden laughter made Tairlaine jump. "He comes as the nemesis of the madhouse. And he finds the mad—person. So he has to die."

"That's ridiculous!" cried Judith. "Guy, do stop putting on airs and be natural! Stop it, do you hear? That's exactly the voice you used to use when you'd tell me ghost-stories about . . ."

Staring uneasily at the table and chairs, her face was again flushed, and she stamped her foot in a curiously childish gesture. She looked appealingly at Tairlaine, who cleared his throat for a mighty, if pedantic, pronouncement. Guy was urbane.

"But you are not a child now, my dear. You are thirty-one. Let me go on. Bender, then, was marked for death from that source. And, in the alleged 'game' to-night, by what seems a curious coincidence he drew the card that would send him for the vigil in this room! Tut, tut. Can we believe that the card was given him *by accident?*"

"Go on," said H.M. in a wooden tone.

"Thank you. You can see, gentlemen, that coincidence is strained to a breaking-point when he receives not only the winning ace, but, by a too-picturesque stroke also receives the significant ace of spades which goes in romance under the name of the death card. It wasn't accident, then. But if it wasn't accident, then how the devil was it managed?

"Think about that for a moment. Cards can be stacked, yes, for a deal in a game. But in this case the cards were simply spread fan-wise on a tray, and passed round by Shorter for everyone to take his or her choice. And Bender was the last to choose. How could a card have been palmed off on him—if he chose the card himself? There," nodded Guy, rubbing his hands, "is as neat a little problem as I have met. What is your solution, Sir Henry?"

H.M., who had sprawled his bulk in one of the satin-wood chairs, stopped with his pipe half-way to his lips. He did not move or blink when he said:

"Masters, I said I was a fool. Masters, my lad, I'm worse than that. I don't even see plain facts to be foolish about." Still he did not raise his voice. "Oh, my God, what an ass. And I saw it, and yet I never suspected.—Get that chap Shorter in here, quick! Tell him to bring along the pack of cards that was used to-night. Don't ask questions, dammit! Cut along and do what I tell you." When the chief inspector had been urged out of the room, H.M. regarded Guy somberly. "For the moment you win, son. My bay-leaves are pretty bedraggled."

"I don't know what you're thinking," said Judith, and stared at him with wide eyes, "but Shorter—that's absurd! He's been with us for years. He was here in my mother's time."

"You don't understand," observed Guy. "But I believe Sir Henry does."

Masters brought in a very much disconcerted Shorter, who nevertheless did not look guilty. He had an air of outraged dignity.

"I don't know what this man wants, sir," he said to H.M. "But here are the cards that were used to-night. I gathered them all up and put them back in the box. If you wish to see them . . ."

"Right," said H.M. drowsily. "Now count 'em."

"Sir?"

"Count 'em! You know how to count, don't you?"

Peering round nervously, Shorter drew out the pack; he fumbled and nearly spilled them, but his count was painstaking. Then he frowned.

"Well, sir? I really don't see what is wrong. There are fifty-two."

"Right. Now go through 'em again, look at each card, and see if you can spot anything queer. Don't ask me what! Just tell me if you do."

"Look here, what the devil is this?" demanded Sir George.

"Easy, now! You'll see. That's right, Shorter me lad; take your time. Easy does it. . . . *Aah!* There we got it! What's wrong?"

Shorter had the look of a performer struck with stage-fright. He said:

"I don't know how this can happen, sir. I may be wrong, but it seems to me there are *two* aces of spades."

"Sure there are. Masters," said H.M. sadly, "there's one of our nice little clews shot to blazes. Oh, Bender put on a good performance. You won't remember because you didn't see it, but the others will. Remember how—when he drew a card at the dinner-table—Bender put it down under the table as though to look at it without bein' seen? Remember that—for all his actin' to avoid suspicion—he couldn't keep a hard little grin off his face when he produced the ace of spades? Remember that earlier in the evening a pack of cards in the hall cabinet was taken out and rifled for no good reason? Ah, you see what happened now. Bender pinched the ace of spades out of another pack. At the dinner-table he simply substituted it for the card he had really drawn. He was last to display, y'see, and he knew nobody had drawn the real ace from the real pack. . . . Uh-huh. For some reason he *wanted* to be the one who came in this room. . . . And that nine of spades was in his own coat-pocket all the time. Notice how crumpled it is? He was reachin' for somethin' in his own pocket when he felt the poison get him, and he dragged it out when he fell. The nine of spades, that we fatheads thought might be a clew, was only the card he really drew at the table. . . . I could kick myself, Masters, burn me, I could!"

CHAPTER EIGHT

Talisman on a Dead Man's Chest

"NEAT!" SAID Sir George.

"Elementary," said Guy, and laughed unpleasantly. "Yes, I fancy that is the way it happened. And it interests me greatly to encounter a detective problem in which the dead man turns out to be the villain. I suppose the fellow didn't really commit an elaborate suicide?"

Masters took longer to chew over and digest all this. He paced up and down, rubbing his heavy chin, and occasionally giving a hopeful glance at his notebook as though for inspiration.

"That's all very well, sir," he pondered. "But I don't see it helps us. Far from it! Frankly, I always thought that nine of spades was a footling little clew to begin with. And now we've proved it's no clew at all, it asks us rather a queer question. Why should Mr. Bender have been so interested in staying in this room?"

"I know that now," said H.M., "for my errors. Son, he hoped the murderer would come and get him! He was putting himself out for bait. And the murderer did come. . . . You know, Bender had his nerve right along with him. I wonder if Bender had a weapon in his pocket, and pulled out the nine of spades when he drew it? If so, it's gone."

Masters was excited. "Stop a bit! This may not be so bad after all. I've *got* it, sir! I've got it, and a little search may be able to prove it. Like this—" He stopped abruptly, and looked round the group.

"All right, all right!" growled H.M. "Go on. I dare say you're among friends. But even if you do happen to be speakin' before the guilty wretch, which is a remote possibility; and even if you do happen to be right, which is remoter still; all the same I'll take the responsibility for your give-away. What's the brain wave?"

Masters peered round the room with narrowed eyes. "It's just this, sir. And, by George, with a little search we may be able to establish the whole thing! I mean there may really be a poison-trap here after all."

"Oh, my God," said H.M. "You don't say so, now? Is that the idea of blazin' originality that's suddenly hit you? What the hell do you think we've been talking about all night?"

The chief inspector was unruffled.

"All very well to rag. But it's my explanation that's original. You proved, didn't you, that the playing card fell out of Mr. Bender's pocket? Just so. And as for that little roll of parchment that's been bothering us—what's to prevent its having fallen out of his pocket as well?"

"I tell you, Inspector," said Guy, "I never gave——"

"Easy, sir. There might be a dozen explanations why he had it. Let me go on. Mr. Bender comes in here hoping to trap the murderer. What he don't know is that the murderer has set a trap, loaded with curare, in one of the ornaments or the furniture or somewhere. Eh? He gets the dose and suddenly realizes what's happened. In his pocket he's got an accusation against the murderer all written out: in that notebook. What does he think of doing? If he can't help himself, of hiding that notebook! Of hiding it somewhere so that they'll find it before the murderer. He has just strength enough to shove it away somewhere—maybe into the bed somewhere, which accounts for his position when he fell. And as he takes it out of his *inside* pocket, both the card and the roll of parchment come with it. The card lands beside him. The roll, by a queer accident, on his chest. And there," said the chief inspector, "is the whole thing."

H.M. sat up slowly.

"Oh, love-a-duck," he breathed in an awed tone. "Oh, Esau, my son! Y'know, I've heard rummy reconstructions in the course of a misspent life, but I still had to wait for one that defied the law of gravity as well as the law of common-sense. Do you really believe that, son?"

"I do. Everybody here has an alibi for the time of the murder. The window is covered with locked steel shutters, and the door was watched by five people. Well, then?"

"If I got to tell you what's wrong with it, I will." He looked at Guy. "*You* see anything wrong with that?"

"But it sounds silly!" protested Judith. "I'm sorry, Mr. Masters; I know you know a lot more about it than we do; but it *is* silly. You mean he had strength enough to rush over and hide a notebook, to take it out of his inside pocket and shove it away, but he still hadn't strength to cry out? I mean, it's like saying that a drowning man has the strength to toss his hat ashore so it won't get spoiled, but is too exhausted to yell for help. . . . And if he pulled out the card and the parchment with the notebook, they'd both have fallen, wouldn't they? And he was lying *on his back;* I saw him. In that case, you see, the parchment would have had to hover about in the air until he had fallen, and then settle down in the middle of his shirt. Sort of like a dicky-bird, you know. . . . Now you're going to chuck me out of the room. But I still think it's silly!"

"Steady, Judith," said Guy. "I shall have to take your side, Inspector. It seems a bit—strained. But even if we do accept everything else, how do you explain the voice from this room?"

Masters said quietly: "I'm not called on, you know, to explain anything to you. If I allow any latitude, it's because Sir Henry exists. But I've heard of mechanical contrivances that could reproduce a voice. . . . All right, all right! Certain people are entitled to make funny faces if it makes 'em feel any better. It's past two o'clock, but I've still a job of work to do to-night. I've got three men here, and in my plain uninspired way I'm going to make *sure* about this room. Hum! Care to stay and help us?"

H.M. said he had other business. He said he was going to Mantling's study, and insisted that the others go with him. Guy, who was watching Masters sharply from behind his dark shield, waited until they were ready to go; then he laid his hand on the silver casket.

"You've examined this box, you tell me, and found nothing wrong with it? Yes. Then, since it's in the clear as evidence, would you mind my taking it along with me? I'm interested. Mere sentimentality, of course, but I think I shall just——"

Masters' hand went out as Guy reached after the box. Whatever Masters thought, not a muscle moved in his face. His voice was colorless.

"Sorry, sir. Nothing can be moved yet. I dare say there's no good reason why you shouldn't take it along, but that's the rule. . . . What would you be wanting it for, just between ourselves?"

"I don't want it particularly," said Guy. He was cool, but a little of that former inexplicable and ugly flare—rage, desperation, fear, or sheer perversity?—stirred in his long face. The sheer repression made him look dangerous, as though he were seeking a loophole. You could never place him. In one moment he was easy and pleasant, in the next affected, and in the next horribly reptilian. His voice shook now. "No, I don't want it particularly. I don't want the box. But there's—there's a miniature inside, I think I told you, that I should rather like to . . . Suspicious? Ha ha ha. What rot!"

Masters wrenched open the lid, watching Guy covertly. He fished out the discolored metal object Tairlaine had already seen. Flat and oval in shape, not more than three inches long, the metal was a sheath for a smaller miniature painted on ivory. On one side was a woman's face, on the other a man's. It was sealed in thin glass with a gold locket-link at the top, so that the rich hues were undimmed and every fine line preserved.

Guy took it gently, and Judith ran to him to see it.

"Charles Brixham," he said, brushing his finger-tips across the glass, "the first who died here, and his wife. Surely I may——?"

"Let him have it, Masters," said H.M.

While they went out of the room, Judith took the miniature and studied it as she walked. It seemed to fascinate her so that she could scarcely let it go. But she handed it to Tairlaine, and for the first time shadows out of the past grew to tangible beings in this house. They peopled that gimcrack room with the ordinary affairs of living, of sleeping and lighting candles and looking into mirrors, which made more terrible the death that struck out of it.

One face was that of a youth in his early twenties, thin,

with the fire of the visionary, gentle to the point of weakness. He wore his own hair in a queue behind, a neckcloth and buttoned-up brown riding coat. His fingers were on his chin as though in thought. Though the pictured face was floridly colored, you suspected pallor; a mind lightly balanced, and liable to snap from sheer weight of dreams. . . . The woman's face was a contrast, gentle in its own way, with a round Latin prettiness and dark eyes, but it had a kind of bouncing practicality which sat on her as firmly as the curls of the powdered wig. Her face seemed naturally florid, her mouth severe.

"Do you think she looks like me?" Judith demanded unexpectedly. "Guy says so, from the big picture of her upstairs, but I'm dashed if I see *any* resemblance. Different color eyes and hair, everything; and if I ever get as fat-faced as that I'll jolly well cut my throat. Why did painters in those days make everybody look so round and goggle-eyed, as though they'd had air pumped into their faces; especially the French ones? No, I'm hanged if I see *any* resemblance."

"She was a very clever woman, my dear," said Guy.

The faces haunted Tairlaine even when they returned to Mantling's study, from the open door of which proceeded sharp rattling noises and a sound of smothered profanity. A constable on guard at the door, peering in with much interest, was dispatched to Masters by a growl from H.M. By the light of the lamp on the desk, Ravelle and Carstairs were bending over a bagatelle board. The former, counting up with fierce intentness, was using some lurid language at having scored only five hundred for twenty balls; Carstairs looked guilty and hastily swept up a pile of silver.

"We had to do something!" Carstairs bawled, glancing at Judith. "They're trying to segregate us or something, and they wouldn't let us out." He was aggrieved. "Dammit, Judy, you needn't look at me as though I were something that had got into your salad! I offered to help you and sympathize with you, I offered to . . ."

"You must not mind him," Ravelle consoled, with expansive indulgence. "He is whiffled, you understand. He has been drinking the whisky-soda. Ha ha ha. He say to me, 'Old man, I offer her consolation, and she spurn my consolation.' Then he take a drink of whisky-soda. I say, 'Yes, old man, but what is it that you have to console her about?' He say, 'It is not that, but it is the principle of the thing.' Then he take another drink of whisky-soda. Blimey! I am like an Englishman myself, but I do not understand the English. Perhaps that it would be better that I have another drink of whisky-soda. Old man, I tell you what I do: I will shoot you ten up for a bleeding tanner a ball, what?"

"You take that damn bagatelle-board," bellowed H.M., "and— Hum! No! Wait a bit. Where's everybody? Where's Mantling?"

"Lying down," Carstairs answered eagerly, as though to reëstablish himself. "Look here, I can't imagine what's happened to Alan. He's the coolest of the lot in a tight place, I can tell you. But he seemed to go all to pieces over this business. I don't understand it. I——"

"Uh-huh. What about Miss Isabel?"

Ravelle said: "She has a fit, I think. Blimey, what is the matter with her? Look at what has happened! While we are in here, she rush in and run over to this desk. *Alors,* she start to pull out the drawers and chuck things all over the floor. There is a bobby on guard at the door. That one jumps after her . . ."

"Stow it, will you?" said Carstairs. He seemed nervous. "It's a lot of rot, but she kicked up a good deal of commotion. Judy, you'd better speak to her. She's got some sort of crazy idea that those little darts Alan and I brought back—not the arrows or the spears, but the little fellers about two inches long—well, that they're poisoned . . ."

"And aren't they?" inquired Guy, very softly. "It seems to me you bragged about them yourself."

"Yes, I know. But it's all very well to say you've got something like that when you know there's a thousand-to-one chance against it. Makes it interesting," retorted Carstairs, with heat. "For instance——"

"They are not concerned with your notions of what is interesting," said Judith quickly, "any more than I am. If you want me to speak frankly, it is bad enough to have you in the house at all. I can't help that, because you happen to be a friend of my brother's. But while you are here, I expect you to show some amount of common decency. Well, you may drink your beastly whisky-soda. I'm sure *I* can't prevent it. You may tell your nasty bragging lies about . . ." She turned, breathing hard. "What was it you wanted to see Guy and me about, Sir Henry?"

Carstairs stopped and stared, as though at a light in his brain.

"Oh, Lord," he breathed. "So that's it?"

There was a flurry of ruffled skirts, and Judith was out of the room. Carstairs remained looking blankly at the door; then with a slow gesture he lifted his arm and brought it down again as though he were shooting dice. Tairlaine, who expected to find H.M. bellowing at this nonsense, was surprised to find him pacifying.

"Well . . . now," said H.M. "You know, I rather thought there might 'a' been trouble somewhere."

"It's those damned spears," said Carstairs. "But how was I going to know that? She never said anything at the time. She only laughed, and so I thought . . . You see, she says she hates sentimentality. And women have such funny ideas nowadays that sometimes that's true. So how are you going to know? Then I was in here one afternoon, you see, pitching her the hell of a yarn about those spears, and whirling one of 'em round my head, and I accidentally stuck myself in the hand with it. I admit I felt queer for a second, but I thought I might as well use it for all it was worth in case it happened to be true. So I said, 'Judy old girl, I'm a goner.' Then I sort of acted a bit, the way they do in the films. By Gad, I was surprised at how eloquent I could get when I had a clear field with no gullies or coverts! I told her how I felt about her and then I said, 'But it's no use, Judy old girl, because my time has come and I'm smacking well finished.' Haa! Then she told me a lot of things," beamed Carstairs, arching his chest, "which I will not repeat, because a gentleman don't. But when I told her the same things a week before, only less so, she called 'em Nauseating Slush. The trouble was, you see, that she went out crying for the doctor or somebody. Then unfortunately she came back and caught me sneaking a quick one out of the bottle, to keep my courage up, when I was supposed to be *non compos* in the chair. That tore it, although I sort of grabbed her . . ."

Ravelle shook his head. He tapped a finger against his nose.

"*Dans l'amour, mon vieux,*" he announced, with that profound and didactic gravity with which many of his countrymen approach this subject, "*il faut s'approcher de la femme avec le plus grand soin, voyez*. You should have been more gradual. I impress upon you that always you must do the thing gradually. And when the time arrive that it is no longer possible to be gradual, then it is too late to bother about it anyway."

"All right, all right," growled H.M. "And then she laughed,

hey, and treated it as a joke and said she knew all along? And you were fine and friendly that afternoon? And then two or three days later she suddenly flared up about nothing at all, breakin' the whole business off? Uh-huh. Now look here, curse you! I'm not here to listen to silly ravings. I want to know about that poison."

"It wasn't poisoned, worse luck," Carstairs said gloomily.

"What about the rest of the stuff?"

"Oh, the spears and arrows are all right. I think Alan's darts are all right, too. But you'll soon know. I told you, didn't I, that the old lady cut up a row? Well, that brought in first the copper at the door, and then a sergeant and another copper and some fingerprint chaps who were comparing results in the front room. They took the darts with 'em. Arnold had to lead Isabel upstairs. I suppose she's all right now."

"That's all, then. Cut along. Yes, get out! You'll know where to go, but don't leave the house yet . . . No, steady!" He held back Ravelle as Carstairs, muttering to himself, was not long in going in pursuit. "No more shootin' bagatelle to-night. We want you here to listen to a little piece of family history."

"Family history? What family, old man?"

"Yours," said H.M. "Y'know, you didn't tell us you were related to the Brixhams."

Ravelle's eyes narrowed a little. But he retained his grinning affability, though his forehead assumed an air of bewilderment.

"I say, old man, is it a joke? I am much honored, of course, but who is it says I am related to my friends here?"

"The police," answered Guy. "And I say so, for another. I traced it back a bit, you see. I don't think anybody else knows. Certainly Alan doesn't. I thought it best to keep my own counsel, because I wondered why you hadn't mentioned it yourself."

"Well, I will be frank," said Ravelle suddenly. "*Tiens,* you need not be so solemn as that! It is nothing. I have heard there is a very leetle relationship, yes. It is so small that we can be very good friends. Now! I tell you. I have come here to buy things, maybe. Well!—would I wish to embarrass my friends? Suppose I say, 'Alan, old man, you have got to let me have this or this at my price, because I am related to you.' No, no, no! That is what we call not to be sporting, eh? So I will not do it."

Guy bowed.

"Since we both know that isn't true," he said, "everything is what we call sporting, and we can let it go at that. I don't mind."

"Good! Thanks a thousand times," acknowledged Ravelle, not at all perturbed, and with a genial return of the bow. "I am too full of the whisky-soda to-night to think of a good one off my hand, eh? Besides, I am thinking of that poor chap who came to the end so damn sinistair, and I am glad it was not me. What have you found, may I ask? The policeman would not tell. I am interested."

"Uh-huh. You had an ancestor who was interested in things like that, too," observed H.M. "Do you know if the eighteenth-century Martin Longueval made any of the things in that room?"

Ravelle raised his eyebrows. "I assure you, sir, I do not know of any Martin Longueval so old. I do not know of any Martin Longueval before my great uncle."

"Then," said H.M. slowly, "if you're not interested in furniture, I wonder if you're interested in *putty,* now? I know Guy is."

There was a dead silence. So long had this shot remained in abeyance that Tairlaine had almost forgotten it, forgotten the words Isabel had said Guy used in her sitting-room. It had a startling effect, but not an effect on the person Tairlaine would have supposed. Guy merely glanced round; after a brief pause he lifted his hands and applauded softly. But Ravelle, who was lighting a cigarette, burnt his fingers with the match. He turned away with picturesque language to hurl the stump into the fire, and also to conceal his face. When he turned back again his face was still amiable as though with a thick plaster, the veins standing out bluish against the temples.

"Puddy?" he repeated. "I beg your pardon, sir, but what is puddy? I do not understand." He cleared his throat. "Some words are harder than others, and I do not know puddy."

"In all likelihood, my friend," said Guy with great urbanity, "you understand better than he does. I like these Merrivale shots in the dark. So well do I like them that, when I tell you about the Widow's Room, I am going to be really frank. I hadn't intended to be frank, but you deserve it. You will see the whole clew to those deaths—if you are keen enough. I give you that challenge." His wrinkled face was delighted as he moved over to the sideboard in the dim light. "A glass of port to keep my throat clear. Let me see. Alan has it in one of these compartments. . . ."

He saw that they were watching him, and had heard a queer note in his voice that made them watch him still more closely. He had the air of a furtive conjuror. Looking at the two lower doors of the sideboard, he turned the key of the right-hand one, still talking.

"You must try Alan's '98. Why do all sideboard doors stick so, I wonder? There seems no reason why they should warp in a warm room, any more than someone's brain. This one—ah!"

It screeched loudly as he got it open. Guy stood back so that his shadow should not block the light from the lamp on the table. And Tairlaine, who was staring over Sir George's shoulder, saw a face.

The face was looking up at them from the inside of the sideboard, its eyes wide open. Tairlaine saw what it was, with a flurry of relief mounting to anger, just as Guy chuckled.

"Must be the other side.—Sorry, gentlemen! I hope that didn't give you a start? Alan has enormous gusto, and a childish robust sort of humor in elementary things. He takes great pleasure in making that dummy tell questionable anecdotes before his friends. . . . Perhaps I neglected to tell you that my brother is an expert amateur ventriloquist?"

He dragged open the other door.

CHAPTER NINE

The Legend

"The story of the Widow's Room," said Guy, "begins in the month of August, and in the city of Paris, and in the year 1792. It begins with the Terror, but it has not ended yet."

He sat behind the desk, in the little pool of light which glowed red through the glass of port before him. The miniature lay there, too. He picked it up, exhibiting the face of the young man to the four auditors who sat about him. And Guy's face looked as fanatic as the pictured one.

"Charles Brixham was the only son of the founder of our house. In that year he was twenty; he had just completed a year of study at Paris, and his letters home (patterned after Rousseau, but with even more flower-choked frenzy) show that the French Revolution was still his idol. 'We have labored for three years'—he wrote this in April—'and the end is not yet, but, please God, what we have achieved we have achieved with less bloodshed than the civil courts of England inflict in six months. Our new Girondist ministry is gently firm. There are, *ça va sans dire,* men of extreme views, in a thrice-damnable club calling itself the Jacobins, but these M. Roland will know how to control.'

"His father at home, a self-made rich man but as fanatical a revolutionist as his son, appears to have derided this view; and in a couple of ill-spelt letters repeats bluntly that you can't kill a goose without wringing its neck. Apparently there was trouble about this, for in one letter Charles declares passionately that he 'will disown him kith and kin, nor accept a penny more' from a father who has such beliefs. That's strong talk, you see, but the pale young fool meant it. In 1792 we have him living at austere lodgings in the rue St. Julien le Pauvre, hard by the river at the Ile de la Cité; wearing worsted stockings and his hair without powder, reading Rousseau by a tallow dip, sharing his bread and cheese, and haunting the rowdy galleries at the National Assembly.

"Any child could have seen the typhoon coming, when the Girondist ministry declared war on Austria. The French army was rotted with treason, without money, and its officers fleeing. When it went to pieces before the enemy, the yell of treason went through France; the Austrian queen was denounced, Lafayette had retreated, and Marat called for heads. They quieted this when the king spoke soft words and wore a red cap before the mob. Then Prussia declared war, and was on the march for Paris.

"The Jacobins uprose in power. Charles Brixham was at the Orléans Gate when the men of Marseilles marched in 'against a yellow sunset, with their drums banging, and singing a catch I could not understand.' He was struck down in the mob for raising a cry for M. Roland, and lay insensible in a doorway while there roared past him the first triumph of the greatest battle-song in the history of the world.

"But he records everything else; he heard it shaking Paris's gables many times again. On the tenth of August Danton swept the Assembly. In his lodgings Charles Brixham heard the firing from the direction of the Tuileries. He ran out, presently heard that the Swiss Guards were slaughtered and the king and queen taken, but could not get near because the bridges were so crowded. Anyhow, the National Assembly was overthrown. With the three props of glory in Danton, Marat, and Robespierre, the guillotine went to work in the Place de la Révolution.

"And then Charles Brixham fell in love.

"I suppose the fool couldn't help himself. He had been too much blown up on airy rhetoric, and too much starved; but the first time he saw Marie-Hortense he seems to have fallen past hope. The circumstances are curious. He had been carried in the crowd up against the walls of the Hôtel de Ville on the day the commune met—this was on the 16th of August, three days after poor fat little royalty had been shut up in the Temple—and Charles Brixham clung to a window with two or three others, listening to the debate. He heard Robespierre speak, urging a Revolutionary Tribunal; 'a prim little man,' he writes, 'with a greenish warty face like a cucumber, standing very stiff as though to balance the spectacles on the end of his nose, and a singularly sweet voice.' Then somebody else spoke, I don't know who, but it was a cry for blood. Charles Brixham tried to shriek out some imprecation, but he was half mad and all French had fled his wits. He gabbled something in English, which was evidently taken for approval. In the excitement he was elbowed off his perch, tumbled into the crowd, and found himself flat against a buttress, the tears streaming down his face, and being helped up by a woman in a hooded cloak."

Guy saw that he had caught his audience. Lifting the other side of the miniature, he displayed the woman's round face with its shrewd merry eyes and hard mouth.

"She said to him, 'I know English, and the milor' must be mad.' To which this fool must bawl in French, 'Down with the damned Jacobin murderers,' and the mob closed in. He was back against the angle of the buttress, the woman behind him, and it was close work, but he held that buttress for five minutes, until his sword was broken on the wall. The surge piled in and must have caught somebody else by mistake. He found little gray-cloak, head down, forcing him out. Presently they came exhausted to the river, and sat down on the steps by the oily water. She would not tell him her name, saying, '*Faut pas faire des bêtises*'; but she kissed him and said, 'I will see you again.'

"Mark the effect on a visionary youth, his brain half turned by the smash of political ideals and fed by love-notions from *La Nouvelle Héloïse.* An unknown woman had become his goddess; she was all he had left. He writes to his father in the wildest style of the day, 'I have beheld an angel's countenance on mortal woman,' to which Brixham senior seems to have jeered and offered crude if practical suggestions which led for a time to the breaking-off of the correspondence. In the ensuing month he left his rooms, left off prayer for the end of bloodshed, only to prowl the streets in search of her; and meantime came the fury of the September Massacres.

"Paris grew slippery with blood, but he was untouched. He found her again on the night the Goddess Reason was crowned amid flowers and caperings, in the new Year I of the Republic. He met her far from the torchlight, slipping out of a door in the rue du Temple with what looked like account books under her arm, so that he vowed she had been on an errand of mercy. Although she seemed glad to see him, she drew back. But they went to a wineshop, where he was dizzy with the sight of 'an angel's countenance on mortal woman,' and her smiles. At her suggestion she accompanied him to his lodgings; they stayed there three days, at the time of the warm rains and the yellowing leaves, and were very happy. She said briskly, 'Yes, now we must marry, but not yet,' and still would not tell him her name. She slipped away on the fourth morning, while he was asleep, but left a note.

"There was nothing he could do. He waited long, and still had not seen her by the raw January day when they cut off the head of Louis Capet, whilom king of France. Charles Brixham saw it done. He saw it from a great distance in the mob, where ladders and opera-glasses fetched high prices. In an interval somebody lent him a glass to see the splashed engine, and the two executioners swathed in coarse overalls to keep their clothes clean. But the glass was jerked away when a tubby little figure was impelled up the stairs, and seemed bewildered. Louis Capet's hair was pinned up under a cap before he knew it; he was hustled forward with expert smoothness, and tilted under the knife. Charles B. shut his eyes; but just before that stupefying roar went up, he heard the three separate thuds with which the engine worked.*

"He stumbled away as the cart drove up to receive head and body. He remembered the curses of an envious neighbor, who said that Sanson the executioner would make a pretty bit from selling locks of Louis Capet's hair. And presently, out of his very horror at this smooth expert butchery, he began to wonder about the mechanics of it; where the dead went when those mounds of

---

* Although it seems unnecessary to insist on historical accuracy, in a story so slight, it might be pointed out here that Mr. Brixham's account agrees with the records of the time in almost every particular. For details as to the managing of the executions, *c. f.* M. L. Lenôtre's remarkable book, *The Guillotine and Its Servants*

heads and bodies were driven away together, what became of their clothes or effects, even how often *La Luisette's* blade had to be sharpened or replaced. They were not good thoughts. You can see this strain weirdly mingled in our family's character ever since, of the visionary with the practical, so that I can be practical about studying magic, and Alan visionary about murdering rhinoceri.

"Charles Brixham's rooms were not far from the prison of the Concièrgérie. Sometimes he went to watch the latest batch brought out to the tumbrils, prodded with musket-butts, their arms bound behind, 'so that,' he writes in his journal, 'they could climb with difficulty into the carts, and many stumbled—feeling keenly this semblance of fear when the onlookers jeered, and therefore pressing their arms tightly to keep from shivering when the day was raw and rainy.' Moreover, he began to drink costly brandy. To a friendly wineshop-keeper of the Quai du Nord he put questions. He is afraid that the man might be suspicious of this unshaven young *anglais,* who has a full purse, wears no cockade, and often forgets to address you as 'citizen.' But he was unimportant, not worth *Luisette's* while as yet, and the shop-keeper was affable. If the citizen wished to see how the republic disposed of its enemies, let him go by night to the hill beyond Père Lachaise—he would find the place easily by the glare of the bonfires—to see for himself.

"The *citoyen anglais* did so, and could not keep it out of his dreams afterwards. The great bonfires gave light as well as drove off infection while lines of long pits were dug. Into these pits rolled what was left of the republic's enemies after they had been stripped of clothing: the clothing sorted into neat piles, checked over for prices by a comptrolleur with a book, and sent away to be washed before the selling. Hence that scene of a fiery devil-camp(the comptrolleur in a dirty blue coat and red cap, with a wart on his nose and a bottle of wine in his pocket, but the only man who had clean hands) began to assume shapes at night. Another image came of the day—it was early February, when there were rumors of war on France by the execrated Tory minister Pitt—that he followed a tumbril to the very ladder. Of the two executioners, the one in charge was a portly dignified young man, a bit of a dandy, who wore his hair in a neat queue and had a rose in his teeth.

"Only one thing kept him in Paris, which he describes as his 'white radiance,' but he could not keep warm. He did not even open letters, including one from his father, which says, 'You must gette *out,* take my warning, I got near S.* yesterday at the play, who was drunk but swore Chatham would make them declair which means war. Have sent draft for £200.'

"For Charles Brixham, the crisis came on February 3, 1793. Two days before, Marie-Hortense had appeared at his lodgings, and he was mad with joy. He poured out questionings, 'to which she appeared much moved, and tearful, saying only, "I had to decide: if you still want me we shall marry, but we must go out of France afterwards." '

"He had himself shaved, and for the first time took from his chest the satin waistcoats of old. They married the same day (it was a simple matter in the time of the Goddess Reason) without witnesses. He did not see the name she wrote in the register, but to him she gave it as Marie-Hortense Longueval . . ."

. . . Staring at the lamplight glowing red through the glass of port on the desk, Tairlaine started a little as a heavy voice broke

* Probably Richard Brinsley Sheridan, then Under-Secretary for Foreign Affairs.

across Guy's smooth one. Tairlaine realized that he was again in Mantling's study, and that H.M. had interrupted.

"Longueval?" demanded H.M. "Sure of that? It's accurate, is it?"

The spell still held. Sir George Anstruther was leaning forward, a dead cigar in his fingers, from the gloom beyond the lamplight. Martin Longueval Ravelle rubbed his eyes with a strange gesture; he was not smiling now. But most of all Guy was affected. This recital, Tairlaine felt, was his life.

"Yes, that was really her name," he replied, "in the sense that she had a right to it. You will see why. You find my little tale interesting, gentlemen? I have rehearsed it many times." He drank a little of the port, and went on like one who goes back into a dream after a small interruption.

"He hired a glass-coach, in which they drove along the river out to the village of Passy. They were to spend a week at an inn there, and then take passage for England. All her possessions she brought in a chest; but when he said, 'Have you no parents, nobody?' she replied that they did not matter. It satisfied our young idealist, who had come into a happiness he could scarcely bear. His journal is incoherent. He says that at night he could sleep; sleep like the dead; sleep in glorious exhaustion, with only radiant dreams of this his wife, and awake refreshed. The weather was mild, and there were already lilacs in the yard; she worshiped him, and he her; from the window of their inn on the hill they would watch the pink twilight descending on the river, and be happy.—Then, suddenly, the idyll cracked to bits. Even in Arcadia they heard the criers. Marie-Hortense came in with a white face, and told him the news.

"War was declared against England. George Jacques Danton

had roared that he would hang the damned *Rosbifs* to every lamp in the rue St. Antoine; red-caps were out, and the innkeeper had bolted to report a *Rosbif* under his roof. Our young fool roared with laughter. He was a new man again. His heart rose up when he thought of Lord Howe's ships in the Channel, to puff away this scum as you blow the head off a dandelion-clock; the tall redcoats on the march at last, with their drums tapping, and huzza for the British Grenadiers! Oh, she cut him off quickly, and contemptuously. She said: '*Tu es fou, imbécile!* We must hide. You will be safe in my house.' She also said a thing that startled him. 'You are my husband now, and I don't mean to let you get away from me whatever happens. What I have, I keep.'

"It was the tone of her voice that surprised him. She hired a fast post-chaise, before the news should get too far; they whipped into Paris towards nightfall, through muddy streets when the rain was blowing, and he was still bewildered about 'her house.' All she said, threateningly, was: 'Don't forget you're my husband.' And, 'Don't be surprised to see a very fine house,' this with some pride.

"He says he had forebodings, but this is undoubtedly an afterthought. Still, when they whipped into the rue Neuve St. Jean, they were stopped by a scouring-party who cried that only aristos and Englishmen could afford to ride. Marie-Hortense put her head out into the light of the carriage-lamp, drawing the hood from her face and saying, 'Do you know me, citizens?' And, to the bridegroom's sudden horror, the man shrank back. The party begged her pardon and splashed away into the dark.

"They stopped in a courtyard of the rue Neuve St. Jean. The house was certainly fine enough, 'though,' he writes, 'with too much vasty disarranged fineness, as though it were new, and large portraits lying in the floor.' Also he was struck by how nervous the servants were, and how softly they trod. It was quiet but for a noise of talking somewhere.

"'My father is here?' says Marie-Hortense, of a majordomo with staff and powder. Charles Brixham thought these were reckless aristos indeed.

"'Monsieur de Paris is dining,' says the man, with another aristo term, 'with Madame his grandmother, and four of Messieurs his brothers from the provinces. The fifth brother is detained, but M. Longueval is here from Tours.—Mademoiselle has not forgotten Madame Marthe's birthday?'

"'I will see him now,' says Marie-Hortense, grimly. And to the bridegroom: 'That is my great-grandmother, the tyrant, who will be ninety-seven or eight to-morrow. You have chosen a good moment to meet all my family. Now you will wait in there until I see them first.'

"He was taken to a chamber whose double-doors evidently gave on the dining room, for he could hear loud talk. Although he felt some trepidation, since he had not known he was marrying an aristo, it did not worry him. From the next room he heard the talk suddenly grow louder and fiercer, the hammering of a stick on the floor; once Marie-Hortense's voice crying, 'He is an English milor', and rich!' Presently she came out, with a flushed face, and bade him go in.

"The room was a blaze of wax-lights and color. Imagine the room you saw to-night, in the freshness of its gold leaf; the satinwood table steaming with food, the six chairs around it. But there was a seventh chair, a sort of throne, in which sat an old crone in lace bonnet, with a high-bridged nose and a painted face: she had one hand on a goblet of red wine and the other on a crutch-stick. Five of the men, short hardy fellows with their queues tied in gay ribbon, were clearly brothers;

the sixth resembled a shifty poor-relation. There was a slight muttering. Then the eldest of the brothers, a sharp-eyed, gray-haired, fastidious man in a green riding coat, rose and bowed civilly enough.

"'You must know, Citizen Englishman,' says he, 'that my daughter's marriage takes us by surprise. The question is now whether you should be given over to prison for trial, or taken into this family. My brothers and I cannot risk our positions, to say nothing of our heads, for the sake of my daughter's caprice. But until that question is decided—' Here he extends his snuff-box, and looks at the shifty little man. 'Martin Longueval, a chair for our guest. Monsieur de Blois, some wine for him.'

"Charles Brixham went cold. He saw all the hard faces staring at him as though they had six dozen eyes, eyes everywhere; and he noticed also how shiningly clean all their hands were, scrubbed clean in a day when nobody paid much attention to this formality. Says one of the brothers, chuckling; 'It will probably be your head, *mon gosse*. Take this wine while you have a place to put it. All the same, faith, I like you! You must have been very much in love. Not many care to join our little circle.'

"The old lady began to curse. 'Speak with pride, Louis-Cyr!' says she, hammering her crutch-stick. 'Our commission was a hundred and four years old last September. It was given to my husband's father by the Grand Monarque himself. I saw him when he was an old man, feeding carp in a pond, and he spoke to me. Yes. He gave it to us because of that fool Legros, who was drunk when he handled the sword, and only split Doverel's head through to the jaw-bone. God damn you, Louis-Cyr! As for the Englishman, why not? *My* daughter married a musician. If the little Marie-Hortense wants him, she shall have him. Besides, I like him. Come here, Englishman, and kiss me.'

"Now Charles Brixham began to feel queer and sick. 'Monsieur Longueval,' says he, addressing Marie-Hortense's father, 'Monsieur Longueval——'

"'Longueval?' says he, sharply. 'Why do you use that old form of our name? None but the doubtful southern branch of our family has borne it for generations. Eh, now, is it possible that the little Marie-Hortense has not told you our real name?'

"Suddenly such a yell of laughter went up from that table as blew the candle-flames wild in their sconces. They doubled up and slapped the table and spilled their wine; only Marie-Hortense's father remained unsmiling, tapping his finger on the lid of the snuff-box. The bridegroom never thought of that scream of mirth but as a noise beating up out of the Pit—though they were, after all, quite good fellows. The lights were distorted to his gaze, and the eyes had multiplied. Then he looked at a door across the room, through which was entering a man with a great smoking joint of mutton on a salver. And to his horror Charles Brixham saw that this was a portly handsome young man, with dignified airs, who had a rose in his teeth.

"Then Charles Brixham found his senses going.

"'In the name of God,' says he, and found that he himself was screaming also, 'in the name of God *who are you?*'

"'That, citizen,' says the old man, nodding towards the youth with the steaming mutton on the tray, 'is my eldest son, who has superseded me in active duty. And we, citizen, are of the family of Sanson, hereditary masters of the functions of execution to the high courts in all France.'"

. . . At this point in the narrative, Guy Brixham stopped,

cleared his throat, and looked satirically round the group of listeners. Nobody spoke. They heard a clock in the hall strike the half-hour.

"You will, of course, have guessed it long ago," Guy proceeded, "but it has been necessary to go into such detail in order to make clear the ensuing tragedy. One thing also I must emphasize. These people were not devils, or even bad men. On the contrary, as I have told you, they were thoroughly good fellows in their own way, who tried to make the stranger comfortable and respected his thin-skinned view even if they did not share it. They voted him shelter when it was very dangerous to do so; even Marie-Hortense's father was persuaded to agree. If it had not been for Charles Brixham's own wabbling brain, or possibly the efforts of old Madame Marthe Dubut Sanson, the marriage might have turned out tolerably well.

"The Sansons had a certain job to do; they did it, they discussed it, and naturally the financial side came uppermost. There was no thought of attempting to prey on his mind, as he seems to have thought. Even at that first dinner, where under Marie-Hortense's hard bright eyes he tried to put a good face on it, they could not be expected to refrain from talking about their business. You may still read many of the elder Sanson's letters to the Attorney-General, which are preserved at Paris. You will find them the most horrifying documents of the Revolution, simply because there is no effort to shock or horrify. He is always bitterly complaining that the Convention does not allow him enough expenses; what about carpenter's services, the replacements of dulled knives, his own and son's clothes irretrievably ruined in the course of duty? They order him to put a man to the torture—very good; but that requires the services of an assistant, and he will not proceed until the money for this is forthcoming. Sometimes these debates sound grotesque to the point of absurdity, yet why? C. Henri Sanson was no romantic sadist of fiction; he was a shrewd business man determined to make some extra bread-and-butter at his job; pleasant enough at home, dignified enough abroad with his pale face and high-crowned hat, but quite certain that twopence-halfpenny is never a matter of sentiment.

"All the same, poor Charles Brixham was to die a madman.

"It does not seem to have bothered him much at first; either he was too dulled by shock, or too obstinate to let it bother him, and—he loved Marie-Hortense. Certainly he had too much pride to say, 'Why didn't you tell me?' For the first two weeks he stayed hid at Sanson's house, there is no word in his journal except that he has written to his father, 'who will find means to bring us out of the country, if the letter be not intercepted.' Then the dreams began to return, and Marie-Hortense's image was mingled with them. *She* never referred to the matter, except to say it was God's mercy he was decently sheltered. The jocose uncles were summoned away, which meant work in the provinces. Shut up among the draggled finery with old Henri, Henri his son, Madame Marthe Sanson, and Marie-Hortense, Charles Brixham found his nightmares coming on him by daylight. One day he comes on a fresh pile of clothes stacked in the kitchen; one day he merely sees his own image in a mirror, and it scares him. He could not help it. Still there was no reply from his father. On the eleventh of March the Revolutionary Tribunal was established, and then began the real Reign of Terror; *Luisette* could not grind fast enough. On the night of the sixteenth, he got quietly drunk alone in the book-room, and went out quietly to give himself up to arrest. But before he had gone a dozen steps he ran into young Henri—a decent sort, who spoke good English. Henri humored him, then struck him senseless from behind, and carried him gently back. Presently Marie-Hortense came to him with a sallow, blazing face, and afterwards they did not speak for days.

"Then he received a smuggled letter from his father's attorney in London. His father was dead, either of apoplexy or false information that his son had been caught by *Luisette;* he was dead, anyhow. Somehow the heir must be spirited out of France. This would be managed, but in such dangerous work he must be patient for further word. When he showed the letter to Marie-Hortense—her sleeves rolled up over her red elbows, bossing the servants as a good housewife should—she only said, 'I will go wherever you go,' and there would have been tenderness between them, 'if it were not for my cursed self, since heaven knoweth she is not to blame, but, God of Mercy, how shall I conquer myself?'

"Or, in my opinion, if it had not been for Madame Marthe. She was proud of the Sanson line. And when she saw the thoughts that Charles Brixham never spoke (it would have been better if he *had* spoken them, to ease them all), then she hated him beyond all belief of younger people. The March winds found her ailing, and she hated him the more because she thought she would die. Hers was the room of the satinwood chairs, the great gilt swanbed. She sat propped up under the bed-canopy, the rushlight beside her shining greenish on a face without paint, and a band of flannel round her throat. When she would insist on seeing him, he had to go. She would tell him of past horrors, when the headsman bungled; of costly gifts given to her husband that he might be swift, which she had yet; of other things you can imagine. Since he was always silent, and bowed courteously when he left her, she raged because she thought it failed. But it was succeeding. He did not forget that shadowy room smelling of medicines, the jar of leeches in the rushlight: with Madame Marthe cackling from under her lace cap, and her hands snake-veined on the pink coverlet.

"Late in April the word came. There was a sloop lying off the coast four miles below Calais. The best that could be done was forged passports to get them out of Paris gates and beyond, but this would have to be risked. Madame Marthe was close to death when she heard that news, because she heard it. She had been spending many hours with Marie-Hortense at her bedside; she knew how to knead Marie-Hortense's mind like dough, 'exhibiting to her singular gold and silver boxes, while cousin Longueval looked on,' he writes at a later date, 'and once making her swear on a crucifix. I had this from Henri, who was disturbed.'

"Her malignant grin went with them when they left in a closed coach. They do not seem to have had much trouble in their flight. You might have thought he would have shouted for joy when the gates opened them out of that murky city, after a brief turmoil of white cross-belts and bayonets at the coach windows, into the green countryside. He writes nothing of it. From his wife we learn later that he was sunk in apathy, his cloak drawn up about his eyes. He was still in that strange mood when, with Marie-Hortense on his arm, he smelt Thames mud once more and from the bow of the sloop saw gray London River become gray London. No mighty uplift of the heart to see St. Paul's towering beyond the spars, or hear the homely familiar speech that is the most soothing of all. He writes only that the attorney met them on the wharf, bowing low; but this Mr. Lavers gave a start at seeing him, and said hurriedly, 'Sir, you went away a boy and are become a man. It is only fitting, sir, that you should appear older.'

"Now that, you conceive, should be a properly happy ending. In time memory will grow thin, and start up only late at night when he has had too much claret at dinner; they settle to a comfortable fortune; Marie-Hortense makes a good if often-sharp-tongued wife. For a while it was true. They shared the same bed, and went on amicably enough. Then, one day about eighteen months after they had come to live in this house—it was broad noon of summer-time, remember—he saw it.

"He was coming downstairs to a sedan-chair waiting outside; and he saw the high corpse-cart coming upstairs to meet him. It was swimming in blood as he remembered it, and the headless things were sliding backwards by reason of its slant as it came upstairs. He ran back up to see whether it had turned towards the bedrooms at the top of the stairs, but it was gone.

"That night the hatred between his wife and himself flared at last.

"Similar visions kept appearing at intervals: he records them all. All that ailed the poor devil, obviously, was a plain attack of the horrors, and at first even he is aware that these things are phantoms. The trouble was that he saw them. One night when he was gaming at White's Club, he saw two or three of Sanson's victims come in through the door and sit down at the table with him. He did not leave the house after this.

"On the second of July, 1796—early in the same year twin children, a boy and a girl, were born to Marie-Hortense—word came that old Madame Marthe had been choked off in a fit of quinsy when just short of her hundredth birthday. She left an odd will. Every stick of furniture in her room was to be given to her great-granddaughter Marie-Hortense. It was to be transferred bodily to England. Before her time came she dictated a letter to Martin Longueval (whom she seems to have left comfortably provided for), and he brought it to Marie-Hortense. Marie-Hortense burnt it after the reading. But she did not forget it, although she mentioned its contents only once.

"Charles made no objection to the furniture being moved in. He had taken to the Bible and saw strange purposes working, nor did he object to Marie-Hortense sleeping there alone with the children. Since she had come to idolize that dead virago . . . well, we don't know.

"The rest I leave deliberately vague, since your imaginations can complete it. We know that she died before him; of what we do not know, but the family records say natural causes. The legend of a curse on the room, so that nobody could remain in it alone, seems to have originated with a housekeeper who attended her in her illness. But in the last interview she had with her husband, the sallow hatred went from her face; she kissed him, and spoke gently some words of which the housekeeper could catch only *'great need.'* Presently she asked for the windows to be set open so that she could look at the sunset. This reminded her of old days by the Seine, the first of her marriage. She seized her husband's hand when she knew that she was going, and suddenly seemed trying to utter a warning. But she did not speak again; and the two children huddled beside her even when they could not make her reply, because they feared their father and the phantom people who followed him in a cart."

CHAPTER TEN

Blowpipes and Ventriloquism

When the soft voice died away, and Guy folded his hands on the desk, Tairlaine had to shake away evil shadows. The thing had been too real, as real as Guy in his dark spectacles, and somehow a part of him. A relaxation set chairs creaking as his auditors settled back.

"Now, gentlemen!" he said, raising his hand before anybody could comment. "You will say there can be no doubt about a death-trap, eh? You will say it was constructed at the instigation of old Madame Marthe, by the craftsman Martin Longueval, and sent to her great-grand-daughter with instructions as to how she could get rid of her mad husband——"

"Well, do *you* have any doubt of it, man?" demanded Sir George. He struggled to light his dead cigar. "At the last minute she tried to warn him about it, and couldn't. Yes, and what about the old lady's having shown her 'a silver box,' or something of the sort, with Martin Longueval looking on. We've had a lot to do with a silver box tonight."

"With which, I think," suggested Guy, "you found nothing wrong?"

"No. No tricks or whatnot. That is, unless—" growled the other, and peered sideways at H.M.

Now if at this point H.M. had uttered an exclamation and dramatically slapped his forehead, they would have known he was off on another of his digressions. He did not. He sat quiet, wheezing, and stared fishlike behind his spectacles, with a dawning look of realization. He said:

"Y'know, that's a pretty good yarn." He seemed to examine it from all sides. "It's a bit of a jolt to realize what gutters and buckets of blood you've suggested, and only once or twice used the word. But that's not the interestin' point. The interestin' point is whether we're supposed to sympathize with that poor crackbrain Charles Brixham or with his wife and family. Now, you don't sympathize with either. All you sympathize with is The Past. That's what fascinates you most about the whole story."

"Well?" inquired Guy, shutting his teeth. "What of that?"

H.M. spoke with a sort of obstinacy, and with apparent irrelevance.

"I'll answer that question like this. You were askin' me, Anstruther, is there anything wrong with that silver casket? Yes, there is."

"But we agreed—" said Tairlaine.

"I know, I know. We agreed there was no poison anywhere about it, and never had been. So in that case, I ask you, what *can be* wrong with it? You're a descendant of this Martin Longueval, Mr. Ravelle. Does anything occur to you?"

Curiously enough, the genial Ravelle had been the one most unpleasantly affected by the story. He still sat holding the arms of his chair, his veined face a mottled color beyond all reason from a mere tale. More imagination, more superstition, more sheer nerves, more what? He seemed to know he cut an odd figure, for he tried to make light of it.

"You think I have the 'obgoblins, eh? Ha ha ha. Maybe, maybe. I do not know anything about any box, but what I do not like is that business about the 'eads. Listen! If you had ever see anybody go to the guillotine, you would not talk so easily about it. I have."

He swabbed his upper lip with a handkerchief, and hesitated.

"You in England can talk very easy about the guillotine. That is because you do not have it nowadays working when a man commit murder. I tell you, you ought to be glad they hang them over here!"

"Why?" said H.M.

"Why? Well, because somebody is going to be hanged, is he not?" asked Ravelle, turning to look at him with the handkerchief against his face: "I say, old boy, do not tell me you think yes about this rot—poison-traps. Ah, *zut!* Did you find any? Did my old man find any years ago? No! Maybe once, yes, though I think not. But now it is different. That chap Bender died of something else. The bobby says he died of that Indian arrow-poison what-you-call-it. Do you think that old boy all those years ago knew about South American arrow-poison? No!"

"That," snapped a heavy voice behind them, "is the first time anybody's talked sense in this house to-night."

Tairlaine whirled round towards the shadows. He had not heard the door open or close, and he did not know how long Alan had been standing there. The man looked still bigger and more ominous in the dim light. He had the rumpled appearance of one who has failed to sleep.

"Sense is what I said, and I meant it. Oh, yes. I heard most of your ghost-story, Guy. It didn't scare me—that." He snapped his fingers. His eyes looked bleary, but he was grinning. He lumbered over to the desk. "Fact is, my lads, Guy revels in public appearances. The only one he can scare with his ghost-stories is little Judy, but he's got it all pat like a lecture. Hey, George? What are you drinking, Guy? Port? Been in my sideboard again?"

Guy looked straight ahead.

"We all revel in public appearances, sometimes. At least I do not imitate the polished wit that passes in your dialogues with that dummy. No, I didn't disturb it. It's still in the sideboard."

"Uh-huh. We were speakin' of that," observed H.M., as Mantling pulled open the sideboard door and suspiciously peered in. "Your brother said you were a pretty good ventriloquist."

Mantling was at first suspicious, then vastly amused. "I say, H.M., you coppers are a queer lot! Daresay it's part of your method to sit here and talk about a ventriloquist's dummy when there's a poor devil dead in the next room, hey? Subtle. Maybe, but—Yes, this is Jimmy. I take him out sometimes. Like to see him work?"

He sat down and fished out the dummy, which had an expression of cheerful witlessness on its red face, a grin, and watchful eyes which it began to twitch back and forth on them.

"I was talkin' to a ventriloquist the other day," volunteered H.M. "The Great Somebody-or-Other. He said this business of 'throwing the voice' was a myth. He said it was absolutely impossib——"

"Stand back, all of you," ordered Mantling. "It won't be effective if you get too close, dammit. Now. Now, Jimmy, I want you to listen very carefully. I want to ask you . . . Well?" he broke off, turning impatiently to the door. "Well, Shorter? What the devil is it? What do you want?"

"Excuse me, sir," said Shorter's voice, *"but you'd better come directly. That police inspector's lying on the floor in the Widow's Room, and he seems to be dead."*

H.M. surged up with a curse, the pipe dropping out of his hands. Tairlaine, whirling towards the closed door, heard behind him a bellow of laughter. Mantling was kicking the floor and chortling.

"That, gentlemen, is my brother's idea of humor," said Guy without moving. "He was giving you a practical demonstration, I think."

Mantling, wiping his eyes from mirth, had folded up the dummy again.

"Right. Got it in one. Hang it, H.M., don't go on like that!" he protested querulously. "I'm not much in the mood to work Jimmy to-night, but I thought I'd give you a taste. Put the wind up you, hey? Ho ho *ho!* Guy's right, though: practical demonstration. I concentrated your attention on the dummy, so you wouldn't suspect me of trying games with the door. Then, when I broke off and spoke directly to the door, you took it as a real thing and the answer as real. . . . Your friend's right, though, H.M. You can't *throw* your voice. What you do is use it like a conjuror. People can't locate sound, and most of it's acting. You speak to a certain place, then you look as though you were listening. Back comes a sound with the right, whatdyecallit, distance-pitch; it sounds as though it came from the place where their attention's been directed, so they believe it."

H.M. glared at him, wheezing as he groped after his pipe. But he controlled himself.

"Uh-huh. All right. So it's acting? But how'd you manage that voice? *That* wasn't acting."

"Interested? Right," said Mantling with bursting complacency. "It wants practice, but I'll give you an idea. That was the down-in-the-cellar voice. Now look here—with my mouth open. I'm going to yawn, d'you see? While my throat's in the position to yawn, I talk through the yawn. Then I curl my tongue back to the back part of the throat. The farther it goes, the more distant the voice is; distant, and deeper, eh? What gives it power is the stomach-muscles: you contract 'em as though you were going to cough. That part's easy. Hard part is forming the words when your lips don't move. Some consonants you can't pronounce at all without movin' your lips. Well, then you have to substitute others that sound like 'em . . . What's the matter with you fellers? You look funny."

"Steady, now," said H.M., blinking at him. "You mean to say you could make that down-in-the-cellar voice come from any distance?"

"No, not *any* distance. I mean, d'ye see, any reasonable distance where I could call your attention to some screen or door, for instance; and speak to it, and make you think the voice ought to come from there. Of course, the voice is never very clear from the way you have to talk. And the farther you seem to send it, the more kind of muffled it gets, until——"

He stopped suddenly.

He stopped, his muddy blue eyes opening wide and his mouth half open. Then the freckles began to start out against his skin as he stared from one to the other of his guests.

"You fool," said Guy very clearly, "don't you see you have described exactly what happened to-night?"

Mantling had taken a step forward when the door opened to admit Masters. Undoubtedly Masters noted the explosive tension of the room; his eyes flickered round, and he shut up his notebook as though to go into action. H.M. forestalled him.

"We've been hearin' some very enlightenin' things, son. All about the past. They can wait. How'd you come out? Did you find that notebook?"

Masters was quietly triumphant.

"We came out very well, sir. We didn't find the notebook, *no.* But I fancy we shall pretty soon prove how the 'voice' was managed. However, as you say, that can wa——"

"You note my brother on the point of apoplexy, Inspector," Guy put in smoothly. He clasped and unclasped his hands. "I think you'd better give us a hint. Was the voice managed by ventriloquism, by any chance?"

Though he controlled it well, Masters' heavy face was for a flash so startled that Alan fell back against the sideboard with a kind of grunt.

"'Ventriloquism,'" Masters repeated, as though he were turning the idea over in his mind. "Hurrum! Ventriloquism. Hem! Just so. Of course you understand, sir, I am not permitted to——"

"What the chief inspector is trying to tell you, son," said H.M., mouthing his pipe, "is that members of the Force ain't allowed to speak even concernin' the things they don't know anything about. He's a smooth one, Masters is. But he hasn't got his eye on you, Mantling. Not yet."

Masters cleared his throat.

"Lord Mantling? Thank you, sir; just so. I have been looking for you. I now have a statement from everyone here, you see, except you and Mr. Ravelle. If we can just get it over with quickly, sir, then I shan't have to trouble you any more to-night. Of course, I'm bound to tell you that we shall be late in going over that room . . ."

Mantling tried to quiet his heavy breathing. "All right! 'Squite all right, Inspector. Yes. Quite all right. I—hum—well, get on with it! What d'you want to know? *I* didn't do it, blast you!"

"No, sir. It's about these darts, now."

"Eh? Darts? What darts?"

"The South American darts, sir, which Miss Isabel Brixham took out of a drawer in your desk and gave to one of my men." (Here Mantling lurched over to the desk, felt along the drawers, and seemed startled to find a key in one of them.) "Did you know they were tipped with curare?"

"Now that's a damned funny thing . . . Hey? Oh, no; not the darts; I mean—sorry, Robert, what did you say?"

"Did you know they were tipped with curare, sir? I warn you they are. The police surgeon had gone, but my sergeant phoned him and had the darts sent over. Dr. Blaine has just phoned back. Well?"

Mantling fretted. "The answer's . . . well, yes and no. I mean, I suppose they ought to be, because what's the bloody use of a blowpipe dart unless it *is* poisoned? That's why I kept 'em locked up. But those chaps in the brush are usually liars. They like people to think their stuff's poisoned; makes 'em respected. And as often as not a cut or scratch will get infected when nothing's wrong with the weapon. Then tetanus sets in, and the poisoned-weapon idea gets a lot more credit than it deserves. *I* don't know, but I kept 'em locked up, and it's a funny thing . . ."

"Just so, sir. How many of the darts were there?"

"Eight. Look here, tell your men to be careful of 'em, will you?"

"Only five were found in the drawer, sir," Masters told him. Mantling jerked up his head, and they stared at each other.

"Well there *were* eight," Mantling insisted, in a rather querulous tone. "Got to be eight! I tell you I saw 'em myself, saw 'em last . . ."

"Yes? Last——?"

"Come to think of it, that's what I can't remember. A week, two weeks; I don't remember. The funny thing is about that key, though. Last time I saw that it was on my ring, and I don't remember how long ago *that* was either, and yet here it is in the drawer. Damn it, why do people— I say, Inspector, it wasn't here earlier to-night."

Masters' face was still wooden as he made notes. He pondered.

"Now, sir, you said 'blowpipe' darts. Do you have the blowpipe there, too?"

"Ahha, so that's it, eh?" said Mantling, and regarded him with an expression of what can only be called stupid shrewdness. He leered a little. "You think that little swine who called himself an artist might have been killed with a blowpipe-dart? It's better than thinkin' a curse did it.—Look *here!* The blowpipe's gone, right enough. I say . . ."

Masters hurried round, and H.M. glowered at him.

"Even the old man," growled H.M., stirring uneasily, "has got to admit that this looks serious. Any reason behind this, Masters? Did you find a dart in your search, by any chance?"

"No, sir, I'm bound to admit we didn't find anything like that," Masters admitted after a pause, and H.M. roared at the anti-climax. "Or any suggestion of a dart. But it's as well to be sure. Hum. No blowpipe. So."

"Look here, son, what did you find?" demanded H.M., studying him as he meticulously noted down the fact of there being no blowpipe. "You seem devilish cocky. Fingerprints, maybe?"

Masters' face assumed a cheerful expression as he went on making notes without looking up. He had at last found a case which had the old man bothered as well as himself, and he appeared to enjoy it.

"Plenty of fingerprints. I should say, just about everybody's fingerprints. They'd all been in there, sir, before—um—it occurred to you to get in touch with me. *And* the person who cleaned up that room so nice and tidy beforehand took care to wear gloves to—keep his hands clean, maybe. But I think we've found a trace or two of him." Here Masters spoke so casually that Tairlaine felt he was speaking to somebody in the room, and driving in a wedge of fear. Quickly on that, he shut up his notebook.

"Thanks very much, your Lordship. I shan't require any more to-night, unless you can suggest? . . ."

"Good God, *no!*"

"Very well. Now, Mr. Ravelle, if you please." Ravelle, who had gone softly over to pour a surreptitious whisky-soda and crept back again, took a deep pull at it. He arranged his face. Masters saw this, and was affable. "Nothing to be alarmed at! We can't arrest on suspicion in *this* country, you know. Just a brief statement——"

"On my oath, sir, I do not know one thing about it! No. I have an alibi, which is bad for me I know. But even though I have an alibi I still did not kill the poor Bender." He shrugged.

"That is all. I sit at table with the rest. I do not know Bender, and I never meet him before. Here endeth. *Voilà*. You do not mind if I drink the whisky-soda?"

"Not at all, sir. . . . But it wasn't about the dinner-table. I want to ask you about afterwards. You left them—when?"

"At half-past eleven, after we hear the voice. God, I do not forget that! I hear he is long dead then, and that is good for me."

"After you left them, where did you go?"

"To my room. I have two cablegrams which I must send to Paris, and a note I must write. The cablegrams I have telephoned to the Vestairn Union from the 'phone which is in my room. I wrote also the note, and this I am taking downstairs to put on the hall-table when I hear someone yell."

Masters studied him, becoming very quiet. The next question he addressed to his notebook.

"I've been looking about, you understand, Mr. Ravelle; and they tell me your room is on the floor just above, at the front . . . on the other side of Miss Isabel Brixham's sitting-room, that would be? Yes. Now, I don't suppose you looked in as you passed, or spoke to Miss Brixham, or anything like that?"

"I did not speak to her, no. The door was open. She was seated in a chair with her back to me—in front of the fire, you see—and her head was *so,*" he bent his chin on his breast with a hideous facial expression which was evidently meant to be slumber, "and I think she is asleep. So I do not disturb her. I go on. Ha! Eh?"

During the profound quiet that came on the room, Masters glanced at Guy. Guy sat bolt upright, gripping his knuckles hard. Masters said softly:

"Just so. And where was Mr. Guy Brixham sitting then?"

Ravelle stared. "I do not understand. Guy? Guy was not there."

"You are mistaken, my friend," Guy told him with great coolness. "You couldn't have seen me, that was all. I suppose you didn't go into the room? If you have any doubt about it, ask my aunt."

The other moved uneasily, began to be deprecating with a flat spreading out of his hands, but he was clearly so uneasy that he burst out.

"Look! I tell you, now! I do not wish to make trouble for anyone, and you are my friend, but I jolly well will not lie to these coppers!" His face grew redder. "They put you in the clink, blimey, and I will not lie. Old man, you were *not* there. I am sorry to say this, but I looked in, and you were not there unless you hide in the cupboard or like that. She sat in a big fat chair with cretonne on it," he declared, as though clinching a point, "and over the back of it I see the top of her head *so.* Eh? But you were not there. No."

"Sorry," remarked Guy, lifting one shoulder. "It's two people's word against one, you know."

"I think we must speak to Miss Brixham again, and make sure of that," Masters said with equal composure. "Thank you, Mr. Ravelle. Now, when you came downstairs to put your letter on the hall table—that was about midnight? Just so—then you passed the door again. Did you look in?"

"Well . . . no. I was not noticing. Hah! I think now the door was closed. Yes, I think I notice it was closed, but I am not sure."

Masters put away his notebook and clipped the pencil to his pocket with an air of finality.

"That's all I need trouble you to-night, gentlemen, unless any one has something to add? No?" He glanced at H.M., who was sulky.

"I'm goin' home," the latter announced, with decision. "I want to sit and think. Never knew a time when I needed so much to sit and think. Look here, it's nearly three o'clock." He blinked at Tairlaine and Sir George. "Which way are you two goin'? I know you're just 'round from me, Anstruther; walk along and smoke a cigar. *And* you're not goin' clear out to Kensington to-night, Doc; take you till morning in this fog. Nonsense! Come along with me and I'll give you a shakedown. I need somebody to talk at. . . . Out in the hall, Masters. Let's have a little *causerie* in private."

Parting words to his host, Tairlaine found, were a little difficult to manage. "Good-night; had a splendid time," seemed somewhat out of place. He shook hands and mumbled something. They were all absent-minded, while Ravelle prowled the room without looking at a stolid-faced Guy, and Mantling growled to himself. The center of all the cloudy hatreds afloat seemed to beat back on Guy, who never unclasped his hands or looked up.

Out in the hall H.M—in a coat with a moth-eaten fur collar, and an ancient unwieldy top-hat stuck on the back of his head—was arguing with Masters when Tairlaine and Sir George joined them.

"Now, sir, you just go home," said Masters, like an indulgent policeman to a wandering tippler. "We haven't finished altogether—not until I can get a description of that blowpipe, which, hum!, I'll bet was a short one. And until I can show you everything I'd rather not speak at all—Tut, tut, such language! I'll come 'round to your office to-morrow, if I may."

"Uh-huh. Then you think you know who did all this, and how it was done?"

Masters waved away Shorter, who was assisting the others into their coats. He walked with them to the door. A thin mist was still ghostly in Curzon Street, muffling the lamps, and Tairlaine shivered as it began to curl in.

"I'm rather certain I do," the chief inspector told them, "and one or two minor points—minor points, mind!—will clear up everything."

"And who's guilty?"

"Mr. Guy Brixham. Look here, Sir Henry," said Masters, beginning to grin, "shall I take *your* attitude, and drop a couple of hints as you would?"

"Well?"

"I know it," said Masters, "first, because I saw some mist—like that. And, second, because I've been in Mr. Guy Brixham's room, and found he owns a real Japanese dressing-gown. . . . I'll bring you the proof in the morning. Good night, gentlemen. Mind the steps."

He bowed like a butler against the yellow light as the door closed.

CHAPTER ELEVEN

The Man at the Window

At H.M.'s insistence, Tairlaine spent that night at the big house in Brook Street. H.M. said he wanted somebody to talk at. He also embarked on a long list of grievances to show how persecuted he was. His wife, he said, was always in the south of France except when she came home to throw the house open to a lot of so-and-sos he did not want to meet. His two daughters pinched his car, went to parties in it, and then came back and hooted the horn under his window at five o'clock in the morning to make him put out his head and swear. At the War Office the thus-and-sos were too parsimonious to install a lift, making him walk up four flights of stairs; furthermore, some dignitary he referred to as Sniffy refused to take his advice about the case of the Rosenthal cipher.

The house, in fact, was one of those ornate chilly places which seem to exist only for the purpose of giving receptions. Most of the time it was inhabited only by H.M. and the servants. But that he should growl about his sleep being disturbed by motor-horns was another thing. He did not allow Tairlaine to turn in until half-past five. Instead he took him to a set of attic rooms, his lair, lined to the low ceiling with books and full of dusty trophies. At that drugged hour of the morning, Tairlaine could not keep pace with the man's enormous intellectual restlessness, which was in contrast to the Chinese-image woodenness of his face, and seemed at first to occupy itself with what looked like children's pursuits.

H.M. dragged out, for instance, all sorts of board-games. They were deceptive. There was one particularly devilish game, a reconstruction of a naval battle, which required as much concentration as chess and was fully as complicated. Tairlaine never forgot H.M. sitting in the firelight, his collar off and a cup of vile coffee at his elbow, his face-muscles never moving except to draw at the black pipe, while he swept down to annihilate the other's defenses. After losing all his heavy ships and also his temper several times, Tairlaine settled down grimly to play. He studied and fought hard and cursed over those little card-board gunboats. And, by the time he could put up a tolerable defense, he was as wakeful as an owl.

H.M. never stopped talking—lugubriously. He switched to some bewildering word-puzzles, in which you built anagrams and acrostics out of people's dying words. He lumbered about the room, taking down books, firing out quotations which Tairlaine, as a professor of English, was expected to complete. Finally the learned doctor got mad, and began unreeling some of his own eruditon, and almost stopped H.M. They went on hammering the table and sneering at each other until half-past five. When at length Tairlaine was handed half a tumbler of whisky and stumbled away to bed, he felt as though his brain had been through a clothes-wringer. He was half asleep before he remembered that H.M. had not said a word about the case at hand.

"You're all right," said H.M. "You're the best Watson I've tumbled across." He added the old Irish motto, which he said held good in this house: "If you want whisky, just stamp twice on the floor. The servants understand."

Tairlaine felt better later, after a few hours' sleep, when he had gone back to his flat for a change of clothes. He was to meet H.M. and Sir George at the former's office in Whitehall at ten o'clock. It was a gray morning, but not cold, when he turned left at the Horse Guards, and penetrated up through the rabbit-warren to another attic room which was H.M.'s lair overlooking the Embankment. It was very much like the one in Brook Street, but dustier with bales of corded papers, and over the mantelpiece there was a tall portrait of Joseph Fouché. H.M. sat with his feet on a broad desk, smoking a cigar and grousing.

"Siddown. Mind the seat in that chair," he said, kicking the telephone to one side. "Look here, I'm worried. I'm devilish worried. It came to me last night, while we were workin' the battleships, that maybe I oughtn't to have done it. Then, after you went to bed, I got to sittin' and thinkin' again . . . maybe I ought to have tipped Masters off. Burn me, I don't know! But the poor feller's the younger son, after all, and I thought I'd give him a chance. I wonder."

"What's all this?"

H.M. made vague gestures. "About Guy. You don't understand, do you? Well, Masters'll be here shortly. I think I can see how his case is goin', and that worries me too. I—Baah!" He growled as the telephone rang, but he subsided at the news that George Anstruther was on his way up. The stocky little baronet stumped in, wearing an even louder overcoat than usual, and at the un-Pickwickian expression of his face H.M. sat up.

"Yes, you're quite right. It's trouble," he said. He sat down to get his breath. "Mantling rang me up this morning."

"Well?"

"He didn't know the number of your private wire here, and there was nobody at your house when he 'phoned there. He said it was none of the police's damned business. I hope not."

"You're not goin' to tell me? . . . ."

"Oh, no more deaths, if that's what you mean; but it looks a nasty game. He wasn't as clear as he might have been. Anyway, it's like this. Last night Carstairs and Ravelle nearly murdered each other."

"Eh? Oh, love-a-*duck!*" said H.M., opening his dull eyes. "Steady, now, son. Sure you got it right? *Carstairs and Ravelle?* Those two are good pals. Unless . . . how did it happen?"

"Masters and his crew seem to have left the place about half an hour after we did. All quiet, and everybody had turned in except Alan, who let them out. Masters—and I think it was fool negligence—didn't leave a guard in that room. Suppose there were any poison-mechanism that somebody wanted to remove? It was a simple precaution. . . ."

"Uh-huh. A simple precaution," H.M. said dully, "which I urged him not to take. H'm. I didn't think he'd agree. Well?"

George shifted. "Alan went on up to bed. He'd taken rather a lot to drink all evening, and he dropped to sleep straightaway. A noise woke him—it had to be a loud and continued one—and, by the time he'd got his wits together and turned on the light, he heard the hell of a row going on downstairs. Furniture knocked over, and smashings and whatnot. This was about twenty minutes past four. He got a gun and went charging downstairs. I gather he nearly funked it when he found the noise came from the Widow's Room, although he won't admit this. Then he heard Carstairs yelling 'I've got him, I've got him,' in the dark. Alan turned on the lights in the dining-room, and went out with an electric-torch. Something was reeling about in there, and crunching wood. As he got the light on them, somebody landed with a straight crack and somebody else went across the table like a spinning plate. Then he saw Carstairs standing in the light, too winded to talk; but pretty well messed up, and with a gash down one cheek. They lit the gas as Ravelle was coming to life on the other side of the table. When he saw who it was, Carstairs couldn't believe his eyes—he said."

Again Sir George stopped for breath. H.M. stared at him.

"I might 'a' known it!" the latter roared, and shook his fist. "I might 'a' *known* it! But I didn't think he'd go that far. . . . And now I'll tell you something. Ravelle had a knife on him, didn't he? and also he probably had a very long steel bodkin almost as thin as a needle, with a sharp point?"

Sir George pushed back his hat.

"How the devil did you know that?—It's quite true. They found both things. The bodkin, if that's what you call it, Alan described as a knitting-needle with a handle. Alan swears it's what Ravelle used to commit the murder . . ."

"Eh?"

"Yes. You remember Ravelle sat next to Bender at the dinner table? Well, Alan says Ravelle had this thing on him tipped with curare; that he stuck Bender with it under cover of the table, just before Bender left. But he only scratched the skin, and the poison took a little time to work, but killed him *before* the first reply was due from the room. Then there was some sort of gramophone-contrivance, that sang out the answers . . . Oh, you needn't look so agonized! I know it's absurd, or sounds absurd.

But Alan's wild about that ventriloquist-accusation, and raving. Besides, there may be something in this business of the bodkin. . . . Anyhow, to go on with the story: There was one thing they found on him that nobody could explain. Wrapped up in a handkerchief he had half-a dozen sticks of that plasticine stuff. You know—the toy modeling-clay you can get at Woolworth's, for children to mess about with? What do you say to that?"

H.M. was getting into a better humor. He surged back in his creaky swivel-chair, and adjusted his feet.

"I say *I* can explain it. Ravelle wanted it to replace the putty, of course. . . . Don't forget that putty you haven't seen, son! It's goin' to be important, although I'll bet it was a washout for Ravelle. H'm! Ravelle knows the secret of that room right enough. He knows the trick mechanism, or rather what used to be the trick mechanism. I wonder . . ."

Sir George looked at him. "Damn it, man," he said, "let's have a little more consistency, shall we? Now there either is a trick mechanism, or there isn't. And you've been going about all the time assuring us solemnly that there isn't. So exactly what *do* you mean?"

"Now, now," said H.M. soothingly. "Let's stop talkin' about what I think of it, and find out the rather more important question of what Ravelle and Carstairs thought about it. How did they happen to get into that scrap? How'd they explain all this? In short, son, what happened?"

"That's what I couldn't get with any clearness from Alan. Apparently Ravelle wouldn't speak. He'd taken a good deal of punishment—and given some, by the way; it must have been a neat battle. He got up with some dignity and staggered away to his room. Alan locked him in, which seems to have made him frantic. As for Carstairs . . ." George peered from under shaggy eyebrows, folding and unfolding his pudgy hands. ". . . as for Carstairs, he wouldn't talk much either. He said he was waiting in that room for the criminal to 'come in and do something——' "

"How'd he happen to be in the house, by the way? He doesn't live there, does he?"

"No. Apparently he sneaked back after he was supposed to have gone, had a duplicate key to the front door, or something. Alan says he talked a lot about 'making something of himself.' Then somebody came creeping into the Widow's Room with a flashlight. So our young hero rose up and pasted him before he got halfway through the door."

"Blasted young fool! . . . Now why couldn't he—haa!" said H.M., giving the telephone a malevolent glare as it rang. "You know who that'll be? That's Masters, full of beans and cussedness, comin' up to say, 'Just so' over the old man's carcass. Burn me, I'll have it out of his hide yet! *All right; send him up, Lollypop!* If he's got that last bit of evidence——"

Evidently he had, for he beamed effulgent with fresh barbering as though to deck himself out for an arrest: his big jowls shining, his hair exuding an aroma of tonic as he majestically removed his hat.

"Ah, gentlemen!" said the chief inspector, putting down a brief-case on the desk. "Good morning to you all! I've been doing a bit more work this morning, gentlemen, as you may guess. New clews, you'll want to know? Well, yes, in a great manner of speaking." Under H.M.'s sour glare, he sat down and accepted a cigar. "To be exact, I've been investigating Mr. Bender's private life. And, while it does not add to, it *confirms,* my case. He lived at a little private-hotel in Bloomsbury, near the Psycho-Therapathic Hospital in case they should need him. I've been talking with his landlady, and it confirms my case . . . confirms it, gentlemen, even on so small a matter as Corns."

"On so small a matter," said Sir George, "as *what?*"

"Corns, sir," explained the chief inspector, lifting a large shoe and examining it affably. "I hope you've never been troubled with 'em. They can be uncommonly nasty things, for anybody who——"

"This," said H.M, and struck the desk, "is the end! Lummy, I thought I'd heard some gibberin' so far in this case, but I never expected to have my ears assaulted with this. I can't bear it. Look here, Masters, are you goin' to tell us Bender was murdered with poisoned corn-plaster?"

"Now, now, sir! . . . I'll come to business. But I couldn't resist using some of your own mystification." He left off smiling and became brisk. "Like this. It was the young fellow's consciousness I meant. You remember, I couldn't get it through my head at first that he would go out of his way to put himself in that room and maybe run into the trap of somebody he knew to be a lunatic? That's what he did—from his own character. Bit morbid, I should think, the lengths he carried it. Once when he had a stomach-ache so bad they thought it was appendicitis, he still went on duty and refused to mention it to anybody; said it would distract the patient's attention in a mental case, or some such nonsense, to have an ailment or pain in the doctor. Even with a little thing like corns——"

"Nothin' really wrong with his appendix, was there? No. Well, then," growled H.M., "why are you makin' so much fuss of all this?"

"Because I know how he did die," replied Masters calmly, and opened his brief-case. "I've got here two pieces of evidence: a bit of fine thread, and a photograph. With them I'll show you how Mr. Guy Brixham did this murder. I daresay he's mad and won't suffer for it.

"But, gentlemen," he continued, with relish, "to, hum, illustrate this, let me first show you my apparent difficulties, and how they helped me. So! Now here's the room."

He pulled over a piece of H.M.'s writing-paper, and on that he drew a perfect square. The side nearest him he marked *Door,* the side just opposite *Window,* the left-hand side *Fireplace,* and the right-hand side *Blank Wall.*

"So, you see, we had straight off what looked like another of those impossibilities. Door watched, window covered with steel shutters unquestionably sealed with bolts rusted in the sockets. First my men and I had a look at the chimney, which was covered with a close grating a little way up, and so choked with soot that it was impassable. Secret passages—none, anywhere.

"And that at first looked as though there *must* be flummoxing somewhere; I mean, a poison-mechanism. Well, gentlemen," announced Masters firmly, "my men and I went over that place—hum—with a comb. And the plain fact is, there's nothing of the kind."

"You're sure of that?" demanded Sir George.

"Absolutely certain-sure. Right! And yet the next difficulty, it seemed, was, though a voice was heard in there, and a man stuck with poison, everybody had an alibi. And, gentlemen, if you'll forgive me for saying so, I went at that difficulty in a common-sense way. The first thing is, break the alibi if you can. And *that* wasn't hard. Because two of 'em hadn't really got an alibi at all. That is, it wasn't supported by a number of outside sources like all the others; it was simply two people supporting each other's word. I was pretty sure Mr. Guy Brixham was lying, and had persuaded his aunt to back him up.

"The first thing I remember was her queer behavior giving testimony. But queer behavior's not evidence. What did strike me, though, was the last thing she said before she left us. All of a sudden she rather had a fit, pointed to that window and said in a (hum! if you'll forgive me) a bit of an agonized way, 'Are you sure it's really locked on the inside?' "

Against the gray light of the windows H.M. sat up.

"That's not bad, Masters," he grunted, and scowled. "I'm afraid you're gettin' the lecturin' habit like me, but still it's not bad. Uh-huh. I thought of that, but—So it led you to the window, did it?"

"Because I also remembered," said Masters, tapping the desk, "where the body was lying. Eh? It was lying on the other side of the bed. Not on a line with the window directly, but close to it between the angle of the bed and that wall.

"Just so! Now, why did she say a bit of a queer thing like, 'Is the window really locked?' So I said to myself, 'Suppose Mr. Guy had been away from her, and admitted he had looked in that window, and saw Mr. Bender die; but swore he couldn't have had anything to do with it, because of the locked shutters—then asked her to give him an alibi so he wouldn't be suspected?' She might have said just what she did, in that case. Hum! And a person outside the window *could* see through easily enough, if he had his eye close against 'em. Because they've got a line of slits, horizontal, to let the air through, and the slits are about a quarter of an inch high. So——"

"Stop a bit," interposed Sir George. "What about the window and window-glass outside them? And yet, come to think of it, I remember——"

"A current of air in the room, coming from there," said Tairlaine, who had a vivid if idle recollection of this. "Some panes were broken."

Masters nodded.

"Exactly so. I noticed it myself, late in the evening, when the mist was thicker and a little drifted in. Well! My men and I broke the bolts and got those shutters open; *they* hadn't been disturbed. The window flat against 'em—a very high window, you remember—was built in a series of panes each maybe a foot and a half square. They were black with dirt, all except one, and that was missing. It had been cut out (neat job!) about half-way up the window. Our hardest job was getting that window raised; stuck like a rock, the thing was.

"And then the business was plain as plain. That's the back of the house. It gives on a little alley, no more than four-odd feet wide, with the blank wall of another house just opposite. Now, from that window it's a little distance down to the ground. But there's the ledge of a wall—big wide thing, built to buttress the place—running right under the window over to the steps up to the back door. . . . See it? Somebody could walk out the back door, walk up to the window, shove his face up against the shutter through that empty space and see everything.

"And, Lummy, then's when it hit me!" said Masters, rattling his brief-case. "If he could see through it, and hear through it, then it's certain-sure he could talk through it. He could give exactly the kind of muffled yell, with no words, that you heard in answer to your hail; and, in a manner of speaking, it would come directly from that room."

After a pause, during which Masters drew in his breath in triumph, he coolly took some sheets from his brief-case. He said:

"Point o' fact, sir, I know he did. Here are the enlarged photographs of the fingerprints. He left two good ones on the messy glass of that window. Later I got in and compared 'em with the prints on that glass of port wine he was drinking in the study. They're the same."

CHAPTER TWELVE

The Vanishing Dart

"Of course, I can't take much credit for it," pursued Masters, who was swollen to bursting with pride. He waved his hand deprecatingly. "Ha ha! Mere matter √of routine investigation—which I know you hate, Sir Henry. Hum. But as to practical considerations, it would have been easy for him. The only slight danger he'd have run was being overheard yelling by somebody *outside* the house, and that was almost nothing. First, he was shouting directly into the room with his mouth against that slit. Second, you know how fog deadens sound, and away back in that little what-d'ye-call-it, *cul-de-sac,* he couldn't have been heard as far as the street. Third, there was a blank wall on the other side of him. Just so."

"Just so, I'm afraid. Yes, you can take credit for it," said Sir George, rubbing his forehead, "and we were fools for not having seen that as it was. It's good, it's amazingly good, it's almost convincingly good. And I still don't believe it. . . . Look here, you've only explained the voice, you know. You haven't said a word about the murder."

Masters was looking at H.M. H.M., still without speaking, hoisted himself up from the chair. In his near-sighted, bat-like way, he blundered over towards the fireplace, a vast figure in baggy clothes. He dropped some coal on the fire with a tongs. Then he stood motionless, his spectacles down on his nose, staring at the blaze. At length he nodded.

"Uh-huh. Yes. It's good. I'm afraid you've got him, Masters."

"Afraid?"

"Well . . . I mean, it don't altogether satisfy me in all things, if you're goin' to develop it as I think you will. But the whole point of that is in the murder. How was the murder committed?"

"It was committed," said the chief inspector, "by a poisoned dart projected from a blowpipe through one of the slits in the shutter."

He relished the word "projected," as though he were already giving evidence before a coroner. He was a good fellow, Humphrey Masters. Also, with a handful of trumps, he was sometimes a little pompous; and why not? He proceeded: "Stop a bit, gentlemen. You'll say, immediately, 'But there was no dart found.' Quite so. There was no dart in the room. And that's what I should like to explain."

Sir George scowled. "I say, Masters, is that why you rang me up this morning, for——"

"Exactly, sir. For a word to get help from the primitive-weapons department at the Museum. The gentleman was most helpful. I have here," said Masters, diving into his brief-case, "two types of South American blowpipe; the shorter one, I daresay, is the one we want. And here are some darts. You needn't be afraid of them. They're not poisoned."

On the desk he laid a tube of what resembled discolored

bamboo, not much more than three inches long. Beside it he put two black slivers of wood, slightly tapering and of an inch in length.

"First you'll want to ask whether a man against that shutter could *see* to fire one of these things. Yes, he could—and it would improve his aim. Those shutters have the air-slits about two inches apart. An ordinary man, with the mouth of his tube against one slit and his head forward, would find his eye a couple of inches from the second slit above; peering into a lighted room, it would be exactly like a rifle-sight. He'd want skill with the blowpipe, that's all. Now look at this dart. It's a duplicate of the ones in Lord Mantling's desk. . . . Pick it up, sir. What do you notice?"

Tairlaine was surprised to find it much heavier than he had expected from a sliver of wood. He gingerly tested the point with his thumb, and found it needle-sharp.

"Yes, it seems to be lightly weighted in some way," agreed Sir George, taking it from his hand. "It might be heavier and give greater accuracy, but what of that? What we want you to explain is how a man shot it through that window, *and then it vanished.* Hang it, Masters, that's worse than the locked room!"

"Think you could give a demonstration of it?" H.M. asked suddenly. He saw Masters' eye gleam, and nodded sourly. Lumbering over to the litter in one corner, he trundled out a tall folding-screen with leaves of some heavy semi-cardboard material. He set it upright and slapped away some dust. "Got a penknife, Masters? Right, then. Cut some slits in it. It's not quite as high as that window, but it'll do.—Sure it'll wreck the screen, and I know your tidy soul revolts; but go on! You stand behind there and pop a dart at somethin.' If you can make it disappear as soon as it strikes, well . . . Think you could do it?"

Masters had almost the air of a pleased clergyman. His head was high.

"I used to be pretty deadly with a pea-shooter when I was a kid. And—I've tried this already. I can do it right enough, sir, because I've got the stuff here. . . . Go you one better than that, gentlemen!" he said suddenly. "This reminds me of that show you staged at Plague Court, Sir Henry. But now the show's *mine*. Eh? One of you gentlemen sit over in that chair with the light on you, now. I'll get behind this screen a dozen feet away, I'll blow a dart, and I'll defy you to tell me how it vanished even after you feel it hit you."

"No, I'll be damned if you will," said H.M. "Now look here, son, that's goin' too far to get some of your own back. Suppose you plop somebody in the eye with that thing?"

"Guarantee to make it just prick your coat, sir! Won't be shot hard, won't even puncture. Well, gentlemen?"

There ensued an argument, in which both Sir George and Tairlaine wanted to get into the line of fire; so, it was obvious, did H.M., who refused to allow the experiment simply because he was not running it. H.M. roared, and finally they matched coins. The lot fell to Tairlaine, as he had uneasily felt it would; while Masters cheerfully went about cutting narrow slits in the screen.

"This is the goddamdest fool Punch-and-Judy show *I* ever saw," growled H.M. "I hope somebody walks in while we're playin' it, that's all I hope. There's a couple of top-hats comin from the Austrian Legation to see me to-day, and if they don't write home to Freud about it I miss my guess. All right, all right. What do you want us to do now?"

"Turn on the desk-light, sir," said Masters, sticking his head out from behind the screen like a photographer. "Just enough so

I can see him clearly. Now, Doctor—take that chair away from the desk; I want a straight line to you. Sit down in it facing the windows away from me. That's it. Don't look at the screen until I tell you. . . . I'll move it back some feet." There was a bumping noise. "You two gentlemen stand to one side, and don't look at the screen either until something happens. Ready?"

It was one of those swivel-chairs which suddenly throw you half-way over backwards when you sit down in them. Tairlaine adjusted himself, staring out of the gray windows in which was reflected the bright light behind his back. He heard H.M. growl, and the crackle of the fire during a silence. Below him he could see the traffic moving along the Embankment, the smoky river as far as its curve behind Charing Cross. The faint mutter grew . . .

Somebody yelled behind him, and then the voice went to falsetto.

"Help! Tairlaine, for God's sake help . . . !"

He stumbled, his heart in his throat; he got out of his chair, whirling round and lifting up his head towards the screen as he rose. And, as his head was lifted to expose the neck just under the line of jaw and chin, something flicked him there with a sharp sting.

For a moment he stood staring blankly at the light, for longer than a moment. Something moved behind the slits in the screen; that was all. Then he clapped his hand under his jaw, and felt nothing.

"I say, I'm sorry, sir!" exclaimed Masters from behind the screen. "My aim wasn't as good as I thought it would be. Yes, I've nicked you there, but it's not even as bad as a nick at shaving.—Point is, do you see any dart?"

With H.M. and Sir George looking on either side of him, he peered. He shook his clothes, looked behind, brushed at the floor, all without result. H.M. lumbered forward and pointed his finger malevolently.

"You did that a-purpose!" he declared. "Masters, you did that a-purpose! You yelled out so he'd look round and raise his head. Then you nicked him——"

"Just in the place where Bender had the only cut on his body," said Sir George.

They looked at each other. The Punch-and-Judy man poked his head out cautiously as Tairlaine began to use some very un-academic language. Masters looked pleased. "I'm glad you take it as well as that, sir," he said heartily. "It's always a good sign when they swear. Sorry! I mean it. But to do it properly, you see, I had to do it just as——"

"I don't mind," snapped Tairlaine, who minded most of all the start he had been impelled to give at that cry, "provided the thing isn't poisoned." He soothed his ruffled dignity by slapping at his coat. "Though I don't see how the murderer could have bawled like that without the rest of us hearing him in the dining-room. The essential point," said he, normal again, "is the means by which the thing was accomplished. Well?"

"Let me show you. No, don't look behind the screen yet, if you please. The medical report came in this morning, and confirmed fully what I'd thought. Mr. Bender died of curare poisoning administered by injection into the bloodstream. The only cut or puncture of any kind on his body was that light nick under the jaw, and it *had* to be that. But I thought it had to be beforehand . . . Hum. You remembered what bothered us a lot, Sir Henry? At least, it bothered me. Even with a poison that acted like lightning, and paralyzed the muscles first of all, why couldn't Mr. Bender have called for help? You see what this means, though?"

H.M., lumbering up and down, made irritable gestures.

"Uh-huh. That was clear enough. It had to be shot into the neck, where the first thing it paralyzed would be speech. But——"

"And it worked, you see," nodded Masters, "while Mr. Bender was still getting over his surprise at being stung. Eh? You saw what Dr. Tairlaine did. He—well, goggled a bit. If he'd been in that room, he'd probably have gone over towards the window to see what was wrong and who was talking to him. And then it got him. . . . Now, gentlemen, look at this. I found it caught in the shutter." Producing an envelope, he shook out something into his palm and held out the hand.

"What are we supposed to look at?" demanded Sir George, after a pause. "I don't see anything except your hand."

"Try it under the light. Here, now—ah, you see it! Texture's heavier than a hair, but just as light, and pliable as . . . This strand is black, and about two inches long. It's one ply, or strand, of real Japanese silk, and strong enough to surprise you."

He replaced it in the envelope, went behind the screen and returned with his hands spread apart.

"Turn the light on me, or you won't be able to see it. I've got here four yards of two-ply silk thread, twice as tough. Put the whole lot on the back of your hand, and you'd feel it not much more than a cobweb. Right! The principle is—like a kid's popgun, you see? My kid has one. To work this trick, you take your light-weighted dart, you wind an inch of silk round the off-end and seal it with gum. You come up to the window. Through a slit you push the slack of your thread, so that four yards of it hang down for loose, easy play. Nobody can see you do it; thread's nearly invisible, and there's only gaslight. One end you hold yourself or tie to something for safety; the other's gummed on the end of the dart. Dart goes fairly loose into your blowpipe, carrying a couple of cobweb inches with it . . . You call out, get your man into exactly the right position and just the right distance away with no furniture between. Then you fire. Dart punctures but won't stick; or if it does stick, very lightly; you're drawing in the slack before the poor blighter knows what hit him. Back through the slit again . . . and you've absolutely proved that he died by an agency in that room; that the poison-trap is working and the curse of the room still as strong as it used to be."

Masters' modest eloquence trailed off into a cough. He folded up the thread carefully with the dart, and put the device into an envelope.

"Hurrum!" he added. "Just so."

"Y'know, Masters," said H.M. meditatively, "the words that've been runnin' through my head are, 'Did you think of that all by yourself?' Son, I might 'a' known that a feller whose hobby is trick spiritualist-devices would hit on that solution. Oh, I'm not disparagin'! So far as I can see at the moment, it's all the more damning for poor old Guy because it's the only way the trick could have been worked. You've broken his alibi. You've proved he was at the window and talked through it, with good, undeniable fingerprints. And, finally, if you can trace this funny dingus to him——"

"I can, sir."

"You said last night," Sir George muttered abruptly, "something about a real Japanese——"

"Silk dressing-gown. Quite so. It's an old one, very frayed so it almost comes off on you with unraveling. I found it hanging in his closet. This piece of silk exactly matches some loose stuff on the edge of the pocket. He could have got as many feet of strong two- or three-ply by unraveling the bottom edge of the gown. And what's more, a glass-cutter, gentlemen! A glass-cutter hid away on the top shelf of the closet. Brings it home to him finally, eh?"

"Sit down, you chaps, and quit wanderin' about!" roared H.M. Tairlaine was rather surprised that they were all moving round in a caged fashion. Why? Why this tacit insistence to protest against Guy Brixham's guilt? Visualizing that bony face, with its too-high forehead and sickly smile among the wrinkles, Tairlaine knew it could not be friendship.

"It's true," he admitted, "that Guy seems the likeliest one to have inherited—a kink. From the story he told us, it's true that he gloats over that room. It's true he might visit it secretly at night, to restore its old appearance; and strangle a parrot that screeched at his passing or cut the throat of a dog that barked at the door and might betray his presence there. It's true he might have killed Bender when Bender discovered his kink, and killed him in just that way. If he's mad, he's at least as shrewd and common-sense as his ancestor Henri Sanson. Yes, he *fits in*. He's the only one who does."

Sir George was dogged. "Fair enough. But you're not even allowing him a consistent madness. What good would it do him to kill Bender? Others could discover that kink."

"Yes. Only—he wouldn't think so."

"And besides, if he's so shrewd and commonsense, why does he stand at the window and sing out Bender's replies long after Bender must be dead? If we accept Masters' solution, why would *anybody* do that?"

Masters smiled indulgently.

"I'm not strong on what you call the psychological side of things, gentlemen," he said. "But, talking of common sense, that part of it's the easiest of all.—He did it because he had to make sure Mr. Bender was dead before you people got to him. Nobody, not even an expert toxicologist, can tell how long any poison must work before any given person is dead and past all antidote. Remember, in the place where Mr. Bender fell he couldn't be *seen* from the window: it was too far to one side. Now, suppose Guy Brixham shot that dart just after Mr. Bender had given his usual reply at eleven-fifteen. The rest ensues, Bender goes down out of sight. At eleven-thirty he may or may not be dead. If you people out there don't hear the usual answer then, you're going to be into that room in a hurry. And suppose this poor chap's just got strength enough to say something before he does die, and blow the gaff? . . . Hurrum! No, no. Friend Guy has got to wait until he's sure his victim is dead as mutton beyond *all* question. Hence the reply at quarter to twelve, after which he bolts. Why, it's plain common sense, if you ask me. And puts it beyond any doubt. Eh?"

H.M., who had dragged back his chair and settled into it, spoke plaintively. "I say, Masters, ain't you forgetting that notebook?"

"Sir, I've worried about that notebook long enough. And what I say now is," said the chief inspector, with an affable gesture, "*blow* the notebook."

"Oh, I admit I'm crushed and humbled. All I mean to point out is that it was pinched."

"Was it? Then let me ask you a straight question. Did you ever see that notebook at any time? Did anybody ever see it? Can you even swear, in fact, that there ever was a notebook?"

H.M. muttered to himself. But he stared at the desk, and did not reply.

"Exactly. You're too good a barrister, sir, not to see what your own evidence amounts to—if you were ever put in the box to give it before cross-examination. An hour or more before dinner, you saw a bulge in a man's breast pocket. You bumped against him, and felt what you thought was a notebook. Which is not evidence. . . . And even supposing something of the sort was there at that time. Very well. Some little time elapses when you do not see Bender——"

"Oh, yes! Sure! I follow the cross-examination," grunted H.M. "'Even if there had been something in the pocket before dinner, what's to have prevented him from takin' it out in the meantime?' 'Since you didn't touch him later, can you swear he had anything in his pocket when he came to dinner?' 'Bulges, you say? I put it to you, sir, when a man sits down to grub in a boiled shirt, is it not true that his chest will bulge considerable?' . . . I can hear old Goopy Howell thunderin' out the questions, and waggling his pencil at me through the blast." H.M. shook his head somberly. "Burn me, you're much too legal to be sensible. I can't swear there was a notebook because I didn't see it. That's like sayin' a man can't swear it was his own wife he, *um,* put his arm around, because it happened in the dark. Pfaa! I tell you, Masters, I *know* it was a notebook. But as for the dinner-table . . ."

"Hesitation," said Sir George, peering at him. "Are we beaten?"

"I'm afraid so. In the study he had a notebook and some-thin' else, but afterwards . . . Quite. The old man's got to concede the match. Masters and Common-Sense score five-hundred for one wicket over. The only thing we can bowl him with is that little roll of parchment. But what's that against all his evidence? By some miracle, d'ye see, that little roll might have been in Bender's own pocket like the nine of spades. By some miracle he might have had it in his hand, and dropped it on his own chest in his death-pains. Burn me, a good counsel like Goopy Howell would argue that was just what he *had* done, to draw attention to Guy as the murderer!—Guy left his fingerprints on the window and his proved thread-mechanism in the shutter. Guy alone can be guilty by every convergin' bit of evidence, and even that little roll of parchment proves . . . even that little roll of parchment proves . . . parchment proves . . ."

Suddenly H.M.'s voice was wabbling and whirring and repeating the same jerky phrase like a phonograph running down. It trailed away. He sat rigid, his hands on the ends of the desk, and stared.

"Oh, my *God,*" said H.M., very softly.

He sat motionless against the darkling sky. Nobody spoke. Nobody spoke for the space of a full minute, when the shrilling of the telephone bell made Tairlaine jump.

The call was relayed from Sir George's offices at the British Museum. Mantling's wild voice squeaked so loudly in the receiver that they knew what had happened before H.M. told them. Guy Brixham had been found dead in the Widow's Room. There was no doubt he had been murdered, for the back of his head was smashed in. He had been rolled under the far side of the bed, and a tarnished silver casket was still lying near his hand.

CHAPTER THIRTEEN

The Secret Drawer

Since Masters telephoned in the report immediately, the police surgeon and squad men were in Curzon Street almost as soon as the group in Masters' car. Tairlaine never forgot that ride through smoky streets, with the heavy-footed traffic refusing to make way, and H.M. piled beside Masters in the front seat. H.M. spoke only once.

He said: "The killer's comin' out in the open now. And I'm very much afraid it's a loony we've got to deal with. But not Guy.—I don't know the truth. For a second I thought I had a faint hazy glimmerin' of what might be the truth, but I'm still far away. What I did guess last night may not bear, really, on the main issue. And yet, burn me, I might still have prevented this if I'd told you last night."

In Curzon Street idlers had gathered, and enterprising newspaper-sellers cried news of the Mantling scandal before Mantling's house. The door was opened by a winded Alan, whose flesh seemed to have gone baggy and wrinkled since last night. He scooped them inside, shook his fist at the onlookers (who enjoyed the sensation to be told at home), and slammed the door.

"Couldn't get through to you," he protested with weak irritability. "Had to fight with the Museum people before they'd tell where George was; then a lot of rot—" He rubbed reddish eyes, and after a pause added: "Poor—little—blighter."

"Let's have a look at him," said H.M. curtly, always uneasy before sentiment. He seemed again his vast and assured self, whereas Masters was bewildered. "You weren't clear on the 'phone. When was he found, and who found him, and why didn't you report this sooner?"

"It was only half an hour ago, I tell you! Bob Carstairs and I found him. We went in lookin' for clews——"

"What clews?" said Masters sharply.

"Well, *any* clews. You know. Clews to prove Ravelle had . . . Tell you about that when you've seen him." He had become grim, and hitched his big wrists out of his sleeves. "We were over looking at the window, and Bob grabbed my arm and pointed. There was the toe of a shoe sticking out from under the bed. Poor little blighter. I—I wish we hadn't tried to yank him out as though we'd caught a burglar. Sat down flat when I saw who it was." Again he dragged a grimy hand along his eyes. "Well, come *on*. You know the way. He's been dead some time. He's cold."

Wheeling round, Alan led them through the chilly over-decorated hall, which looked more bleak by day. That house had a bad atmosphere of instilling suggestion, as it had done ever since the first Charles Brixham saw his first phantom on the staircase. In daylight Tairlaine could see by the condition of the woodwork how old the place was.

Carstairs was waiting for them in the dining-room, pulling at his toothbrush mustache. When Masters saw that one side of his face was swollen and discolored, the chief inspector began to wake up. When he saw a bandaged cut along the temple, he stared.

"Would you mind telling me, sir," he said, and rounded on Alan, "exactly what's been going on here? You report a man with his head beaten in, and then I find somebody who looks as though he'd been in a fight——"

Carstairs, haggard as he was, hopped up with a kind of protesting yelp which reminded Tairlaine idiotically of a well-meaning dog. Alan forestalled him. "Oh, *that's* all right," he said, contemptuous of the whole business. "That was last night, when he knocked Ravelle out. Tell you about that in a minute. Why do you want to fool about with things like that, when poor old Guy—? Come on."

Although the shutters sagged back against the walls of the Widow's Room, the clouded grime of the window-panes still made it shadowy. One square bar of light from a missing pane slanted to the floor, and dust motes moved in it. The part of the room nearest the door showed wreckage. One satinwood chair had its legs smashed off, another was split down the back and gouged along the satin seat, the table heeled far to one side on an already rotting carpet ripped as though by crooked plowing.

"Ravelle and I did that," said Carstairs. "Not—" He pointed beyond the pale beam of light. Then his hand seemed to pain him, and he dropped it.

When H.M. and Masters tramped over into the shadows on the far side of the bed, Tairlaine followed them; but he did not remain long. The figure that had been dragged from under the bed lay almost where Bender had lain, except that this time the feet instead of the head pointed towards the foot of the bed. It was smeared grotesquely with dirt and that feathery lint which accumulates under beds left shut up for even less a period than sixty years. And, since it had stiffened before it was hauled out, the legs were still twisted together and hands flattened against its breast where the murderer had rolled it under on its face. Except for the lower jaw pushed sideways, the face looked very peaceful in the shadows. The dark glasses, broken and shrouded with dust, lay on the floor; but the eyelids still hid the gaze the glasses had kept from the world.

H.M.'s foot knocked against something near Guy's side.

"Y'know, Masters," he growled, "I'm almost saying 'poor devil' myself. Dying under a bed; I dunno why, but it seems as mean a thing as dyin' in the gutter. What's this? Dammit, can't we have some light in this place? Aha! It's our old friend the silver box." He put on a pair of gloves and lifted it carefully. "What was used to do the business? See anything?"

"I can tell you that," Alan said dully. He would not come near the bed. "I struck a match and looked under. Remember that hammer I brought in here last night, when I thought we'd need it to open the door? Look under the bed and you'll see it. I—I can't remember where I left it. I'd forgotten . . ."

"Never mind. *I* can remember," said Masters, who was groping under the bed with a gloved hand. "We used that hammer and chisel to break open the shutters and pry up the window. We left 'em on top of this bed—all covered with *our* fingerprints, I daresay. God!" muttered the chief inspector, whose face was heavy with rage. "This business . . . How long has he been dead, Sir Henry?"

H.M., on his knees, called irritably for light, and Masters raised the loosened window. For the first time the crumbled splendor of the room was made raw by daylight; gray daylight, but a human illumination at last. Beyond, across the narrow alley, Tairlaine could see a blank brick wall. Faces looked washed-out in this daylight, the room as tawdry as morning in a theater. Glancing down, he saw H.M. lift the thing's head to feel the back of the skull; and he looked away again.

"Humph. Ha. Time of death—" grunted H.M. presently, "time of death, offhand, I put between eight and nine hours ago, but a good deal nearer eight. The time now is . . . let's see . . . few minutes past noon. This feller was killed round about four o'clock, more or less."

"Four o'clock?" cried Carstairs. Horror grew in his face. "You don't mean four o'clock this morning?"

"Presumably," said Masters. "Why should that surprise you, now?"

Carstairs groped back after a non-existent chair, seemed surprised not to find one, and stared at the body. "You mean—he was lying under that bed, dead, all the time I was waiting here in the dark for somebody; and I never knew it?"

"That's right, son," nodded H.M. "Bit of a nasty thing to look back on, ain't it? If you had your row with Ravelle at twenty minutes past four, as I seem to have heard somewhere, that's just what did happen. Better tell Masters about it. That smashed furniture is loomin' up to him as bad as a smashed head."

Carstairs came nearer the window. Never an especially handsome specimen, and now with his face discolored and his lank figure clad in a dusty brown suit, still there was something honest and sound and likable about him. He was incongruous in this room. Tairlaine thought that in the young man's blundering, amiable way he felt Guy's death more deeply than Mantling. Mantling was the bass drum; Carstairs was only Tommy

Atkins muddling along behind. He shifted, looked at the body, and away again.

"You see," he said hesitantly, "I thought somebody might sneak back here in the middle of the night to get something. . . ."

Masters got out his notebook. "And what might make you think that, Mr. Carstairs?"

"Well, dash it, I heard *you* say so! At least, one of you did, when you and the sergeant and somebody else were in here messing about with the room, and taking down the shutters. But then you decided that everything was all right, and you wouldn't bother to leave a guard. I say, you're not suspicious of your own statements, are you?"

"Never mind that, sir! You mean you were listening?"

Carstairs flushed. "Uh—well, yes, in a way! I was mooching about. . . ."

"Why?"

"It was like this, if I've got to tell you. I had another row with Judy last night. We hadn't been on good terms, you see, ever since I stuck myself with that spear and said I was poisoned. Last night she was mad at Arnold, and every time she gets mad at anybody she hops on me. She comes straight back to the old subject. Last night again—this was just before she went up to bed—she got back to, 'Why don't you make something of yourself?' Then she said, 'But I suppose you can't make bricks without straw; in fact, *you* can't even make a scarecrow.' And that made me mad, because Arnold was standing by with that damned superior air of his, as though he always had his bankbook in his hand——"

"Steady, Mr. Carstairs. I want facts, if you please. When did this happen?"

The other pondered. "Have to get the times straight, what? I've read that. I'm pretty sure it was just after the three of 'em had left." He nodded towards H.M., Tairlaine, and Sir George. "That would be about ten minutes to three. I remember, because I didn't have a chance to say so-long. Judy and I were in the library. We came out into the hall just as Ravelle was going up to bed, and Guy went up not long after him. Then after a while Arnold came down—he'd been soothing the old lady, or some rot. That was when Judy made the remark about the scarecrow. Then was when I got the idea, 'Suppose I could find the murderer?'" He clenched his hands. "While Judy and that— while they were saying—what they had to say to each other, I went out to the dining-room to think it over. And maybe get a line on what the police were doing, which I did. And all of a sudden I thought, 'Good God, suppose Arnold did that murder, and I could pin it on him!'"

Masters looked up.

"You think Dr. Arnold—?" said Masters. A curious thoughtful gleam began to show in the chief inspector's eye.

"He's as much under suspicion as any of us, isn't he?" Carstairs protested. He fidgeted and then wavered. "Yes . . . No, I don't suppose I believed it really. Trouble is, he's much too smart even to commit a murder, and that's one of the things I don't like about the swine. But I *wanted* him to be guilty, if you've got to have the truth, and he could just as well be guilty as anybody else. Then was when I thought of waiting up all night in this room. Of leaving the house openly, you see, and coming back——"

"Just so. But how did you mean to get in?"

Mantling interposed with heavy impatience, to brush away these irrelevancies. "Dammit, that's all right. 'Squite-allright.

Bob's got a key. When we're plannin' a trip somewhere, there are a million little things to attend to, and we hop in and out twenty times a day."

"If you say so, sir. . . . When then, Mr. Carstairs?"

"I said my good-nights, and left the house with Arnold. Then I told him I was going in another direction, and hung back in the fog and trailed him——"

"Trailed him?" demanded H.M. "Burn me, what for?"

"Well, I was playing detective, wasn't I? I thought he might do something suspicious, and besides what else could I do? I had to wait until everybody here went to bed. He went home, curse him. . . . When I got back here again—it was nearly half-past three—Alan was just letting you out," he nodded at Masters, "and a couple of others. So I turned up my collar and stood in a doorway across the street until the house quieted down. When I'd given it a good half-hour, and everything was dark, I started across the street. And just as I was nearly to the door, a light went on in a room on the second floor."

"In whose room?" H.M. asked sharply.

"In Guy's room. I . . ." He hesitated, and his eyes widened. "Look here, I never thought of it until now! That was a few minutes past four o'clock. But if Guy——"

"Uh-huh. Y'see, son, it wasn't Guy who turned on the light. What then?"

He seemed to review a memory a long time before he spoke. "I ducked back again. I felt rotten; I was cold and damp clear through; and I almost chucked the whole thing. The blinds in the room were down, and I could see somebody's shadow moving back and forth. . . ."

To Tairlaine, the vision of those yellow windows above the misty street, with a shadow moving back and forth that was not

Guy's, made the terror at Mantling House more vivid than even two dead men. Carstairs gestured.

"Then the light went off. I thought, 'Only Guy up for a moment or two, and probably half asleep. I'll risk it.' So I did. But even so I was worried for fear Guy"—he flushed again—"that is, for fear . . ."

He paused again. "Yes, sir?" prompted Masters.

"Tell you later. Well, I got into the house. It was all dark and quiet. I'll admit I had the wind up then." He stared aggressively. "You try going back in a place like this, in the middle of the night, without a light . . . I struck a few matches, that was all. Everything seemed right enough, but I decided I wouldn't sit down or stand against anything. So I waited here." Walking to the middle of the room, he looked round slowly, as though he could not reconcile its present dingy appearance with last night's terrors by the light of a match. "And, by Gad, I hadn't been here ten minutes before I heard somebody coming—along that passage. Chap had a flashlight. I felt cooler when I saw it was . . ."

"Was who? Go on!" said Masters.

"Was human," Carstairs replied. He nodded, and his brown eyes were slightly protruding. "If you know what I mean. I suppose I wasn't cool, because I let drive at him straightaway. He dropped his torch, and—" He grinned faintly. "I like old Ravelle, in spite of what Alan says. He's jolly good on the in-fighting. Hang it, Alan, he *didn't* go at me with that knife! He had it in his hand, and the thing was accidental. He dropped it. . . . Besides, if he killed Guy at four o'clock, why did the fathead come creeping back twenty minutes later?"

"You're a stout fella, Bob," Mantling said indulgently. "But you're not long on brains—eh? Are you, now? You waited for somebody to come back, didn't you? That's why you were here."

His big face hardened. "Let me tell you, Inspector, what he had with him."

He detailed the finding of the knife, the sharp 'knitting-needle with a handle,' and the sticks of modeling-clay.

"Any idea," said Masters, "what he wanted with that rum lot?"

"Not a ghost, my boy. But if we simply took Mr. Ravelle, you and I, and gave him a little third-degree—he? *Ha!*"

"We'll omit that, if you don't mind, sir. Now, you heard this row at twenty minutes past four and came downstairs. How many of the others in the house heard it and got up?"

"Everybody, except Isabel. She'd taken a sleeping-draught. I sent the servants back to bed, and Judith and I patched up old Bob as well as we could. But, my Lord, we never suspected—" He pointed, and swallowed hard.

"Didn't it surprise you that Mr. Guy wasn't there?"

"Haa, no! He wouldn't have bothered.—I mean, don't misunderstand. I don't mean anything against the poor devil." Mantling dug his hands in his pockets. He walked over to the bed. Unblinking, he looked down at the body with a sort of curiosity. "And we owe him an apology. He didn't mean anything, either."

"I don't think I understand that, sir."

"Old H.M. will, if you don't," said Alan, nodding without lifting his eyes. "But I'll try to explain. I know I'm supposed to be about as good at thinkin' as a bull is at mathematics, or at least with the hide and the imagination of a bull. I admit that last night I roared like one. But imaginative people are usually pretty intolerant and narrow-minded about imagination; they can't think of it in anybody but their own clan, and they get startled when they suddenly discover a clerk or a coster thinkin' the same things as themselves. Maybe I've got too much imagination, and have to conceal it. Maybe that's why I was afraid of this room.

"Look at him." He pointed to the body. "I thought he was crazy. Or at least—touched a bit. I still don't know what to think, except I know he didn't murder anybody. But I'd be a filthy hypocritical swine if I pretended I'm not a little glad he's dead—restin', sort of. He didn't *fit,* anywhere. It wasn't that he always made me nervous; he made everybody nervous, and himself, too. Why, dammit, you talk about 'atmosphere'! Can't you feel the whole place is lighter, there's more air, you feel freer, now that you know he can't speak?"

Masters said doubtfully: "This is all very well, sir, but to go on with the facts——"

"Facts?" demanded Mantling, starting with the bull-roar again, and then trailing off. "All last night I thought Guy was crazy, and crazy to the point of murder! *My* brother, with my blood and my father and mother! I don't for an honest fact hate doctors, or I wouldn't tolerate Arnold, and I'd have spotted that fella Bender right away. Guy spotted him. I was afraid of what they might find in Guy. Last night, after Bender was killed, and Bob Carstairs told me on the quiet about seeing Bender sneak out of Guy's room . . . and we learned Bender was after somebody . . . well, I had to lie down."

"What's that?" asked Masters sharply. "Mr. Bender sneaking out of where?"

Carstairs shifted. "Can't do any harm to tell it now," he said. "Tell the truth, when I saw the chap's face I thought he'd been up to some sneak-thieving, and I forgot it. I say, what's the matter? It's not important, is it?—It was last night a couple of hours before dinner, when I'd gone upstairs for a brush-up just after

I got here. I saw Bender stick his head out of Guy's room, and take a quick look to each side as though he didn't want to be seen, and duck out. I walked straight into him. He had a funny look on his face, I noticed. Fella was fiddling with the buttons on the sleeve of his coat. That's why he didn't notice me. He'd got a long piece of thread or hair or something caught in the button——"

"Thread," repeated Masters in a curious tone.

"Thread," said H.M., and they looked at each other. "What'd he do with it, Carstairs?"

"Do with it? Nothing. He just broke off the long bit and brushed it off him, way anybody would. Then he hurried off. Why?"

"Listen, Masters. And don't deny this, because you especially stressed it yourself," said H.M., pointing at the chief inspector. "Guy's dressing-gown is old, and comin' apart. The edge of the pocket is full of unraveled threads. Oh, Gor'! No wonder you could match so exactly the little piece of one-ply thread you picked off this window-shutter. It came from that pocket. Bender was looking for something in Guy's room; he stuck his hand in the pocket, he got a sleeve-button tangled . . . Where'd you find that thread stuck in the shutter, man? Quick!"

"It was caught over a jagged edge in one slit. It—hur-rum! You don't think," the chief inspector muttered, scowling, "that Mr. Bender caught it there himself? He had part of it still tangled in the sleeve-button. And then maybe—mind, I say maybe!—when you gentlemen left him in here, he came over to make sure the shutters were tight-bolted before he settled down? Is that what you think? And he caught it in the shutter himself."

H.M. lumbered out and stared at the gray light from the window.

"Shot to blazes," he said. "Masters, this kind of awes me. Whole great big beautiful bloomin' theory cleared out by a ten-strike straight down the middle of the alley. What price fiendish murderer hauling back his dart on a cobweb line? What price the whole bloody hypothesis *now?* It came from nothin', and it's gone back to the same."

Masters cleared his throat.

"Don't deny it," warned H.M. He lifted a heavy fist and brought it down. "This is a new experience, son. I've met tricky murderers before, but Bender takes all prizes for being the trickiest corpse. He burked us by leavin' that nine of spades here himself. He probably burked us in the same way over the roll of parchment. And he's certainly left us for dead with this new stunt."

"Mind telling us," said Mantling, "what the devil you're talking about?"

"I would," said H.M. with some fervor. "Not for worlds will I ever be persuaded again to utter one word about the sinister episode of the boomerang dart. Boys, we sat in my office not very long ago and played a game that the old man blushes to remember. Henceforth, I'm goin' to trust my own judgment.—Has anybody got any practical suggestions?"

Mantling's sluggish anger stirred again.

"Gone blind, hey?" he snapped. "Can't see the plain flat fact in front of you? *Nail Ravelle,* that's what to do. There's been a lot of talk about mad streaks in our family. All right; but Ravelle's connected with it, too. Guy told me that last night. He told me to watch out. And that was the last time I saw him alive. He warned me. Why fasten on one of us, when Ravelle was in this house when the dog was butchered and the whole filthy business *began?* Hadn't been anything like that before, mind. Why is he here anyway? Three weeks off his business to buy up a couple of pieces of furniture that can't be worth a hundred quid for the lot. Well, then? And, last of all, can't you see anything queer in what he did last night? What was he after?"

"I can tell you that," answered H.M.

He spoke with such dull, bitter anger that the others swung round. He pointed a gloved finger at the silver casket on the bed. He added:

"That was what he was after. Only he didn't know it."

"Didn't know it?"

"He was lookin' for something, and he would have looked in the wrong place. What he was after had been moved. Want me to show you?"

Lumbering over, H.M. picked up the heavy casket and returned to the window. He stood silhouetted, in his ancient top-hat and fur-collared coat, staring down at the tarnished metal.

"You've asked over and over, all of you, why Ravelle sneaked into this room in the middle of the night. Hasn't it occurred to you to wonder why *Guy* did? You've asked what Ravelle was after. Then ask what Guy was after, so that he slipped in here without lights, and somebody was able to collar him and smash his skull from behind. You won't have to think hard. Masters, you were here and saw how Guy nearly had a fit of hysteria when he walked in last night and saw us tinkerin' with it. Burn me, didn't you notice how hard he worked to persuade you to let him take it away with him? You wouldn't. So he came back after it.

"Why? I kept tryin' to call it to your attention. Over and over I kept saying there was something wrong with this box. All you could persistently and fatheadedly answer was, 'But there's no poison-trap in it.' Quite right. In that case, what else could there be wrong with it? What sort of casket, d'ye think, is the blasted thing anyway?"

"*Well?*" said Masters.

"It's a jewel-casket," said H.M., "and it could have a false bottom."

He swung it up sharply against the light, yanking his hand along the under side. A shallow drawer sprang five full inches from the carving, and something jumped out of it like a toad . . . The group jerked backwards until they saw a leather pouch strike the floor, bursting its string and spilling. In the glittering heap Tairlaine could count five diamonds, two in heavy gold settings, a shoe-buckle set in rubies, and——

"The trinkets given to the Headsman, that old Marthe Sanson bragged about," snapped H.M. "That's what he was after."

CHAPTER FOURTEEN

Marthe Dubut's Chair

"If that's the doorbell I hear ringing now," proceeded H.M., "it'll be the police surgeon and the fingerprint gang, and they'll invade us. So, providin' you want to hear the whole story of the curse on the room as I got it worked out, let's adjourn somewhere. . . . Uh, wait! First, somebody pick up that chair that's got 'Monsieur de Paris' engraved on it—it's the one with the legs broken off now—and bring it along. It'll figure in the reconstruction."

Dazedly Mantling bent over to pick up the leather pouch. It was a new pouch. He scooped up its contents, whose colors shifted and burned in his palm as he spread them out: a core of light for the shadowy room. Although Tairlaine knew nothing of diamonds, he saw that the two in gold settings were about the size of pigeons' eggs, and seemed of the finest water; two more were of a bluish cast, set as ear-rings; and the last an enormous plain stone cut into dazzling facets. The ruby-set shoe-buckle was bent nearly into a half cylinder. Finally, there was a sapphire shaped like a rose, with a broken silver pin as though it had been torn away from someone.

Mantling touched the largest diamond. He said hoarsely:

"That thing must be eighty carats, maybe a hundred. It's what the diamond fellas call the 'brilliant.' Chap at Karnul took me round once. Manalive, how——?"

"Put 'em in your pocket," H.M. cut in gruffly. "They're yours now. I was goin' to let Guy have 'em for having found 'em, and I let him go to his death instead." He rammed shut the drawer of the box. "So you see a hundred carats, do you? I got a funny kind of brain. I see some poor chaps with fine clothes, and shakin' knees, climb up on a scaffold and tear off something to make the Headsmen do their business with one swing. There was a woman among 'em; see those ear-rings? That's your heritage, son. Do you want it?"

"And *I* was thinking," muttered Sir George, "whether we weren't all wrong about the motive for these crimes . . ."

"Motive?"

"Yes. It isn't necessarily a madman who kills for a fortune like that."

"Uh-huh. That's what I thought of. But it's a madman who kills and then lets the fortune alone. Pick up that chair and come along. Somebody get Ravelle; he's got to be in on this."

A silent group, they tramped out. Carstairs caught up the chair that had only one stump of a leg remaining, and looked at it curiously as he followed. In the outer hall, where a very frightened Shorter had just opened the door to the police, Masters stopped to give a few instructions. Then he joined the others in the study. Mantling turned on the center lights. Carstairs went to get Ravelle: 'show there are no hard feelings,' he insisted. When Mantling emptied out the jewels on the desk-blotter, H.M. sat down behind them with his tall hat beside. For a time he sat ruffling his hands across his big bald head.

"It's like this," he went on. "I been sittin' and thinkin', ever since I heard a short outline of this business. And one thing bothered me: the thing that wasn't consistent with a casual curse striking at random. I mean the young woman who suddenly chose to spend a night in that room just before her wedding in December, 1825. She'd been brought up in horror of that room by an insane father, although she was the hard-headed gal who took care of a soft-headed twin brother. Now—what was the answer to that?

"Allied to that was the biggest problem of all: Why did sudden death hit only somebody who was *alone* in that room? Now that didn't work either accordin' to the rules of demonology or the rules of sense and probability. Even if you wash out the supernatural, and agree on a poison-trap, the thing is just as mysterious. The trap must be stationary, ready to sting anyone who accidentally stumbled on it; it couldn't walk about to pick and choose a victim, or be coy enough not to let a second party watch it work. Yet with more than one person there it was always harmless.

"I saw the answer. That girl in 1825 had a *reason* for such a queer act, and a reason for wantin' to be alone. In fact, everybody who died there must have had the same purpose. It wasn't the trap that wanted each person to be by himself; it was each person who wanted to be alone with the trap. They looked for something, something nobody else must see—and died tryin' to find it. Find what? Humph! Well, I remembered two things, which might or might not have been important. December, 1825, was the month of one of the worst financial panics in the nineteenth century; and Marie Brixham's intended husband was a jeweler whose business later went bust."

"But look here!" protested Sir George. "We've established

that there's no poison-trap there. It was established as long ago as——"

"Steady. I'm comin' to that. (Anybody got a match?) Now, what about the subsequent victims? In 1870, over from Tours comes a furniture dealer named Martin Longueval. He's related to the former Longueval who made some of the stuff in that room, and probably has family records; but he doesn't say so. He comes ostensibly on business . . . with your grandfather." H.M. stabbed his finger at Alan. "He insists on occupying that room. Everything goes well while he and old Mantling talk there for hours; but he's left alone, and he dies.

"Meantime, Grandpa Mantling doesn't seem to suspect anything for a few years. But all of a sudden the hard-headed old boy, the grind-their-necks ogre of the mills—*he* seems to go romantic, spends a night in the room, and dies. He's got a clew. What clew, we'll probably never know. The important point is: There's something hidden there, of enormous value.

"Now comes the answer to what's puzzlin' you. The representative of the next generation, later to be known as Buy-the-Best Mantling, knows there must be hanky-panky somewhere. He summons his contemporary, Ravelle of Ravelle et Cie., to examine the furniture. Ravelle does. He even takes some of it away for better examination, as we heard . . ."

"And found nothing wrong with it," said Alan.

H.M. wheezed as he took out the pipe he seldom smoked.

"Ain't it struck your simple mind yet, son?" he inquired.

"We don't know he found nothin' wrong. We only know *he said he didn't.*"

After a pause, while he vainly tried to light the pipe, H.M. went on:

"Burn me, I can't see Buy-the-Best Mantling poking about

in a trunkful of family records! How was he to know the Ravelles were closely related to the Longuevals, and the Longuevals to the Brixhams? But Ravelle knew it. *He* wasn't to be caught by any poison on guard over a treasure. He meant to have the hard-and-salable. Hand me that chair, somebody."

Masters, who could not seem to keep his eyes off the hypnosis of the stones, and was clearing his throat with great frequency, took up the broken chair for a quick inspection before he set it flat on the desk. The discolored brass binding of the satinwood gleamed by lamplight. Bending over it from behind, he ran his hands over the faded red of the seat. They stopped on the outer edge of the seat, where the bottom of the chair was several inches high, and traced a *fleur-de-lis* design on the outer face.

"Give me your penknife, Masters," said H.M. "The part we're goin' into I can only guess. I had a look at this last night, when I thought that if there were any flummoxin' it would be with the head-of-the-house's chair. But I found no trap, because there isn't any *now.* Ravelle senior fixed that.—Watch!"

Snapping open the knife-blade, he moved it gently round the *fleur-de-lis* design. It caught somewhere, lightly. He pressed a little harder, and the knife-point began to enter. Tairlaine saw a faint outline growing against the wood, a circular outline as though a tiny trap-door were being pried open. It was a circle of such size, say, as would contain a man's bunched fingers if he were thrusting them into the opening . . .

Something began to crack.

"Got to break this, maybe," grunted H.M. "Putty's stickin' to the wood inside. It's fairly fresh putty, you'll notice. Got it!"

The circle split halfway just as it flew upwards and outwards on an inner hinge. In the group somebody cursed involuntarily. Releasing his breath, H.M. lumbered round and moved the little trap-door up and down. Inside they could see only a flat surface of putty.

"Neat little gadget, hey?" inquired H.M. "The eighteenth-century Martin Longueval knew his business. This is where you were supposed to put your fingers in and draw something out . . . And, sixty years ago, Ravelle *père* drew its fangs and sealed it up so that nobody'd know."

"You mean, sir, that there'd be jewels in there?" demanded Masters. "In that case, if he wanted the jewels, why didn't he take them? They're still here. They're not only here, but they're in another box."

H.M. began to dig with the pen-knife.

"Uh-huh. Guy, good old Guy, saw to that; that's why the putty is fresh. As to why Ravelle senior didn't take what we see, suppose you dig out this putty and we'll see if we can make a guess. . . . You may need a light chisel there; it's strong stuff." While Masters went to work, H.M. went on talking drowsily. "Naturally I didn't get a clear glimmerin' of the business until we heard Guy's story about old Marthe Sanson.

"Remember that bit about the old virago showing Marie-Hortense Brixham 'gold and silver boxes'? That didn't suggest poison-traps; it suggested jewels and the 'costly gifts' she bragged about. Besides, if you merely put a deadly needle in the lid of a box, you'll probably only kill the wrong person openin' it by accident; and, above all, what's the good of putting jewels inside when he can't even see the bait until after he's caught? This had to be a real trap—with bait out in the open for the right person. Remember those words '*great need*' that Marie-Hortense, under orders from her old harridan, said to Charles Brixham on her death-bed? I got an idea they were the only kind of words any man would sooner or later be bound to fall for: *'If you are ever in great need of money, do such-and-such a thing.'* And good old Charles, with his methodical habit of writing everything down, probably made a note of that. Burn me, if he ever sneered at the Sansons' love of money, old Marthe paid him back! She could wait in her grave till *he* went downhill financially, and— Well, Masters?"

"Putty's not very thick, sir. Take a look now?"

The space was not broad or deep, at first sight. You could put two or three fingers in as far as the knuckle-joints, and it tapered back funnel-fashion to a smaller opening that the putty still obscured. H.M. whistled.

"Give me that largest diamond, somebody! Got it, of course! A big beauty of a sparkler was wedged in there. You pried open the outer trap, stuck your fingers in to pull the diamond out—and the old finger-nail trick was worked again. I told you it was Martin Longueval's specialty. The needle jumped out, and— Uh-huh. No wonder no mark was found on 'em. The diamond was wedged so tightly you couldn't pull it, and before you'd stopped trying the poison got you. The outer trap fell again . . ."

"That's no good!" bellowed Mantling, who was excitedly trying to fix the diamond inside. "It's too small. It'll go clear back through that choked opening at the rear——"

"Right," said H.M. "And that means only one thing. The biggest one of the lot is missing. Ravelle bagged it sixty years ago."

Behind them there was a snorting noise. Tairlaine turned to see Ravelle junior swagger in at the door. He wore a lurid-colored dressing-gown; and, despite his swollen jaw, his face was not so badly damaged as Tairlaine had expected. But he did look flushed and half-drunken and uncertain; as though he did not know whether to laugh or snarl. But he studied their faces, and something bubbled up. He laughed, genuinely. He roared.

"Goblimey," he said, with an air of relief, "you are a funny lot. And I have give you an awful lot of trouble, eh? From the 'eart I apologize. But there is one thing. You say my old papa, who is dead the many years, has pinched something. I do not like that, and besides you will never be able to prove it."

"Steady, you fool," H.M. said to Mantling, and seized Mantling's arm. He added to Ravelle: "Well, rest easy. I don't think anybody's goin' to try to prove it. Friend Alan's found enough to compensate him . . . that is, if you're willing to tell the truth."

Ravelle was affable. He put his hand on the shoulder of Carstairs, who accompanied him.

"Sure, I will tell you, old boy, since you have found out anyway. I do it besides for the sake of my good friend Robert, to whom I do not owe the malice for socking me so well in the jaw. I do it, *enfin,* because I jolly well am not going to be accused of murder." His affability faded, and he grew nervous. "That is bad! Look now! You know why I took those tools last night to that room. The knife to open—that. What you call the 'knitting-needle' to prod in and be sure there was something there. The clay to replace the putty if I find it."

Again H.M. silenced Mantling. "Now, son, we won't say one single word against your old man. We'll say that he never even thought of a diamond, and that what he found in this chair was a large pebble. But look on this desk and see what a haul of pebbles we got. The little ones must 'a' been lined up in that narrower opening behind the Great Mogul, like a jewelry display for the unwary. So why didn't your papa help himself to the rest?"

Ravelle's face darkened.

"The old beggar! He do not think! He do not think anybody is such a fool as to put in more things when that one big one is all she need. He do not know old Marthe has promised to give *all* the—pebbles, you say, to Marie-Hortense if she will tell the mad husband to go look for them. . . . And I can tell you how I think the old beggar my papa overlook it. Tell me, now! In those other pebbles you have found, there is one or two with a big flat gold setting?"

"There is."

"Ah! *Justement!* There is a list of everything, which I have seen at Tours. When he has seen the list later, he know that the little things have joggle about. That gold setting is wedged in front of the rest at the back of the small opening, and he think it is brass like the trimmings of that chair, and it is decoration too; so he think there is nothing but the big di— Ah, bah!" said Ravelle, waggling his head and folding his arms in a rather Napoleonic attitude.

"And don't you think," said Mantling, his breath beginning to sound noisy, "that maybe you have a hell of a nerve to stand in front of a police officer, to say nothing of me, and admit——"

Ravelle looked him over. "I am not afraid of you. And as to the law, myself what have I done? I have entered into a room in the middle of the night, and since I am your guest what is wrong with that? I take a knife with me. Well? Maybe I mean to eat pie, eh? If you do not know about the pebbles, that is your look-out." Suddenly he turned fretful and angry. "Look at you! Look at my friend Carstairs! Now you will lecture me about the sportsmanship. Ah, bah! We are the different races, and what is the use we try to understand each other, I ask you? When I win, I crow. When I lose, I swear. This sportsmanship is like the good advice; which everybody admit is jolly well, but nobody think of taking. It is very nice, but it is not practical."

For some curious reason, this remark seemed to lighten the tension. Mantling looked at Carstairs, and abruptly they both began to laugh. It was the first time Tairlaine had seen his host roaring with a genuine, startled, spontaneous mirth.

"All right, Frenchie," said Mantling, with grim concession. "If you admit that—matter of the pebbles is closed. Got any practical suggestions about the murder of Guy, which you probably did do?"

"You think that?" cried Ravelle, turning to Masters.

"I think, Mr. Ravelle, that you've got a lot to explain; and if there's anything else you can tell us you'd better do it," snapped Masters. "You were after those jewels. So was Mr. Guy Brixham——"

"And do I have them? No! He beat me; that is all. He has taken them out of the chair and put them in the silver casket . . ."

"How did you know that?"

"My friend Carstairs tell me, just now."

Masters wheeled. "I think, Mr. Carstairs, and you too, your Lordship, if you will, that you can give us a bit of help. Will you please go and find Miss Isabel and Miss Judith, and tell them that I should like to see them here? I daresay they know what has happened?"

"In other words—clear out," said Carstairs meditatively. He scratched his head. "Sorry, Inspector. Yes, Judy knows, poor little devil; but I don't think Isabel's awake yet. Come on, Alan."

When the door had closed Masters turned on H.M. "I'm not denying you've done a clever bit of work with the chair and the jewels and whatnot, sir. But do you realize where it leaves us? Just exactly nowhere—with everything. The last chance of a poison-trap is washed out. And we'd just finished washing out any chance that Guy did the murder by standing at the window and . . . you know." He caught himself up as he looked at Ravelle. "Then where does it leave us?"

H.M. had lifted the chair off the desk, and sat down again.

"Think so?" he inquired. The fish-like eyes wandered round. "Oh, I dunno. It puts us a good deal forrader. Be useful, Doc. What do we know?"

"If Guy took those jewels out of the chair and hid them in that casket," said Tairlaine, "then he was really the one who opened the room and visited it secretly at night——"

H.M. was impatient. "Sure he did! Who's ever doubted it all along? He's the one, the real one, the only genuine candidate! *But it never did prove that because of that he was the one who killed Bender.* A man visits an old room secretly and polishes up its furniture: well? That's not necessarily lunacy. It's only eccentricity. *I* wouldn't do it, but then I don't paint cubist pictures or play contract bridge or go in for nudism, either. All them pastimes might seem a little dotty to a normal man, but there's no law to send you to a madhouse because of 'em."

"Just so. But what about the killing of the parrot and the dog?"

"Ah! Sure! Yes! *If* you could prove it. But you can't prove it on Guy. That ingenious method of the boomerang dart, now. That's blown up. Let's see, now, what we unquestionably can prove." He held up his blunt fingers and ticked off the points, "(1) That he visited the Widow's Room at night, polished the furniture, and hid the diamonds in the silver box. (2) That, by the unquestionable evidence of your fingerprint-men, he really was standin' outside the window of the Widow's Room when Bender died."

"What?"

"Dammit, man, it's your own theory and your own proof. Simply because your imaginative addition of the dart on the thread turned out to be wrong, don't discard the really vital part of it. Don't discard the part that really tells us somethin'. . . . Do you realize the big thundering inference from that? Watching outside the window; of course he was watching outside the window! You'd be there yourself, if you had a fortune in diamonds hidden there in what you thought was the safest place in the house, and wanted to make sure the exceedin'ly snoopy Mr. Bender didn't find 'em. Do you understand why Guy was so cocky last night? So shrewd-sighted over the evidence, knowin' so much and patronizing us poor fools? Man, Guy wasn't the murderer—*but he saw the murder done.*"

Masters faced him with a kind of wild sanity.

"Now, sir," he said, and swallowed, "now! . . . I've taken back my own theory, you know. And, if he saw the murder done, you're not prepared to say, are you, that he would not only stand there without doing anything, but would also call out Bender's replies after Bender's death?"

"I do," said H.M. coolly.

"But . . . stop a bit, sir! You mean he was in collusion with the real murderer, as accessory before and after the fact?"

"Not at all. I say that he saw the murder done and saw the trick worked. I say that for purposes of his own, working independently of the real murderer, he gave the answers. I'm telling you, son," said H.M., putting his hand down flat on the table, "that the vaguest germ of an idea's got lodged in my mind, and part of it's growin' every minute. I begin to see who's guilty. I begin to see why Guy did an apparently insane thing like imitating a dead man's voice—with cold hard sense behind it. I see why he was shieldin' the murderer last night. But, d'ye see, the murderer didn't relish that kindliness. Guy wasn't killed for the jewels, or they would have been stolen. Guy knew too much, and he had to die."

Sir George Anstruther made an angry gesture. "You say that helps us? It makes the thing worse. If you had an impossible situation before, look at it now! The window not only inaccessibly bolted, but guarded by somebody who didn't do the murder. The door watched—and the rest of it. So, if Guy saw the murderer in that room . . ."

"I didn't say he saw the murderer," H.M. interrupted sharply. "I only say he saw how it was done, and therefore knew who the murderer was."

"Do you mean to say, then, that we're circling straight back to some trick that didn't need anybody present to work it?"

H.M. nodded somberly. "And in an absolutely harmless room, my boy. Find the trick, somehow. *I* don't know what it is."

In the course of the debate they had forgotten Ravelle, who was fidgeting. He coughed loudly. He said:

"The discussion of the technical is quite nice, although I do not understand what is talked about. But do you wish to ask me questions? If not, I shall go and get something to eat. But if you do," his face hardened a little, "then I shall be frank. I am not welcome now in the 'ouse. I have no reason for being here, and I can be frank."

H.M. opened his eyes. "Meanin' that you know something?"

"That is as may be. I am never such a fool as to volunteer information to the police."

"But that we can extract it from you under pressure? Uh-huh," agreed H.M. drowsily. He stared at the jewels on the desk. "Let's take your story of last night at its face value. You sneaked out of your room between quarter and twenty minutes past four, to go downstairs. Did you meet anybody else wanderin' about the house?"

"Eh? Good God, no! Or I would not have gone."

"Your room's at the front of the house, you said last night. Would that be anywhere near Guy's room?"

"Just *en face*. It is across the hall. Why? I did not see *him*, I tell you!"

"No, but I suppose you had your eye on it? Didn't notice any lights, any moving about, anything like that?"

"You can jolly well bet not, my boy, or I would not have gone, *hein?*"

H.M. checked Masters as the latter was about to speak. "That's all, Ravelle, except . . . what's on your mind?" H.M.'s little eyes became sharp. "What have you been burstin' to tell us? Dammit, don't deny that! I've been watchin' you all along. You want to tell us, and you've been weighin' pros and cons to see whether you'd better. You got an ugly look about you. And why did you follow so close when we spoke about darts? *Speak up!*"

His hand came down with a flat crash on the table. It roused the other to snap in reply, as Tairlaine thought it was meant to do.

"Very well. I tell you. Why is there reason for me to conceal a truth? Last night I pretend I was surprised at the fuss that was made over the darts—the darts from that drawer. I speak about the fuss, then, that Miss Isabel made. But I was not surprised. Miss Isabel only guessed something, but I knew. Now I do not mean to conceal the dirty linen in the closet. There were one, two, three darts and one blowpipe which were pinch from that drawer. I know who took them. I saw it done."

"You know—" said Masters, and gulped. "Who took them?"

"It was the little Judith Brixham," said Ravelle. "I saw it done."

CHAPTER FIFTEEN

Last Clew Gone

In the shock of that statement nobody, not even H.M., could take his eyes from Ravelle's flushed face. They did not hear footsteps coming across the room. Now that the words were out, Ravelle's wrath seemed to dwindle with a sudden puncture. He looked stubborn, and nervous—and ashamed. Slowly he drew the back of his hand across his mouth.

"Yes, I know what you think," he said. He began to hammer the desk. "And it is what I think of myself. I did not think it could hurt, but all of a sudden I find it does hurt. Yes! I am not the sportsman. I really tell you that because I get knocked all over the room by the man she care about, and I have not forgotten that. Otherwise I never tell you. Now I wish I could say I have lied. But, God help me, I have not lied at all."

"The man she cares about?" repeated a voice behind him. "Exactly what is all this?"

Slowly Ravelle's hand ceased to pound on the desk. He stared over his shoulder towards the direction of that calm, assured voice, whose owner's presence made itself felt before you saw him. Dr. Arnold, in correct morning-coat, his hands brushing gently before him, his cold eyes thoughtful and his large handsome face bent as though he were listening to a confidence, stood at Ravelle's shoulder.

"I overheard what you said," he continued. "But I am still not sure that I heard quite rightly."

"Quick, Masters!" said H.M., so rapidly that Tairlaine scarcely heard him. "Get Judith. And Carstairs. Get 'em quick! I got a fancy to see how this triangle works. And then hold 'em at the door within hearin' distance until I cough."

Arnold was staring at the blaze of diamonds and rubies on the table, which H.M. owlishly stirred with one finger. Arnold's gaze moved down to the shattered chair, and then up towards Ravelle, who was regarding him contemptuously.

"So you are the doctor of the brain?" he said. "Then tell me what is what you call sportsmanship and when is it a disease? Yes. You heard rightly what I wish I had not said. I said——"

H.M. made noises. "Just a little discussion, d'ye see, that can come in its proper turn. Not very important; only whether Miss Brixham prefers you to young Carstairs. It can come in its proper turn."

Arnold controlled himself. The others he greeted civilly. Towards H.M. he was courteous to the point of—not obsequiousness, Tairlaine thought, because that would be incompatible with his dignity, but to the point of being confidential. Nevertheless, his nostrils tightened at this.

"Is that what you choose to call unimportant, Sir Henry?"

"Depends. I suppose you've heard about Guy's death?"

"Judith telephoned me, naturally. I came over as soon as I could."

"Uh-huh. Sad business, ain't it?"

"Frankly, Sir Henry," said Arnold, and dusted his hands, "I

don't think so. In fact, I hinted to you last night what I hoped you would see for yourself before I took steps. In my opinion, given offhand, Guy Brixham was probably suffering from idiopathic morbid action—complicated by epilepsy and ending in hyperæmia."

"Dangerous?" asked Sir George.

Arnold was courteous but impatient. "My dear sir, why do all laymen assume that every form of mania must be homicidal mania? I meant, of course, dangerous in the sense that it jars the body social, makes for a wrong state of things, and should be cast out. Whether Guy's hyperæmia might have taken a physically dangerous turn is, of course, possible. That is not the point. I believe in an Ideal State. I am a Shavian or a Wellsian or what you like. In a properly managed state, those whose brain-illnesses lie in the disintegration of physical tissues—that is, which do not respond to therapeutic treatment, and are incurable—would be destroyed. Painlessly, of course."

H.M. sucked at his pipe. "Oh, certainly. Without pain. Yes. We'll judge him by our own crystal-clear brains, shove him into a lethal chamber, and over his grave we'll write, 'God showed you no mercy, and therefore man shall show you none.' I say, you're pretty ruthless, ain't you?"

"I am not sentimental, if that is what you mean. . . . Shall we get away from this discussion? There was something I wanted to tell you, but Guy's death has fortunately made it unnecessary. I presume you know Dr. William Pelham?"

"Pelham? Harley Street? Uh-huh. Bit of a pompous ass, but he's pretty sound. What about him?"

"I had asked him to call here at four o'clock this afternoon, to have a look at Guy. I was willing to assist, but as for taking the lead—" He shrugged.

"Bring him," said H.M. quietly. "Bring him, and both of you might give a medical opinion on somethin' else. Son, I'm curious to see how far your un-sentimentality can go." He leaned forward, his elbows on the desk and his fists against his cheeks. "How would it strike you to hear that your *fiancée* is accused of murder?"

Arnold stood motionless. He had been brushing at the sleeve of his coat, and his hand stopped a second before he dropped it. His voice was cold.

"It would strike me as an absurdity."

"H'm. Bender was poisoned with curare. We have a witness who saw Judith take three curare darts and a blowpipe from the drawer in this desk. . . . No, I see what you're goin' to ask, but you ought to know better than to waste words askin' it! It's no joke."

Arnold cleared his throat. He was not sure of himself now.

"This—this is! . . ."

"Madness, were you goin' to say? It might be, you know, in a literal sense. Or mightn't it? That's what I want to know."

"It's beyond—all *belief,* that's what I was going to say. Judith shooting poisoned darts? Good God, man, you might just as well accuse me. I was with her, you know."

"Why not?" H.M. asked urbanely. "You have been accused, son."

"Well, I can't help that. Never mind about me, but get back to Judith!" snapped Arnold. There was a flush on his face, which somehow seemed to disarrange it. "So that is what Ravelle was saying when I came in here? I tell you——"

"Good boy," said H.M., and snapped his fingers. "I was hopin' to hear that. What about your sense of social justice, though? What if she happens to be guilty?"

Arnold stood back a little, lowering his head to debate something and give an impression of coolness while he did so. His hands twitched a little. Then he decided to speak. When he spoke, it was in a low and repressed voice—but with a kind of naked sincerity that startled them.

"Professionally I've failed with you," he said, looking round; "with all of you. A match can't strike on every box, and you dislike me. I can't help that; I don't even object to it.—But do you happen to think I'm made of stone? In spite of all your beliefs to the contrary, I love that girl. I am absolutely certain she has done nothing, and in any case that does not matter."

H.M. coughed.

Remembering the signal, Tairlaine glanced at the door. Masters stood out in front, looking at the two groups. Judith walked slowly towards them, with Carstairs behind her.

Her prettiness had become almost beauty in the bright light of the room. The very clear skin was contrasted with the gold-brown of her hair; the blue eyes were level, without expression, although the lids were reddish from past tears, and she wore a dark frock. She did not seem alarmed. Her hands were crossed before her, and she moved the palm of one up and down the other arm.

"I hear I am accused of something," she said. "What is it?"

"Steady, Ravelle," H.M. said under his breath, as the latter was about to burst out. He did not take his eyes off her. "I'll handle this. . . . It amounts to something like an accusation of murder, ma'am. But we can't go so far yet. You're accused of takin' three poisoned darts out of this desk. Did you?"

Although she flinched, a strange thought seemed to come to her, and she kept herself well under control. The eyes remained motionless, and the hand stopped brushing.

"Who says I did?"

"I do. I do," said Ravelle. "I am sorry! But I saw you."

Carstairs stared. She turned to look at him as he took a step forward, but he stopped. Her inscrutable look went past him to Arnold—and Arnold was smiling broadly—then to Masters. She asked:

"I say, Inspector, am I bound to answer that straightaway?"

"It won't take up much of your time to deny it, miss; now will it?"

"True enough." The eyebrows wrinkled. "Well, I suppose I had better answer. Yes, I did take them, and the blowpipe, too." After a heavy pause she went on: "I took them a week and three days ago. It was in the afternoon; Mr. Ravelle was passing in the hall when I came out, and, to tell the truth, I was afraid he *had* seen me. I stole the key to the drawer off Alan's ring one morning before he was up; I knew he wouldn't notice it being gone. Then last night, after I heard Bender was dead, I got frightened. In the commotion I went upstairs, and got the key and the blowpipe and the two remaining darts . . ."

"The two remaining—" cried Masters. He fumbled in his pocket for his notebook, and it nearly dropped out of his hands.

"Yes. I was going to put them back in the drawer, and I sneaked down here with them. But that key sticks. Just as I put it in the lock, I heard somebody coming. So I left the key in the lock and hid the rest of the things just as Guy came in." Her color had been rising as she spoke, but her clear voice kept on steadily. "Then we were both told we were wanted in the Widow's Room. Afterwards this room was full of people and I didn't get a chance to return the things to the desk. I suppose I rather forgot it. But I did it, and I might as well admit as much."

"My God, Judy, you *didn't!*" said Carstairs.

"I did. And what of it?" She looked at him. He sat down slowly in a chair. He first returned her look, and then shifted.

"Well . . . I mean to say . . . shakes you up. I mean, having it sprung on you like this—what's a fellow going to *say?* I mean . . ."

He stopped, after a trailing mutter. Arnold was laughing.

"Your indiscretions, Judith," he observed, "are going to get you into trouble one day. I do not approve of practical jokes; in fact, I think you are a fool. But what amuses me is the psychological study,"—his mirth rang a little untrue, but he was very easy,—"on the faces hereabouts. Well, well, let's clear up this nonsense, and let the police get back to their real business."

"Exactly," said Masters. "Where did you hide the stuff, miss?"

"Behind—behind that picture of Alan and the dead rhinoceros on top of the bookcase there," she said, and suddenly began to laugh hysterically. Tairlaine had a sense of an emotional crisis passed in fierce tensity and now relaxing. She whirled round on Ravelle, Carstairs, and Arnold. "Get out, all of you! Please go. Yes, I mean it, I mean it! Go on! I've got something to tell these people I don't want you to hear. You go on, or I'll scream the house down! . . . Yes, you too, Eugene. But all the same, thanks, *thanks.*"

"Look here, I don't believe—" began Carstairs.

"Have you made up your mind?" Arnold asked curtly. "Then come along."

Afterwards she stood alone in the middle of the room, and her eyes brimmed over.

H.M. puffed and blew, Sir George made vague noises, and Tairlaine on a sudden impulse got up and took her hand.

"Thanks," she said, and gripped his arm. "I shall be quite all right in a moment. I hate to make a fool of myself. I was watching your face, and I know what you were thinking. Of course that little show was put on, but I wanted to see something."

"That's better," growled H.M., as she grinned and dabbed at her eyes. "I hate a weepin' woman. Seems as though you were putting on a little test for somebody. What I want to know is, why were you silly ass enough to pinch those darts?—Find anything, Masters?"

Breathing heavily, the chief inspector returned to the desk and laid on it two darts and a short blowpipe very similar to those in his brief-case.

"Now we'll have a bit of explanation, miss," he announced, with grim briskness. "I suspected those darts all along, and it seems we're getting back to them. Here are what you call 'the two remaining.' Pretty easy to draw an inference from that, you'll admit. Where is the third?"

"At the Home Office Analyst's," said Judith. "Sir Barnard Temple, the chief government medical examiner, still has it."

"At the—?"

"Yes. You didn't really think I used any of them, did you?" She sat down in the chair Tairlaine drew out for her. A weary, amused cynicism still wrinkled one eyebrow, but her flushed face looked half ashamed. "It—it sounds so confoundedly silly, now, that I hate to tell you. But I was furious at the time. That's how I got the idea. Did Bob tell you about the trick he served me? It was with one of those spears on the wall. The villain pretended it was poisoned, and deliberately jabbed himself in the hand with it, so that I . . .

"Never mind." She looked up whimsically. "But I thought, 'Very well, my lad; you're going to pay for that.' Then I remembered the darts, which he really did believe were poisoned. First

I stole the key and had a look at them. Five of them had a little brownish-black hard coating on the tip."

"That's the curare. And," said Masters, "those are the five we have. They haven't been tampered with. Well, miss?"

"The other three looked clean, but I had to make sure. Oh, hang it, don't you see what I was going to do? After I'd got a dart I knew wasn't poisoned, and made sure there was nothing wrong with the blowpipe either, I was going to replace the lot. Then I'd get Bob in here, lead the talk round again, make him show me how the blowpipe worked and, accidentally, stick him with one of the innocent ones. *Then* I'd see how Mr. Brave Hero felt when he wasn't swanking it, and thought he'd really been poisoned!—and don't you think I had a right to have my own back?" Her lip twisted. "But I didn't need to do that. I know—now."

They all looked at each other. Masters cleared his throat.

"All very well, miss. But can you prove that?"

"Absolutely. You see, I got a note to the Home Office Analyst, and went to see him. (You can ring him up now, if you like; there's a phone.) When I went back to him, he said that two of them were entirely O.K. and virgin-clean—whatever that means. The other had a trace of curare; he said he'd like to keep it for an experiment, if I didn't mind. Of course I let him, and brought the two harmless ones back. There they are. He'd even had them boiled and sterilized." Her voice rose with angry weariness. "Oh, I know it's horrible to sit and tell you this, when that poor chap really was killed with the stuff! And Guy—Guy dead. Every time I think of that I believe I'll go mad myself. But when you seemed to think *I* killed Bender, especially with that curare poison . . ."

With an uncertain air Masters picked up one dart, looked at

Judith, put the dart down again, and in a sort of despair glanced at the spears on the wall. He said, violently:

"This isn't sense. 'Tisn't *sense,* I say! Look here, I'm beginning to wonder how *anybody* killed Mr. Bender with curare, let alone you. Where did the stuff come from? All eight darts, if this is true, now accounted for. Not tampered with." He swung to H.M. "Realize what this means, sir? First: the darts hadn't anything to do with the murder. Second: neither did the dart poison. So—what?"

H.M. saw that Judith was looking in a sort of horrified fascination at the jewels on the desk, which she had been furtively examining all the time. He growled and pushed them towards her.

"Dunno, Masters," he answered. "Bit of a facer, ain't it? I say, you'd better get your own analysts after some more of these weapons in here. But the more I think of your ruddy darts and your ruddy theories, too, the more I'm inclined to go back to my original judgment. I mean the notebook. I mean the roll of parchment. You say one's a phantom and the other's a hoax. But they're the key to this business just the same." He peered at Sir George. "Nearly forgot somethin'. Did you turn a copy of that inscription on the parchment over to any of your experts at the Museum?"

"I've found the right authority, and forwarded it. Bellows is our man; he'll spot it if anybody can. But he lives somewhere in the wilds of Dorset, and it may take a couple of days to get an answer. Besides, he's one of these scholarly humorists. . . . Why not forget Bender for a while, and concentrate on poor Guy?"

Judith blazed. "That's what I say. Who cares about Bender? All you can talk about is your problem of how this was done or that was done; but do you think it was ordinary behavior, and simple behavior, to kill Guy with a commonplace thing like . . . you know!" She was on the verge of tears again, and pointed to the jewels. "Alan told me about those. If I have my way we'll chuck them in the dust-bin. Guy was going after them when he died. Why don't you ask us something about last night?"

"All right, if you like," agreed H.M. patiently. "You hear any suspicious noises, or anything like that, after you'd gone to bed?"

"No."

"See any lights? Notice anybody prowlin' about?"

"No. I was so dead exhausted I didn't notice anything; I went straight off to sleep, and only woke up when I heard the noise of the fight downstairs."

"Quite so. And there you are; what more can I ask you? If we want to get a trace of this murderer, we got to examine his tricks when the lights are on and he's in full view of the audience. We'll go back to Bender unsympathetically, if you prefer, but we'll go back to him. Ever notice if he carried a notebook?"

She pushed back her hair. "I—oh, I don't know! I don't remember, and I can't seem to think. I never noticed him particularly. He . . ." She jumped a little as Alan burst into the room with his usual tempestuous entry.

"I say, H.M., you told me to get Isabel, but can't you postpone it until a bit later?" He sounded querulous. "She's still pretty weak, and Arnold says she ought to be quiet. Duty done; there! Now, dammit, what's this rot I hear about somebody accusing *you* of pinching my darts?"

"Steady, old boy," said Judith, and grinned at him. "It's quite all right, really. I've cleared myself. Or I shall clear myself when Mr. Masters puts in that phone-call he's aching to make. But they won't pay any attention to Guy. All they're doing is asking me about notebooks."

Her brother stopped short. "Notebooks? What notebooks?"

"I'm gettin' sick of the word myself," remarked H.M., who was dourly trying to fit the sapphire pin on his own coat, "but I've got to go through the rigmarole. I don't suppose *you* noticed whether Bender carried a notebook, did you? No. Probably not. Well . . ."

"I don't— YesbygadIdo!" said Mantling, suddenly. He peered in some suspicion, but H.M.'s manner seemed to reassure him. "I did see it at that. It was a big leather one, and had his initials on it. I noticed it on the table when he was dressin' last night."

"Go on, then! Quick, let's have it!"

"Don't jump like that! What's queer about a notebook?—It was when I went upstairs to dress last evening, rather early. I wanted to tell him dinner'd be late on account of the experiment, and if Arnold saw him when he came to take Judith out, not to blow the gaff. I stuck my head in Bender's room. There's a bathroom adjoining. He was in there. I saw his clothes laid out, and all his pocket-things on the table: watch and keys, you know, and there was a big notebook there." Mantling's face darkened. "I thought he used it to sketch. He said he was an artist. Fella was as jumpy as you are. When I looked in the bathroom door, he was shaving, and when he heard my voice he jumped about a foot and cut himself a hell of a dig with the razor . . ."

Evidently Mantling did not understand the effect of this casual statement on four of his auditors. When Masters had fully digested it, Masters said:

"Now—haa!—careful, sir! You're sure he cut himself?"

"Certainly I am; why not? What about it? I stuck some iodine on it for him. It looked like only a little dig with the corner of the blade, but there was quite a bit of blood in the washbowl. He didn't make a row, but I wondered why he was so nervous."

"Think carefully, sir!—You'd have noticed, then, whether this dig was in the neck just under the jaw-bone on the left-hand side of his face."

Mantling reflected, considering a memory and fingering both sides of his own jaw. "Right! The left side! I remember, because I was on the side of the tub away from him. But what about it?"

"This," said H.M., "is the limit. I am past pain and sorrow. This is the utter and absolute limit."

Masters' tone changed' to a gruff patience as he studied the sincerity of the other's bewildered expression. "You see, your Lordship, this puts us in a bit of a mess. The only mark on Bender's body was a little cut under the jaw. Mr. Bender (no doubt of this) died of a puncture that introduced the poison into the blood-stream, and killed him in ten minutes. But if he cut himself shaving hours before—well, it couldn't have been introduced there, could it? Eh? Just so." He turned to H.M. sadly. "Well, sir, I joked with you at the beginning of this case. I don't joke now. First we find the darts couldn't have been used. Then we find there's no poison to go on 'em if they could have been used. Now we find there's no puncture for the poison to enter even if there had been any poison to use. Anything to say to that?"

"Just so," said H.M. "Will somebody pour the old man a long, powerful drink?"

CHAPTER SIXTEEN

The Hypodermic Needle

TAIRLAINE AND the old man had lunch at the Diogenes Club, where H.M. had slumbered away many a peaceful afternoon. The Diogenes is in Pall Mall just opposite the Senior Conservatives Club, which is viewed suspiciously by most members of the Diogenes as a rather rowdy and uproarious institution that would bear watching by the police. A good many of the stalest jokes about clubs have originated here; and there is, it must be admitted, a good deal of cataleptic sleeping in its armchairs. But its cooking is excellent and its cellar better. In the downstairs rooms—except the Visitors' Room—there is in force the Diogenes' inexorable rule: 'Herein the brethren shall speak Latin or else keep silent'; consequently, H.M. said he found it useful for sittin' and thinkin' or else merely for sittin'.

After a strong lunch, well-fortified with Beaune, they ensconced themselves in a window-embrasure of the Visitors' Room with a card-table between them for notes, and began to argue again. Outside the March day had turned raw again; spatters of rain blew along Pall Mall so that passing clubmen ducked their heads bravely against it without ever thinking of opening rolled umbrellas. H.M. was hoping for a phone-call from George Anstruther, with news from the *savant* in Dorsetshire.

"Not that I think it'll do us much good," he commented. He was drawing pictures on a note-sheet with a blue pencil, all of them libelous caricatures of Chief Inspector Humphrey Masters. "But at least it's somethin' to go on, and it might be a clew to the method. Burn me, that's what makes me sizzle with bright murderous flames! I can't see how the trick was worked, although I got a pretty good line on the person who did the murders, and——"

"And it's no use asking you who?"

"Not a bit," grunted H.M. Viciously he added to the latest picture of Masters a pair of ears which struck even Tairlaine's uncritical eye as being somewhat large. "You wouldn't believe me. I mean that. Got any suggestions?"

"I have been thinking," said the other, who had grown philosophic with wine and whose pipe was drawing well, "of applying the possibilities of literary suggestion.—No, the idea does not call for such forceful comment. Remember: 'What song the Syrens sang, or what name Achilles assumed when he hid himself among women, though formidable riddles indeed, are not beyond *all* conjecture.' Have you observed, by the way, that Miss Judith Brixham is a damnably attractive young woman?"

"Look here, you old rip," said H.M., opening his eyes. "Have you——"

"I am not an old rip," said Tairlaine with dignity. "I am fifty; she is thirty-one, and my feelings towards her are those of an indulgent uncle. That is all. It's only that I rather dislike seeing her waste herself either on that top-heavy prig of a doctor or the likable but wabble-necked young elephant-killer. I am going grayish; I once told myself that after my youthful days I had ceased to be interested in what a prudish modern age chooses to call That Sort of Thing. All the same, I tell you this: if Judith Brixham had ever looked at me as evidently she looked at Carstairs when he cut himself with the spear, I think I could be seen dancing the rhumba in the middle of Harvard Square with a bottle of champagne in each pocket." He drew reflectively at his pipe. "Nevertheless!—Let me see if I can put any ideas in your head about this murder-case."

"You're puttin' a lot of ideas in my head. But go on."

"You're trying to find what killed Ralph Bender. Very well. Why not approach the problem from a literary angle?"

"Hey!" roared H.M. "Now look here, Doc. You either need another drink or you've had one too many. What do you mean, the literary angle?"

"Like this. You've decided that Guy Brixham stood outside the window, with his eye to the shutter, and saw Bender's death. You say he did not see the murderer; but he saw how it was done, and also something that later enabled him to guess the murderer's identity. *Soit!* Now, a sound principle for writing description is this: You walk into a room; what immediately strikes your notice or takes your eye, what thing or group of things, color, furnishing, illumination, or the like? That will be the essence of a vivid description. . . . Then, when Guy Brixham looked in at the shutter, what did he *see?* What could he have noticed that we didn't notice from the other end? If you look at it in that way, your search is narrowed. It is narrowed by the limit of Guy's vision. He could only have seen a small part of the room. The poison struck Bender in that narrow area. So," concluded Tairlaine, rather pleased at the way words were flowing, "let's look for it there."

H.M. put down his pencil. "That's not half bad," he said,

nodding. "H'm. Lemme think, then. I haven't been outside that window. But I've stood back against the shutters. Therefore I can see . . . Aha! There's the feller we want!" He broke off his concentration to point out of the window at Masters, who was trudging towards the club steps with his head down in the rain. "He's been outside. He'll tell us."

Masters, brought in after H.M.'s sketches had been turned face downwards, caught at the idea.

"You mean, sir," he suggested, pinching his chin, "what *action* of Mr. Bender's showed him the means of the crime, and let him guess the murderer. Showing also that the means point directly to the murderer once we find 'em. That's assuming, of course, that the murderer himself was not actually in the room?"

"It seems to me that we've *got* to assume it," insisted Tairlaine, "or we're left with nobody to suspect. Let's get the area first. You're standing outside the shutter, with your head through that broken pane which fixes the only point of vision. What do you see?"

Masters was silent for a time, a film over his eyes. His hand moved left, right, and then clenched. "Devilish little! Lummy! A straight path—widens out, that's true, but not much—a straight path to the door opposite. You can't see the bed on your left, or anything there; you can't see the fireplace or dressing-table or anything on the right. All you can see, except the door opposite, is a strip of the carpet, and . . . Stop a bit, sir! When you took Mr. Bender into that room, and left him there, what did he do?"

"He pulled out a chair from the table and sat down," H.M. replied. "It was that chair labeled 'Monsieur de Paris,' the one we took apart. It was at that end, if you call it an end on a round table, directly on a line with the window. And when we went in and found him dead, the chair was in the same place. Only it was turned facin' the table, and pushed back a bit." A vague gleam stirred in his dull eyes. "Go on, son!"

The chief inspector nodded. "Just so. And, through the shutter, you could see just that chair and a couple of feet of the round table. The door, the carpet, the chair, a little of the table, *nothing more.*"

"Then whatever got him," said Tairlaine, beginning to catch the excitement, "got him in just that space, and in sight of those things. To be seen from the window, he could move only in a straight path towards the window or towards the door. By the position of the chair, suppose him to have been sitting at the table, writing, with his profile towards the window. . . . That seems to end in a blank wall," he added dazedly, "in more senses than one. You've examined all of those things, haven't you, and found them all right? Table, chair: even carpet, door, and shutters."

"But the important thing about it is," argued Masters, "what could there be about any of those things *which could make Guy suspect somebody was guilty when nobody else had been in the room before that, except Guy?* And more! Whatever kind of action the chap indulged in, it had to be something pretty definite that could give Guy a clew. Hum! I mean, sir, he couldn't just sit up all of a sudden and look round him. The thing had to be as definite as a smash in the jaw or a stamp on the foot or . . ."

Now at this point occurred the thing which came close to causing a scandal at the Diogenes Club, and the request of the secretary for H.M.'s resignation. It is not true to say he shouted. It was a mild enough exclamation, not at all like the blast which scattered his lady typists like autumn leaves, but it brought the hall-porter in to see what was wrong.

"Corns!" said H.M., getting up from the table. His succeeding remarks were not much more intelligible, to Tairlaine, at least, for he continued: "That's the secret, but only a part of the secret. Blood in a bowl. Stern duty. And particularly the clew of the chicken-soup . . . Gents, I been an ass. I been such a howlin', blazin', eternal scarlet fool that, if I ever get a case of swelled head in the future, just come up to me and whisper, 'Corns.' My head will dwindle *instanter.* No, Masters, I'm *not* goin' to tell you! You had your little joke with that corn business this morning, and, burn me, I'm goin' to be the one to return it! Ho ho ho."

Masters sat back with a jerk.

"I don't know what you're thinking, sir," he returned, and released his breath, "but I don't mind if you go on whooping. What I do know is that you see daylight." He grinned. "And, so long as I don't have to worry, I'm not curious. Unduly. I'll only remind you that it's now more than half-past three, and we promised to be in Curzon Street before four. Whatever you have in mind, hadn't we better be moving along?"

"Right. First, though, I want to make a phone-call; don't ask me what for. What's the name of that private hotel Bender lived at?"

"The Whitefriars, Montagu Street. I think the phone number is Museum 0828. Ask for Mrs. Anderson." When H.M. had gone waddling out, rubbing his hands, Masters turned back to Tairlaine and grinned again. "The old boy's looking up again, and I'm glad to see it. I haven't seen him so bothered since that Royal Scarlet case.* If he gets his confirmation, he'll be his old self straightaway."

* Masters was here referring to the murder of the American millionaire, Richard Morris Blandon, at the Royal Scarlet Hotel in Piccadilly, and the singular puzzle of the triple impersonation. It is a record which may one day be published.

"What's on his mind, do you think?"

Masters made a parody of a shrug. "Can't say, sir. All I know is it doesn't bother me now. But you're quite right in what you said about the things in the room being harmless. I wouldn't admit it in front of him," conceded the chief inspector, shaking his head, "but I've fooled about with all sorts of mad ideas. I thought about there being something wrong with the carpet: poison in it, or a poisoned pin, or the like. No good. I thought of a knife or needle or sharp edge in the chap's own notebook—which we can't find. That was prompted by a wild story I road about somebody who poisoned the pages of a book; the victim kept moistening his thumb to turn over the pages, and conveyed the poison to his mouth. But that's out, because he could have swallowed a gallon of the stuff without danger; and, as for the sharp edge in the notebook, there's absolutely no mark to indicate it. Of course there's a mark *somewhere,* only we can't find it; if we could find it, we should know."

Tairlaine stared out at the rain. "It's an idea, though!" he said. "Why is the notebook missing? By the way, did you ever cut your finger on a sharp edge of paper? It's thinner and cleaner than any steel-cut; it can hurt plenty but no one else could see it there at all unless there was a little smear of blood. Did your police surgeon look for anything like that?"

"I don't know," said Masters uneasily. "And, by George, you've got me worried! Quite possible. I've heard of so many trick contrivances in this case that (between ourselves) I'm half afraid to touch anything in that blasted house without a pair of thick leather gloves on."

"Well, let's get back to Guy, then. You stayed at the house after we left—did you learn anything fresh?"

Nothing whatever, Masters explained. He had questioned

everybody except Isabel Brixham. None of the servants, who slept belowstairs, had heard or seen anything during the night. Judith and Alan had heard nothing until the noise of the fight. Questioned further about the light which Carstairs had seen in Guy's room at four o'clock, Ravelle replied that he had not seen it; but, since he had not left his own room until nearly twenty minutes past four, and the light had been turned on only for a brief time, this was not to be considered suspicious. As for the medical evidence, Masters concluded, there was no revelation there. Guy Brixham had died of cerebral fracture resulting from two blows of a heavy hammer, the hammer found under the bed. On the hammer were discovered three sets of fingerprints: those of Alan and Shorter, who had handled it earlier in the evening, and of Masters himself. One new fact alone had been learned, an inexplicable and horrible one which explained the curious dislocated position of Guy's lower jaw. The jawbone had been smashed with the hammer—apparently by a deliberate blow, after Guy had been felled.

Tairlaine was still uneasily considering this piece of savagery when H.M. returned from the telephone. He was in ghoulish good spirits, his hat stuck on the back of his head, and he had ordered a cab to take them to Curzon Street. But even he was silent during that ride in the rain, because they had come to expect some new development each time they stepped into the atmosphere of Mantling House, and to flinch from it.

All seemed quiet enough, although Shorter looked excited when he opened the door. Judith was waiting for them in the hall, keeping down hysteria.

"Yes, I've got something for you," she said, in reply to H.M.'s glance. "Maybe—evidence. Come with me. . . . No, not in the library! Guy's in there." She said this in a curious voice, as though she were referring to a living person. "The undertakers are with him. They're so good in talking to you that you almost forget what they're here for, but I can't stand much more of this."

She led them to the drawing-room, which was solid with its heavy Victorian furniture, full of the ticking of clocks, and lighted only by a coal fire.

"That Dr. Pelham is here," she went on. "The Harley Street man. He's in the study with Alan now, and he seems to have got round Alan beautifully. Alan's—well, he's a new man. But there's one thing I've got to know: why did you insist on his coming here, when there was no need after Guy's death?"

"Wasn't there?" asked H.M. in a dull voice.

They heard the clocks ticking in the silence, and saw her white face. She stood by the fire, her head up but the muscles showing tight in her neck. She said: "You know what that makes me think. There's somebody in my family you still want to prove is mad."

"No!" H.M. answered, with a sort of queer, dogged stupidity. "That's the idea, but you've got it the wrong way round. There's somebody in your family that I *must* prove is sane. Ma'am, I'm serious. Pretty terribly serious. My whole case, d'ye see, must depend on somebody in this house being utterly and absolutely sane. Some people might think it would be better to demonstrate that person is crazy, and therefore can come to no harm. I don't. And if you can't understand what I mean, you will presently. . . . What's this about new evidence?"

She reached up to the mantel-shelf. Her voice was jerky.

"We shouldn't have found it at all if it hadn't been for Isabel's housewifely instincts. Isabel is down and about now. She looks like a ghost, and she's got something on her mind, and can't speak. But she couldn't keep away from her housewifely instincts—that's Isabel. When she saw the old bedclothes and hangings . . . you know where . . . she decided they must be taken out and burnt. They're full of bugs, and she said the house would be infested with bugs. The servants flatly refused to touch them, until she bribed Shorter, and Bob gave him a hand. When they hauled the mattress off, it was so rotted that something fell out through a slit in it. It'd been put there recently." She stood back with a jerk and pointed to the mantel-shelf. "It's there. Get it. I can't touch it."

Masters reached up on the high shelf and groped. He brought down a slender object wrapped in a handkerchief.

"It belonged to Guy," Judith added. "He had it for some kind of vaccine injections long ago. I'd forgotten all about it."

Unfolding the handkerchief in the firelight, Masters exposed a hypodermic needle. The plunger worked through a slender glass valve which was a third full of a thin liquid colored a watery yellowish-brown.

CHAPTER SEVENTEEN

Hanging Evidence?

"Bob said he knew you were supposed to take care of those things for fingerprints," she went on. She stared at the glass, through which the firelight glowed a poisonous yellowish-brown like the colors of a spider. "So we wrapped it in a handkerchief."

"Good, miss!" said Masters, in a tone which he tried to make appreciative. He lifted the needle. "But no prints on this glass, I'll swear. Smudges. That's gloves for a fiver. Is this——?"

H.M. lumbered over and took it from his hands. Pulling out a chair, he sat down in the firelight, doubled the handkerchief several times, and put the folded lengths across his knee. Upon the linen, his spatulate fingers surprisingly delicate, he worked out two drops of the yellow-brown liquid. He sniffed it, and then tasted it.

"Curare," he said. "That's the powder in an alcohol solution. Easy enough; scrape the stuff off a weapon in cakes, mash it, and dissolve in a little hundred-proof from the chemist's. This is what you want, Masters."

"You mean that thing killed Mr. Bender?"

"That's not the point," insisted H.M., with a kind of obstinacy. "This is very revealin', but you miss the point of it. Why wasn't it used to kill Guy? If the murderer wanted to keep up the legend of the curse on the room, why not give Guy a shot of this and let him die in the same way? Why up and bat him with that hammer—which wasn't premeditated. Y'see, the murderer didn't bring the hammer along to use. The hammer was already there, lyin' to hand on the bed after Masters had used it in opening the window. But how would the murderer know that?"

"He would know it, for instance," Masters answered very quietly, "if he'd been the one who brought the hammer to the room in the first place. But never mind that. Sir, this turns the whole case upside down again! Don't you realize that, if this hypodermic needle killed Bender, the murderer must have been on hand to do the job himself? Stop a bit! Unless that's such a weak solution that the murderer could have jabbed him before he left the dining-room . . ."

"Jabbed him *where?*" asked H.M.

In the pause he wrapped the handkerchief round the needle again and returned it to Masters. He continued: "I didn't say this was used to kill Bender. I didn't say a word about Bender. All I'm askin', in case it'll give you a hint of the truth, is why it wasn't used to kill Guy? Use what I like to call imaginative common-sense. Guy sneaks down last night after those diamonds. The murderer—whom we'll be fanciful and call Sanson—sneaks after him with the little hypodermic. All of a sudden Sanson realizes, when face to face with Guy or creepin' up behind him, that something's been overlooked for all the careful planning. Suppose Guy kicks up a row at bein' stuck, and alarms the whole place? Good! There's a hammer lying providentially on the bed. Stun Guy with one blow, and then go to work; the curare will do the rest. But it didn't. Sanson merely used the hammer. Note the understatement of that 'merely.' Uh-huh. Well?"

Masters was impatient. "I don't see that it matters, sir. Maybe he was interrupted."

"Might 'a' been," said H.M. musingly. He stared at the fire. "Entirely possible as a contributin' cause, although you'll notice Sanson had time for some good hard smashes. But I think that maybe one realization of something overlooked brought on another. Suppose Sanson stuns Guy; the bruise never shows or is thought of afterwards; it's merely curare poisoning injected, say, under the skin of the scalp where the hair will hide it. Very well. Next morning Chief Inspector Masters arrives, sees the body, *and what does he think?* Quick!"

Masters frowned. "Why, sir, at that time I should have thought that Guy himself——"

"Exactly. You were convinced Guy had killed Bender; in fact, all of us had a strong suspicion of it. You'd have said, with logic on your side, 'The murderer has either committed suicide or got caught in his own devilish trap. Thank God, the business is closed.' Why, man, do you think that with the apparently hole-proof case you'd already built up against Guy, you'd ever have bothered to go on with it? Not you. Or me. . . . And, burn me, Sanson realized that too."

"Then it's a damned funny murderer," snorted Masters, "who isn't satisfied with the proof of somebody else's guilt!"

H.M. became wooden again. He only said in a dull voice: "It happens sometimes, though. Never mind. Let's go along and talk to Doc Pelham. Humph, ha! Steady; you stay here, ma'am. I'm goin' to tell your brother you want to speak to him. Does he know about this hypo? Good! Take care of it, Masters."

An air of amiability pervaded the study as benevolently as

the rich cigar-smoke. At ease in the largest chair sat Dr. William Pelham, who was plump, bland, and kindly, with silver hair and the manners of a prime minister. Dr. Pelham could squeeze the last drop of politeness out of a conversation to such extent that he nearly squeezed the listener dry. A Havana was between his fingers, a glass of sherry at his elbow. His only touch of professionalism, a pair of black-ribboned eyeglasses, he tapped on the arm of a chair as though deprecating their presence while his smooth voice flowed on to Alan opposite him. Dr. Pelham was sometimes a trifle pompous; but he was very capable. Alan, in fact, blundering round to thrust cigars at everybody, was so impressed that he did not seem to relish H.M.'s message from Judith. It was Dr. Pelham, also, who prevailed on him to leave. When he had gone, Dr. Pelham put up his eyeglasses, took a slight whiff from his cigar, and sat back with an affable expression on his comfortable ruddy face.

"Ah, Merrivale!" he said, raising dark eyebrows. "Delighted to see you. Even under such sad circumstances." Immediately his face became grave, but lightened as though at the thought of H.M.'s presence. "We haven't seen you in a dog's years, you know. Not since you confirmed my ideas in that Grandaby business. And you never show up at Association meetings."

H.M. sat down untidily.

"Well . . . now. I'm old-fashioned, Bill. You've had the sense to move with the times and the diseases, y'see. Burn me, look at you!" He blinked down at his own unpressed trousers, and tried to squint at the shabby bow tie skewered under his collar. "Your sartorial elegance is convincin'. Mine ain't. Never mind. You've seen Mantling. Anything wrong?"

Pelham allowed one eyelid to droop.

"Bosh, my boy," he said. "Utter and absolute rubbish." He

smiled. "Arnold told me I should find nothing wrong, but somebody else seems to have insisted. Mantling? Nothing seriously wrong with that chap. A slight neurosis, of course, which we may have to clear up, but as for the rest of it——!"

"The key-word," said H.M. blankly, "is 'of course.' That's what's wrong with you chaps, and why I hate you like hell: you can't find a thoroughly sound person anywhere in the world, and yet nobody can show any proof against you if you commit a mental murder. But I'm satisfied. I want your opinion, Bill, on a real and physical kind of murder. Answer me one question, like a good feller.—If Mantling stood in the dock, with an absolutely perfect case against him for the killin' of his brother, would you hang him?"

H.M. had hardly raised his voice, but Tairlaine went cold. These intangible moves, this sense of H.M. moving on steadily through a mist, culminated in a real horror. Something had stirred in this house, that might have been buried since the eighteenth century. Something as thin as a blood-stream from generation to generation: that at one end touched a painted old harridan gloating over gold boxes in the Paris of the Revolution, and wound on into Alan Brixham, Lord Mantling, walking to the rope for murder. The chill in the room was like a physical chill. Even Pelham felt it. He sat up slowly. He put down his cigar on an ashtray, carefully, and had opened his mouth to speak . . .

And then somebody cried out.

"No, you wouldn't," said Isabel Brixham's voice. "You wouldn't really, would you?" It groped out on a note of entreaty, and then became reassured. "Of course not. Nothing really bad can happen to him? I mean really bad?"

She looked ill and frail. It was as though some inner torture had brought her to a determination in spite of herself; as though she must speak, and would not rest until she did. Also, she had now the dignity she possessed early last night, before it crumpled at the death of Bender. Tairlaine tried to find a word for the expression of those pale blue eyes. Dazed? Not complete enough. 'Haunted?' Too theatrical, too suggestive of loose cloudy sorrows for blank verse, and not of that straight bitter sincerity. She stood bolt upright, the silver hair molded into neat waves against her long head. Her mouth showed a hatred, possibly of herself.

"I heard you were here," she said to H.M., and then to Masters. "I had to see you. Nothing can happen to him, can it?"

"To Alan? I promise you, ma'am," said H.M. calmly, "that nothing's goin' to happen to him. Yes, by God, I promise that!"

She seemed relieved, and sat down in the chair he drew out for her; but, curiously enough, the hatred of her mouth grew.

"I have decided to tell you. I can't rest until I have. Sometimes I think I shall never sleep again. . . . I know who you are." She broke off to look at Pelham. "I can guess why you are here. But it is the business of the police, for the moment.

"Don't interrupt me while I tell you what I have to tell. I lied to you last night, about Guy. He begged me to tell you he was with me, and I did, because I was fond of Guy; terribly fond of him. But you know now he didn't—" She made a slight gesture. She was dressed in black, thinner black than her niece's, which showed her sharp bones. "What I am going to tell you now I must tell you.

"My nephew Alan killed Guy. I know now that he cut the throat of that little dog, too, because I have seen the knife he did it with, and it has not been washed. But that is not the same thing as murdering his brother."

H.M. , his eyes fixed on her, made a savage gesture to the others behind his back.

"Did you see him kill Guy, ma'am?"

Her face went more gray. "No, because I did not dare follow him down. Besides, I did not know what he meant to do. But I will tell you what I did see.

"I went to sleep last night, finally, but I did not sleep all night. I seldom do. When some of you are nearly seventy, as I am, you will know what it is to have every bone in your body as light as a feather and yet feel like fire. I woke up gradually, with a parching thirst. I would have given anything I possessed to have someone bring me water while I lay in bed. Not a little water, a pitcher of it. I wished to glut myself with it, and I knew I must get up and go out to the bathroom if I wanted it. Finally I got up and put on my dressing-gown. When I opened my door——"

"The time of that, ma'am?" said Masters. He had the sense to speak very softly. "Do you recall that?"

She seemed startled at the interruption nevertheless.

"I—I don't . . . or yes, I do; near enough, I think. I have a luminous clock on a table. It was shortly before four o'clock. And, when I looked out into the hall, first it was dark; then I saw a light at Alan's door.

"Now what I am going to tell you will sound absurd and far-fetched and—and *affected,* if you understand me. But you must know it so that you can understand what held me in such terror that I could not move, or make any effort then or afterwards. When I was a little girl, and my own father had just died of black poison in that room, someone gave me a book of fairy tales for Christmas. I daresay it would be harmless enough to most children. But it was a long time before I could read it, and

I always studied those horrible distorted illustrations. To me, under the shadow of that room and of living terrors, it was *real.* The murderings were not pleasant idle stories, as they would be to most children; the woods were dark and marshy, like real woods; the witches were malignant things that looked at me; the bright-colored wine was poisoned; the robbers were not men, they were monsters. There was one particularly hideous story of a young bride going through the forest to meet her bridegroom, and coming to a cottage where——"

She gripped her hands together.

"I will not go on with this, except to say that I used to people this house with those robbers reveling at their round table, with their poisoned wine and the bride they intended to butcher. A dream, a—I do not know! But it has never left me. And what I saw last night was not a dream.

"I looked out in that dark hall, and saw a light in the door of Alan's room. Alan was carrying a little electric lamp, the long cylindrical kind that miners use. The wire round it made little shadows all over him. He looked twice as big and broad as normal; he had on a black dressing-gown with a red collar, and he was peering round the hall. A little of the light shone up on his face when he moved it; I could see his freckles and his bull neck, and his red hair damp with perspiration. But most of all I could see his eyeballs, a sort of horror like oysters, turning from side to side. He was not smiling, though he looked as though he meant to. And then I knew he was mad. . . . He moved out, very quietly. He had the lamp in one hand, and in the other I saw he had a hypodermic syringe with some yellowish-brown liquid in the glass part. He had on black cotton gloves, and he was muttering to himself as he started downstairs.

"Now ask me!" she cried suddenly. "Ask me why I didn't

call out, run after him, alarm the house? I only tell you that I could not. I was physically incapable of it. I may have fainted, although I do not think so. The next certainty I had was that the hall was darkening again, with the little light dwindling down the stairs. All the old horrors had come back. It was like one of the pictures in that book.

"Then it came to me—Guy. Where was Guy?"

Dr. Pelham had picked up his cigar again. He was studying her, curiously.

"You were worried about Guy, Miss Brixham," he stated rather than asked. "Why?"

"I am telling you," she answered, rather forlornly; "I am not explaining. I don't know. All I know is that somehow I groped my way down to Guy's room. At first I was afraid to turn on the light. But I found the switch under my hand; I shut the door, risked it, and turned on the light. His bed was empty." She drew a deep breath. "Then I knew that I *must* go downstairs after Alan. Yet I could not. I sat down in a chair and looked at Guy's empty bed; I tried to nerve myself, and still I could not. My brain was all fiery again, and I could not see very well. But I turned out the light, crept out in the hall again, and tried to nerve myself again to go downstairs. Then it came to me as a—a sort of compromise, a catching at straws, that everything might be all right again if I could go into Alan's room, and wait for him to face him when he came up. That was the worst of all. I thought that I would turn on the light in his face when he came in, but I could not stand the dark. Also, there was a queer smell in the room. So I shut the door and turned on the light. Then I saw the open drawer."

"The open drawer, ma'am?" asked H.M.

"The lowest in a chest of drawers. It was standing out so far that it took my eye. It had a key in the lock. I went over and looked—then I couldn't stand any more. First, there was a knife inside; a big hunting knife of the kind Alan brought back from a trip. It had not been washed. Some of the dog's silky hair—it was a reddish-brown color—was still sticking to the bl . . . Oh, yes! And a notebook. It was a black leather notebook, with all the pages ripped out, and on the cover there were the gold letters, 'R.B.' "

Masters ripped out an exclamation, but she did not appear to hear him. She put her hand to her head as though it hurt her.

"I—you see, I could not stay there after that. The very air was heavy with. . . . I turned off the light and got outside, but just as I was halfway to my room I saw the lamp coming upstairs again.

"Fear? I was insane with terror. I felt as though I had been caught in an open place, against a wall, before rifles. I quite literally could not walk, and I did go down on my knees by the wall, because I thought he was coming after *me.* He did not see me, although he passed within a couple of yards. As he was shutting the door of his room I saw his face again; now he was smiling, and I heard him say, exactly as though he were addressing me: 'That's done for him, right enough.' It was the last I heard or saw, gentlemen. I do not remember getting back to my room, but at least I must have done so unaided. Because, you see—I am alive now."

She rested her head, wearily, against the back of the chair. Her breath was drawn in gasps; she looked as though it would be a relief for her to cry, but that she was past crying. H.M. studied her, his hands folded over his stomach.

"Right you are, Masters," he said in a colorless voice. "Hop upstairs and have a look at that drawer."

She flashed open her eyes as Masters hurried out, his own face rather pale.

"You do not believe that the things are there, Sir Henry?" she asked.

H.M. nodded gently. "Oh, yes, ma'am. I rather imagine they are, and maybe other things too." He turned round. "Uh-huh. Got any questions you want to ask, Pelham?"

"My dear Merrivale . . ." said Pelham, and cleared his throat. He seemed composed. He was not composed. "My dear Merrivale, this is your province, not mine. Rather—the province of the police. For the moment, no."

"Well, *I* only wanted to ask, ma'am: You had a pretty strong suspicion, didn't you, that your nephew was guilty long before you saw that last night? You thought he was the mad one? And, when you saw him come out, it terrified you but it didn't surprise you. Eh?"

"Yes. I may as well admit that now."

H.M. twiddled his thumbs. "That's what I thought. Y'know, you've told this story before four witnesses, ma'am; but it may not—in fact, it won't—be the only time you'll be expected to tell it if Masters finds his evidence. Could you repeat it in a coroner's court? In the witness-box at the Old Bailey?"

"Oh, God, no! I couldn't tell it again! I——"

"But it's true?"

"It's true, and I had to tell you. But now that you know, now that you're sure and no real harm will come to Alan, must I say it again?"

"H'm. That depends."

She stared at him. "You don't mean that you'd *arrest*—? You don't mean, like a common criminal, to be taken? . . ."

The door banged open. Tairlaine saw the end of the chase in

Masters' face, and Masters was carrying a large handkerchief in which were wrapped metal objects that rattled together with an ugly suggestion. Isabel sprang up and turned her face away.

"This was the lot, sir," said Masters rather hoarsely. "Everything in the drawer. We've got him."

Unfolding the handkerchief, he spread out on the desk a heavy double-edged knife whose discolored blade still bore the evidence that it had been used to kill the dog, a black leather notebook, a small stoppered bottle, and a nickeled flask. H.M., using the handkerchief, snatched up the bottle and sniffed its contents.

"Potassium cyanide," he growled. "Quite a maniac's den, with gadgets to murder all at hand. Secondary weapon, I wonder?" He took up the flask, unscrewed its top, and sniffed again. "Cherry brandy; about a third full. Can't tell anything else, but cherry brandy'll cover up the bitter-almonds odor of cyanide neat enough. Notebook——?"

It was of the loose-leaf variety, with nickeled rings inside from which the sheets had evidently been torn, for a shred or two of paper still stuck to one of them. H.M. turned it over and over. Then he drew a deep breath and blinked up at Masters.

"Well, son? It's your move now, and for the moment I'm not goin' to interfere with you. What do you mean to do?"

"There's only one thing I can do, sir. This is clear enough, I fancy. Of course, I haven't got a warrant, but I shall have to ask Lord Mantling——"

"Ask him, then," said H.M., nodding somberly. "He's just behind you."

Mantling stood in the doorway. He looked a little dazed. Carstairs stood at one side of him, and Judith clung to one arm.

"I *say*—" blurted Mantling. His face went a muddy color. He looked round. "What . . . Shorter said you'd gone rushin' up to my room . . . You were . . ." Suddenly he pointed. "Where'd you get—*that?*"

"Out of your room, sir." Masters spoke heavily. "Did you ever see any of those things before?"

"That's my kni—" said Mantling, and could not go on. He stared at Judith, then at Carstairs. "Out of my room? Where?"

"Bottom drawer of the bureau, sir. I repeat——"

"But I haven't used . . . Bottom drawer of the bureau?" cried Mantling. His big fists opened and shut. "But I don't use it, I tell you! I don't *use* it. It's too hard to open easily; it sticks. You know it sticks." He appealed to Judith with a kind of weak fierce persistence. "It sticks, don't it? You'll tell 'em that. I don't use it. I——"

Masters held up his hand. "One moment, sir. I am bound to tell you that your aunt, Miss Isabel Brixham, has just given us evidence to prove that you are guilty of the murder of your brother. We have found these articles in your room to establish certain other charges. . . ."

Mantling turned slowly and looked at her. She switched round, refusing to return the stare, and she was crying now. Mantling began to breathe hard. He lowered his head and regarded her with small reddish eyes. Then his fists commenced to open and shut again, and he moved forward slowly. . . .

Judith screamed. Carstairs made an ineffectual grab for him, but Masters with smooth ease was in front of him. The chief inspector was a good two inches shorter than Mantling; Masters' hand rested only lightly on the big man's arm, but Tairlaine saw his lowered shoulder and understood the readiness that would break Mantling's arm if he took another step.

"Now, sir," said Masters soothingly. "You're not going to cut up rough, I hope, because *I* don't want to use force. Hum! I was saying, sir: it is my duty to tell you I have no warrant. But I must ask you to accompany me to headquarters for questioning with regard to the murder of Mr. Guy Brixham. You will be allowed a solicitor and no formal arrest will be made unless my superiors advise it, but I advise you to come quietly. Eh?"

Mantling stopped. All the danger had gone out of him like air from a tire; his big shoulders sagged, for he looked curiously at Masters as though he had never seen him before. When he spoke, it was with that strange, rather childish plaintiveness.

"What do you want me for?" he asked in a low, puzzled tone. He shook his head and peered round. "I say, Isabel . . . why do you want to tell lies about me, now? I haven't done anything. Why do you want them to hang me? God help me, I—haven't—done—anything—at all."

Masters was brisk. "Just so, sir, if you can prove it. I'm sure we all want to help you. Are you ready?"

"Ready?"

"Your, um, hat, you know, and the rest of it? Eh?"

Mantling put his hand to his head, exactly like a child. "Er, yes. My hat and coat. Where's Shorter? Get Shorter. My hat and coat to go to jail. You needn't worry; I'll come quietly. I'll . . ." While the others stared at each other, he turned round and moved towards the door. While the heavy footfalls echoed in a damned house, they still heard his strange voice going on: "I say, why do you want them to hang me? I—haven't—done—anything at all."

CHAPTER EIGHTEEN

Blood in a Washbowl

WITH THE formal detaining and informal arrest of Alan Brixham, Lord Mantling, for the murder of his brother, the case that came to be known as the Red Widow Murders entered its last and most terrible phase. It was still kept quiet; no evening newspaper had a word of the fresh development, but London was afire with rumor. The collapse of Mantling was in a sense the collapse of a house, and worse. Tairlaine, who was to meet H.M. and Masters for dinner, was despondent as the gray rain that still fell.

Towards seven or eight o'clock in the evening, you will find no place more deserted than Fleet Street. The City is empty; the narrow little thoroughfare that curves down the hill towards Ludgate Circus is filled only with the rush of an occasional bus or the loud footfalls of an occasional pedestrian. Little noises creep out, but you cannot identify them. The morning newspapers have not yet begun to bustle and grind, and most restaurants have shut their iron gates. Of the few that remain open, the *Green Man*—which is tucked back in the smoky tangle of eighteenth-century passages behind St. Bride's Church—is much favored by H.M.

Tairlaine's cab splashed up to the curb at half-past seven. The bar windows of the *Green Man* were cheerfully alight, and a fire-glow played on the blinds of the supperrooms upstairs. Tairlaine tried to arrange his thoughts, without much success. The scenes in the house that afternoon were too vivid for thought. H.M. had been a disappointment. H.M. had said nothing. To Masters' questions and worried looks about the advisability of taking Mantling into custody, he had replied only with a grunt. He intimated that it did not matter, and wandered off to interview the servants. And the others in the house? Judith and Carstairs refused to believe Alan had had anything to do with it. Isabel had gone immediately to her room, and Ravelle never left his.

Tairlaine, in his cab bound for the dinner rendezvous, had felt only that stark despondency which comes to those in a strange harsh city during night and the cold rain. The smoky blue twilight of this town, the mushroom crush of umbrellas gleaming under the smeary lights of the Strand, the clash and roar on wet pavements round Charing Cross, had made him feel lonely for—it surprised him to think thus—for the first time in his life. Lonely? Previously, his life had been self-sufficient. He watched, and was not touched. It was different now; not pleasant; but why?

He felt better when he mounted to the upper rooms of the *Green Man,* where he found H.M. blinking at the menu and Masters warming his hands before the fire in a private room with a sanded floor. Masters also was disconsolate and nervous.

"This, I tell you," he insisted, talking over his shoulder, "is playing the devil. I talked to the Commissioner; he's worried because he'd have done what I did, but he still doesn't like it, and therefore he's taking it out on me." Masters turned round. "Lummy, sir, how can you sit there like a toad on a log?—and as cool as cool! I'm blinking certain *I* can't. Do you realize what this means, if we put that gentleman under arrest? It means a full-dress trial before the House of Lords—trial of a peer for murder—biggest sensation and only sensation of the kind for I don't know how many years. The point is: Did I do *right?*"

H.M. scratched his nose. He was soothing. "Well, now, you ain't done wrong yet, have you? I mean, the chap's not under arrest, and you haven't made a bloomer until he is. Besides, you won't."

"Make a bloomer?"

"Make an arrest. I phoned old Boko myself, just before I got here. He was havin' a conference with the Home Secretary; he said he'd told you to go and roll your hoop until they thrashed it out." H.M. paused to bellow for the waiter. "I'll give you five to one he's out of quod by tomorrow at the latest. . . . What about some turtle soup?"

"Then you think, sir, that Miss Isabel Brixham was lying?"

"No, I don't," said H.M. unexpectedly.

Masters jumped away from the fire as though it had burnt the legs of his trousers. "But, hang it, sir, that's the real test! If we can show she's not lying . . . well, I mean, I've had doubts of it myself, you know. She obviously hates Lord Mantling. But if she was telling the truth, then the physical evidence, the circumstantial evidence, does the rest."

A waiter arrived with glasses of sherry; H.M. said, "Honk honk," waited until the others had sipped and the waiter had gone. Then he said:

"I'm afraid you don't see the interestin' part of the testimony this afternoon: not to say the revealing part. Let's examine it impartially without including the personal element. Let's say, as a workin' hypothesis, that the old lady invented the whole story about seeing Mantling go downstairs last night. Let's say she wanted to see him shoved in the lunatic asylum as criminally insane, and therefore was out to plant a facer of a case against him. . . . Masters, if that woman lied, she lied in a very rummy way. Look here. She knew this morning that Guy had been done in with a hammer. Well, if she wanted to put the blame on Alan, why does she make out such a luke-warm case? Why does she say she saw him sneakin' down with a hypodermic which he didn't use?—that, and nothing more. Why not go the whole hog and say she saw him do the murder with a hammer? As it is, she says nothing but that he was wanderin' about the house in the middle of the night. Which is not hangin' evidence."

Masters gestured. "Come, sir! A subtle trick, naturally . . ."

"Rubbish, my lad. Rubbish. What's subtle about smackout accusing him of murder? If you say she was lying and Alan's not guilty, then you must say she planted all that stuff in his bureau drawer. What's subtle about a bloodstained knife, a stolen notebook, and a bottle of cyanide? If you're goin' to pile on the evidence as thick as all that, then why not make a thorough job of accusing him of the only crime he can be hanged for?"

The chief inspector stared. "You talk as though all those things in the bureau drawer didn't matter a——"

"*They don't!* Not a whoopin' damn, son," declared H.M. "Exactly what have you got? You've got a knife stained with dog's blood; well? Granted you prove that case up to the hilt, you might get him a couple of months in clink for wanton cruelty to animals, but I doubt it. What else? A bottle of cyanide, which proves absolutely nothing. . . ."

"Don't forget the notebook."

"Our little old friend," observed H.M. rather tenderly. "Once your phantom terror and *bête noire,* now your stanchest ally. What of it? Are you prepared to accuse Mantling of Bender's murder? Because, if you are, you've got to show how the trick was worked; otherwise you'd never dare go to a jury. And that's exactly what you can't do. Mantling's alibi is still as sound as ever for that, and you won't establish your case merely by proving a reasonable doubt against it. Notebook stamped R.B.! What of it? Suppose the feller swears them initials stand for Robert Browning or Rule Britannia or anything he likes. Who's to prove it's Bender's notebook, especially as the only person who ever saw it—the only person who can testify Bender ever had such a notebook—is Mantling himself! You've got plenty of evidence, yes. But every bit of evidence proves a reasonable doubt against you."

Masters used bad language fluently. He added: "Then, sir, if you thought I did wrong to arrest Mantling, why didn't you stop me? Why didn't——"

"Because it won't do any harm, and it may do a lot of good. Because by to-morrow your official head may be crowned in bay-leaves instead of dropped in the basket. Because," concluded H.M., consulting a ponderous gold watch, "it is now nearly eight o'clock, and before midnight you will probably have the real murderer under lock and key."

Tairlaine and Masters stared at each other. H.M.'s moon face was split with fantastic jollity.

"Uh-huh," he agreed, flourishing a spoon as the waiter appeared with the soup, "that's what I mean. I've dropped a word, in your name, to have the whole parcel assembled at the house to-night. I'm goin' to try a little experiment. You'd better have a couple of men on hand, Masters, and it won't do any harm to have 'em armed. This person's a killer . . . and *may* bust out. This person, I say in all admiration, has done one of the finest bits of actin' ever seen on any stage. Ingenious!—haa! But don't let it spoil your appetites. Eat hearty, me lads. Salt?"

The drizzle of rain went on monotonously, and the wind had turned colder. Despite H.M.'s efforts to enliven the conversation, his almost ghoulish good spirits, neither Masters nor Tairlaine talked much. The top of Masters' car was leaky; they were in no very good humor when they swung into Charles Street at a little past nine o'clock to pick up Sir George. George was excited when he climbed into the back of the car, and his voice had grown hoarse. From his pocket he dragged a telegraph-form and passed it up to H.M.

"From our expert in Dorset," he explained, puffing. "Just got it forwarded ten minutes ago. Part of the explanation seems as muddled as before. For instance, what the devil is 'The Red Dragon'?"

"Red Dragon?" repeated Masters. As they skidded round into Berkeley Square, Masters tried to peer over the shoulder of H.M., who was reading the telegram by the dash-lamps. "What red dragon? What's a red dragon got to do with it?"

"Ho ho ho!" said H.M. "No, you don't, Masters! Keep away, dammit! You got to let the old man have his show, now, and the cat may be out of the bag if you get a look at this." He folded up the telegram jealously. "Matter o' fact, we don't really need it at all. Obscure scholarship ain't fair to introduce, Masters, and this is only confirmation of something I'd spotted before. Burn me, and I was mentionin'——"

"But exactly how does it fit in?" demanded Sir George. "I believe I'm beginning to see a part of the truth. Look here, H.M., I'm just beginning to see why there was so much blood, or seemed to be too much blood, in that business. You see, Masters, that inscription *'Struggole faiusque lectuate,'* and the rest of it, is really a medieval charm against——"

"No!" bellowed H.M., turning to glare. "Didn't I tell you fellers to keep quiet? If you got an inkling, keep it to yourself."

Tairlaine sat in bewildered silence while the car swung up before Mantling House in Curzon Street. There was another blue car a little way down, and two men got out of it. Masters spoke to them briefly while H.M. punched the doorbell. Then H.M. looked the two plain-clothes officers over. He drew one aside, and gave rapid instructions—which seemed to startle the officer—just as Shorter opened the door. Judith, resplendent, came out to meet them.

"Have you heard?" she demanded. "They're going to release Alan! The Commissioner himself phoned us." Her voice choked with eagerness. "He'll be here any minute; I'm even keeping dinner for him. He's *free,* do you hear? They said there wasn't enough evidence . . ."

H.M. was gentle. "Now, now! You needn't go on. I rather thought they would, y'know; in fact, I advised Boko to do it. You told the rest of 'em?"

"Yes—certainly! Shouldn't I have?"

"By all means. And how'd they take it?"

She opened her eyes. "Take it? They were delighted, of course! That is, all except Isabel . . ."

"Uh-huh. Where's Isabel now?"

"Upstairs in her sitting-room, with Dr. Pelham and Eugene. Just as you ordered. The rest are still at dinner. Will you come along?"

They got rid of their hats and coats, and Tairlaine's hands shook when he tried to get out of his coat. The atmosphere was back again, but this time the clock-hands crawled towards finality. His throat felt dry, although he smiled back into Judith's bright dry eyes. Following H.M., Sir George, and Masters, he hurried out to the dining-room.

It was as though last night were being exactly repeated, except for the empty chairs. Candles burned on the table in the diningroom, burned down crookedly as before; the fire had fallen; and Ravelle and Carstairs sat on opposite sides of the table—but with hostility between them now, and no other guests. The white double-doors to the Widow's Room were closed. Ravelle's fork went down with a clatter as he saw the newcomers in the doorway.

"Good evenin'," said H.M. with studied unconcern. "Finished eating? Then will somebody hop into the Widow's Room and light the gas? I'm goin' to show you how poor old Bender died."

There was a silence. Judith, rather pale, moved back from him until she touched the table.

"This isn't——?"

"It won't be a joke for anybody," said H.M., "and especially not for somebody. Better go in and light that gas, Masters; find something to stand on. You got all the exhibits in that briefcase? Good! In there, all of you."

Tairlaine was growing more and more uneasy. He saw that Masters himself had little liking to go into that room in the dark; although Masters tried to grin when he set wide the double-doors. They waited while they heard him fumbling in the dark. Then a harsh glow shone out of the room, there was a heavy thud as Masters jumped down off the table, and he reappeared wiping his forehead.

"Stage all set, sir," he said gruffly. "Now, then?"

"Me, I do not *like* this," Ravelle announced with a sort of abrupt decision. He flung down his napkin. "It look tome like—like a trap. I mean that somebody is for it, and I do not know which."

"Yes, somebody's for it," agreed Carstairs. He gave them a hard grin. "But you can't tack it on to Alan now, my fine fellas. We've heard from the Commissioner. Right you are; I'm ready."

They trooped into the room, but Judith would not let Tairlaine take her arm. The room had been set to rights, all except the scarred carpet. The denuded bedstead had the look of a dismantled boat; the broken furniture had been removed and the table set straight with the remaining chairs about it.

"Four chairs left," said H.M. drowsily. "Bring some more from the other room. I want everybody to sit down. I want everybody comfortable. Wait! The 'Monsieur de Paris' chair is smashed; put another out just where that one was last night. At the end of the table . . . in line with the window . . . so. H'm. Mr. Ravelle, suppose you sit in it, eh? Right! Now you're sittin' exactly where Bender was when the poison struck him——"

Ravelle jumped up. His scarred face was pale again.

"It's quite all right, sir," said Masters in a colorless voice. "Sir Henry says there's no harm in it."

His big hand pushed Ravelle down again, steadily, like a jack-in-the-box. Then he opened his brief-case, and began to lay out an assortment of articles on the table while Carstairs went after more chairs. It was a weird assortment on the polished satinwood. It consisted of the hypodermic syringe, the dark-crusted knife, the stoppered bottle, the flask, the crumpled nine of spades, the roll of parchment, even the bit of black thread; all the twisted clews in the twisted business that was coming to an end.

H.M. spread himself out in a chair, really succeeded in lighting his pipe, and pointed its stem towards the exhibits.

"Look at 'em," he suggested. "Sweepings and refuse of two of the meanest crimes I ever had the disgust of investigating. But they reveal things, ladies and gentlemen. I'm goin' to show you what they reveal."

"Don't you—don't you want the others here?" asked Judith in a small voice. She was some distance from the table.

"No," said H.M. "No; not now. After a few minutes—maybe more, maybe less—all of you are goin' upstairs, and somebody's got to speak to Isabel. That conversation, if it ever takes place, will be interestin'. The results of what Isabel says may be even more so. But, for the moment . . .

"It hit me this afternoon, all of a sudden. It wasn't logic, I regret to say. It might 'a' been, if I could have put the facts together properly, but all the time I was only sittin' and thinkin' the facts muddled me up. It was a crazy association of ideas. One little point—only one little point—has been confusin' the case from the beginning. It's so damned simple, the trick of Bender's murder was so simple, that we refused to look at the truth when it came up and kicked us.

"When Masters came bursting into my office to-day, and told me about Bender's conscientious way of treating things like corns and appendicitis, I still didn't see it. I howled at Masters, who had the whole answer to the puzzle even if he didn't know it. Bender has a bad case of ordinary corns—and refuses to mention it to anybody. Bender thinks he may have an inflamed appendix—so he still kept his jaws set, the blasted fool, and went on his rounds in fatheaded glory.

"And yet I might 'a' seen it last night. That jumpy air of his, like one who's had a drug shot into him. That expression of—

hurrum—not nervousness, exactly, but a kind of crazy *unhappiness.* That trick of rolling his tongue in his cheek. And then, when I saw him eatin' dinner——"

"But he didn't eat any dinner!" cried Judith. "That is, nothing except soup."

"Except soup. Of course, except soup," said H.M. in a hollow voice. "Yet I was still fool enough not to see it! But didn't you see it yourselves, this afternoon? Didn't you understand what happened when Mantling told his story? Mantling comes in unexpectedly on Bender while he's shaving. Bender jumps, nicks himself with a razor . . . and yet the washbowl is stained with blood! Can you imagine any little shaving nick that would splash a washbowl and yet not hit the man's clothes? Why was there *so much blood?* Where did it come from, then, and what was it that Bender wouldn't tell you?"

His voice snapped across the quiet room.

"Well?" said Masters.

"It came from Bender's rinsing his mouth out," said H.M. woodenly, "and he wouldn't tell you that was because he'd just had an inflamed gum lanced by the dentist."

CHAPTER NINETEEN

Handcuffs

Masters got to his feet as though lifted by a sort of slow explosion.

"I begin to see—" he muttered.

"Yes. Easy, ain't it? I've told you several times to-day; I've repeated over and over; that last night Bender not only had that notebook in his breast pocket, *but he had something else.* Not till this afternoon did it dawn on me. What would go into a breast pocket; what is flat, and in shape like a large notebook; what was behind that notebook in his pocket, and concealed by it? Speak up, somebody! If you looked at the bulge in the feller's breast pocket, what would you naturally think it was?"

Tairlaine's memory flashed back.

"I know what I thought it was," he answered, "the first time I saw Bender. I thought it was a pocket-flask."

"Uh-huh. Better if you'd spoken up. But see how clear, how simple and heartbreakin'ly easy the whole business is now. I steered myself wrong from the first; I insisted to myself and everybody else that the curare could never have been swallowed, because it wouldn't have hurt Bender. And I was quite right.

Under ordinary circumstances it wouldn't have hurt him. But what I didn't realize, and what nobody else looked for, was a small puncture in the gum, toward the wisdom teeth, probably, where the gum is so apt to get infected—a puncture made the afternoon of his death. Blood-stream! Of course it poured right into the blood-stream, and killed him quicker than any injection. We look all over his body, and find absolutely no wound by which you could shove in the poison; but how are we ever to spot a little thing like a lanced gum? What post-mortem man would ever spot a little thing like that, even if he noticed a slight inflammation of the gum? Once the poison's loose in the blood, you can't spot where it came from.

"But, burn me, *I* should have spotted it! Don't you remember, Masters," growled H.M., struggling to relight his pipe, "how we agreed in my office to-day that the poison must have been introduced through the little cut in the throat he got from shavin'? We said it must be that, because it went straight for the vocal muscles and paralyzed speech immediately. See it? Of course it did—because it went in through the gum. But I went gropin' and stargazin' after some unholy clever device, and never thought about the simplest device of all: a man who takes a flask out of his pocket and drinks, not knowin' the brandy in the flask is loaded with curare.

"Look at it there on the table! Harmless-lookin', ain't it? I could take a swig of that brandy right now, and it wouldn't hurt me. But, because there was cyanide in one bottle and cherry brandy in the flask, fool's cleverness instantly connects the two. There's no cyanide in that flask. But there's curare. Bender sat here at that table, and Guy Brixham looked at him through the window. What Guy saw, as somebody remarked, must have been as obvious as a blow on the jaw

. . . it was a man drinkin'. Guy knew what it might mean when he saw Bender collapse and run about blindly till he fell. Guy overheard the talk when *somebody* gave Bender that flask on the evening of the murder. And what happens to all the pretty alibis now? Of course, a crowd of people could be sitting outside the door of this room, chattin' away as merrily as you please, with a shining alibi for the world. Bender carried the death-trap on him. And, when the injection of cocaine or novocaine the dentist gave him had worn off, and the pain began to come on, sooner or later Bender would drink. He would drink because *somebody* had told him there was a deadener and antidote for that pain in the brandy; that's what *I* think. But we're goin' to know very soon. And *somebody* told the truth. There was a liquid in that brandy that deadened pain forever."

Sir George stared at him, his face a mottled pallor.

"But how the devil," he cried, "could this somebody be sure Bender wouldn't take a nip of the flask before he came into this room? And how was the flask stolen afterwards; yes, and the notebook?"

"Miss Isabel Brixham can tell you," said H.M., very quietly.

In the terrible silence the singing of the gaslights was loud. A board creaked under Masters' foot as Masters got up again.

"Then the old lady—" he said; "the old lady, after all? . . ."

H.M. lumbered to his feet.

"We're all goin' upstairs to see what she will say," he replied. "Yes, *all* of us. Don't back out. Don't even back away. Can't you rest easy now? Here's a hollow shell of a room, no more deadly than any set of furniture or old wall-paper; endowed with a curse by your imaginations, and full of bogeys that never existed. The curse is ripped out of it. It's harmless; it's even a bit forlorn, burn me, when you've taken away its only claim to interest. Aren't you glad of that?"

Judith Brixham had moved away, biting the back of her hand. She was pale, but yet there were sharp spots of color in her cheek. Ravelle sat blankly staring at the table, and Carstairs' face was as wooden as H.M.'s. Masters shepherded them out somehow, and they did not protest. Tairlaine had a feeling that the real terror was yet to come; that the memories would not let go their hold on a damned house, but would cling to brains and make one last effort to poison them now. Yet the lights were calm, the ancient wood of the outer hall had no menace. They were up a big carpeted staircase: *the* staircase . . . And then in the upper hall they heard a voice speaking.

It was Dr. Pelham's voice. It went on smoothly, weirdly, and it seemed all the more uncanny because they could distinguish no words despite its precise utterance.

H.M. fiercely gestured them to silence. He moved towards the front of a spacious hallway, where electric candles burned dimly against chill white walls, and the carpet was a deep scarlet. Through that dimness the smooth, eerie voice rose and fell. A word or two became distinguishable, and Tairlaine went cold. Judith was on one side of him, Ravelle on the other. Judith nearly screamed out just before Masters, losing his head, seized her and clapped a hand over her mouth. Before Tairlaine could protest they stood at the door of Isabel Brixham's sitting-room, and they stared. . . .

He never forgot that scene. She was sitting with her back to the door, before a low fire. She sat in a large upholstered chair of some patterned material, and her crinkled silver hair showed over the back of it. Above her on the mantelpiece was the clock whose hands jumped at a minute a time. The room was in darkness but for the glow of the fire, and a shaded lamp on a table some feet away. Then, facing Isabel in the shadows by the fireplace, they saw Dr. Pelham. They could see only a gleam in his eyes as he leaned forward in the chair.

The hands of the clock jumped, with a sudden motion like someone's spring. Pelham leaned a little further forward, his smooth face intent.

"I am anxious to spare you pain, Miss Brixham," he said, "so I ask only for brief replies. You told the police this afternoon, did you not, that last night you had seen your nephew Alan go downstairs with a hypodermic in his hand?"

"I did."

There was a strange, dull, mechanical quality about the voice. The head did not move.

"Was that the truth, Miss Brixham?"

"Only in a sense. I had to tell it."

"Had to tell it? Then you did not really see your nephew go downstairs as you said?"

"No."

"Or find those articles in the bottom drawer of his bureau, as you described them?"

"No."

The clock-hand jumped, and so did something at Tairlaine's side. He heard hard breathing. And he realized now that Pelham, as a part of his profession, had induced hypnosis.

"I will tell you what happened, then, Miss Brixham, and you shall tell me if I am correct. In a sense you were forced to say those things. You were given the story, with full details, exactly as you were to repeat it. You were told to say this to the police officers at exactly five o'clock this afternoon. You could not help yourself. *Who told you to do this?* Will you tell me?"

"Of course. It was——"

The crush at the door smashed through and something leaped in the shadows across the dim light of the lamp. A sharp slap of hands cracked near Isabel's face. She screamed, and her twisted face rose over the chair-back.

"In you go, Masters!" roared H.M. *"Over there!"*

Something was running about the room, blindly. For a flash Tairlaine caught sight of the face of one of the plainclothes men, flicking in and out of shadow, and the gleam of handcuffs. Propelled from behind, Tairlaine stumbled on a hassock, fell against the chair, and was borne forward in the crush. Somebody had thrown open a side door, and he followed Masters through into a front room where streetlamps through the windows made a blurred glow in the rain. A shadowy heap reeled across it, rattled against a dressing-table, and came down with a crash.

"Got him!" panted a voice out of the dark, sharp on the click of a handcuff lock. "Lights, sir! Get those lights on——"

Nearest the switch, Tairlaine fumbled automatically for it. He blinked against the glare, and saw first of all a room full of staring faces. Then he saw the silver toilet-service of a dressing-table spilled across the floor, thirty pieces from an elaborate service. Masters and the officer were helping up a figure that had a dignity of its own, and was brushing its trousers despite the manacles on its wrists.

"We'll take care of him, sir," Masters said smoothly to H.M. "You said he was a killer."

And, leaving off slapping the dust from himself, Dr. Eugene Arnold straightened up with an expression of indifference on his calm, pale, handsome face.

CHAPTER TWENTY

H.M. Sits and Thinks

London had blossomed into something like a spring night, although that is the way of March. The windows of H.M.'s long attic room in Brook Street were open. H.M., hunched up in one corner of a tattered sofa, his collar off and a cup of bad coffee smoking at his elbow, drew at a dead pipe. Masters sat near him with a glass of beer. And, across the table from him, Tairlaine glowered at a board full of small cardboard pieces bearing numbers and the names of warships. A clock perched on a topheavy pile of books said that it was half-past three in the morning.

"'Attack,'" grunted Tairlaine, moving out a submarine. "Look here, you don't mean to say the fellow's confessed?"

H.M. called on Omnipotence. "That's got me," he admitted sourly, exhibiting a light cruiser and tossing it off the board. "What d'ye mean, confessed? Who the devil's this? What are you talkin' about?"

Masters sat back wearily.

"Why pretend you don't know?" he demanded. "The doctor and I have been sitting here all evening, listening to you grouse (if you'll excuse my saying so, sir), just so you would open up about Arnold. There are a lot of things I've got to have for my full report." He turned to Tairlaine and spoke grimly. "He's confessed, sir, in the only way he ever would—because he thought he was going to die. Otherwise he'd have fought us through the courts; and, I don't mind admitting, probably beaten us in spite of Sir Henry. Actually, we had less evidence against him than the evidence he planted against Lord Mantling . . . But he got hold of a bit of jagged tin, and slashed his wrists; he never had much nerve in a pinch, except when it was the nerve to kill. He thought he was dying. He called in the chaplain and the governor, at Holloway, and announced as cool and business-like and smug as you please, that he thought he'd better make a statement. They didn't tell him he wasn't going to die. He'll hang now for a certainty. And I can't say, between ourselves, that it's ever likely to weigh very heavily on my conscience. . . . The point is, Sir Henry, *how*——"

H.M. pushed the board to one side.

"I'll give you ten minutes," he said, with a querulous air, "and talk about it. But I don't *want* to talk about it. No, Masters, that ain't affectation; I really don't *want* to talk about it. This case is far from bein' one of my successes. Not only did I mess up that business about the gum, but in such a clumsy trick as Arnold played afterwards I should have spotted him straightaway. To my crushin' shame, I didn't. You'll have realized, won't you, that there was one fact—one single, concrete, absolute point—indicating beyond all question that *Arnold was the only person who could have committed the murders?* Uh-huh. Daresay you have. But, to give you a chance to think it over, I'll give you an analysis from the beginning."

He blinked round as a muffled and irritable calling began to blunder through the house below, and footsteps stumbled on the dark attic stairs. Sir George Anstruther poked his head in.

"Here I am," he grunted. "You said not to come until late. But what's the game? Don't you keep anybody in the house? I had to find the way up here myself—"

"So," said Masters with malicious enjoyment, "you don't really want to talk about it, Sir Henry? You didn't arrange this little party, and wait until you'd given up Sir George's presence before you started?"

This was a tactical error. They presently contrived to soothe down H.M., who howled about ingratitude and shook his fist under Masters' nose; but calmness was restored after some effort, and H.M.'s pipe relighted.

"All right," he said darkly. "I'm goin' on now, because it's my duty, but don't think I enjoy it. Hum, ha. Harrumph. Well, then.

"Eugene Arnold, my lads, is mad. I don't mean mad in any legal sense, or even according to his own tinpot rules. He can't be certified for it; he can't even, under the present social order, be called eccentric. When his kind of brain keeps within the law, we very often call it admirable and exalt it first to Rolls-Royces and presently to statuary. His kind of ailment is only a copy-book maxim gone diseased and decayed like his brain. In short, lads, he had General's Disease without any army to command, and Financier's Disease without any industries to manage.

"I'd call it the disease of One Idea. All his life had to be regulated like a chart. Things to him were either common-sense or not common-sense. If they were not, they jarred and had to be thrown out. He decided what he wanted, and whatever it was *he meant to get it.* He was for facing facts, and for plumping out with the speakin' of facts—provided, of course, that they were not about himself. No prophet of common-sense and realism ever is very fond of such facts. Certain things he wanted, for a good reason. Uh-huh. If he violated bourgeois moralities or bourgeois conventions in attainin' the ends, what difference so long as the Superman followed his code and was shrewd enough to gull the poor mugs who were dancin' attendance? He'd got accustomed to tellin' so much truth about everybody else that he hadn't any left in himself; and the poor fool hadn't realized that if all mankind shares a folly or an illusion, and likes to share it even knowin' what it is, then the illusion is much more valuable and fine a kind of thing than the ass who wants to upset it."

"And yet," Tairlaine said thoughtfully, "he stood up for Judith when she was accused of stealing those darts. . . ."

H.M. was dour. "Uh-huh. If I hadn't been already certain that he was guilty, that by itself would have given me a pretty strong hint. He stepped out of character so flatly and jarrin'ly, and the actin' was so lousy, that I nearly told him flat to draw it mild. Y' see——"

"Steady, sir. Take it from the beginning," suggested Masters. "When did you first suspect him?"

"The first time I talked to him. Not, I'm admittin', a definite suspicion, because I couldn't think how the trick had been managed and everybody had an alibi. Simply because I lost control for a while of my sittin' and thinkin' apparatus, I didn't attach the weight to it that I did later. But yet in the things he told us—in the very fact of Bender's presence in the house—I sniffed an incongruity, an improbability, so strong that I can only repeat I don't want to talk about it.

"He had put Bender in that house. He was Bender's chief,

Bender's overlord; somebody there was suspected of bein' mad; and Bender had been there quite a little time—certainly enough to get a good line on the mad one. Yet Arnold said he had no idea of where Bender's suspicions lay. I might by a long jump o' credulity believe Arnold had never made any inquiries of Bender (especially when it concerned the girl Arnold was engaged to). But I could not believe Arnold had no inkling of the little game in the Widow's Room they were goin' to play that night. Dammit, wouldn't Arnold be the first man Bender would consult, when the plan of opening that room had been under discussion for a week? A whole cloud of improbabilities begins to gather round. *Why* was Bender so dead set on bein' the man who sat in that room; so dead set that he took a long risk of hocusing the cards? 'Conscientiousness' wouldn't do it. If they all believed there was a trick mechanism in that room, how would it help Bender in nailin' his lunatic if he exposed himself to it? It had a queer look and a queerer smell, and behind all that I thought I could see somebody's hand workin'. You know, it's remarkable just how little Arnold did know!—or profess to know! After all the time he'd spent in that house, after all the times he'd been with that crowd, he still hadn't a good idea whose brain was cracked. It didn't seem reasonable to believe that Bender had discovered in a little over a week what Arnold, his brilliant superior, hadn't spotted in over a year. You saw how keen he was on preservin' social justice? I can see him with his chin tilted up, and that common-sense-modern Utopia stare in his eyes, sayin' with calm deliberation, 'If there is a madman in this house, that person must be placed under proper restraint.'

"As I say, I was sittin' and thinkin'; and I said to myself, 'Look here, is it possible Arnold don't *want* the loony discovered?' Of course it was, if he'd been a human being and wanted to hush the thing up. But he put Bender in that house. Why? Why?

"But I thought to myself, 'Without sayin' a word against Arnold, let's see how it would affect him if either Guy or Alan were certified as mad. Let's see what changes it would make in the life and future of Dr. Eugene.' Well, now, if Guy were pronounced mad, it would be a sad event; younger son clapped into an asylum, poor feller without any patrimony. In that case, Dr. Eugene's future and prospects would be exactly where they had been. . . . I mean, with a vigorous, probably long-lived elder brother *standin' between Judith Brixham and the fourth or fifth greatest fortune in England.*"

Sir George accepted the cup of coffee Masters handed him.

"Then you mean," he said, "that the whole point of the scheme was to have Guy—the real touched-one—dead, and his elder brother Alan certified as insane for having killed him? Alan was to be put away so that Arnold's *fiancée* could inherit the money Arnold wanted?"

"No. No," said H.M. somberly, "that's exactly what I don't mean. That's the part that was common-sense, that's the part that was so devilish, and should have given you a clew as to where to look. Alan was to be certified as *sane.* All things depended on provin' Alan was sane when he killed Guy. . . . Know anything about the lunacy laws?"

Sir George looked at Masters, who shook his head.

"I'd always had a bit of an idea, sir," the chief inspector answered doubtfully, "that a madman was—well, in a sense regarded as dead, and his property turned over to the next of kin; to be managed by the next of kin, anyhow."

"No, my boy. That's exactly what it ain't. That's what led to all the trouble in the bad old days, before the law was made. The best way to tie up a man's money so that *nobody* can ill-manage it, or manage it at all, is to have him certified. His property is then controlled by the Commissioners in Lunacy; sort o' Chancery Commission tyin' up the bulk of it so that no funny games can be worked by lovin' relatives. . . . *See it now?* If the purpose of these murders had merely been to get somebody put in an asylum so that Judith could inherit, *then Alan would have been killed and the blame put on Guy, the really cracked one.* But suppose that had been done? Alan is dead; the crowd believes Guy is guilty, and, just as Guy inherits the Mantling fortune, he's put away by responsible doctors and the fortune goes to a standstill until he recovers or dies. In other words, it wouldn't do to have a real madman as the murderer."

"But where did Bender come in, then? Why kill him?"

"Steady!" growled H.M. "Easy now! You're a rotten audience. You're makin' the old man get far ahead of himself. Lemme go back to my first suspicions of Arnold and work 'em out in the proper order. Them suspicions—as I admit—stayed static for a little while, until Guy was killed.

"But I found myself playin' with the theory of Arnold's guilt, and I asked myself, just to test it: 'If he's guilty, where did he get the curare to work with in Bender's case? The only curare we've heard of,' I said to myself, 'was on the darts—and yet all the darts are accounted for and that poison wasn't used.' And there," roared H.M., pointing his pipe malevolently, "is where I was stumped for a minute simply because I didn't know what you knew. I found it out later. I found out what Alan told you the night of the party, just before I'd arrived. Think, now! Isabel was talkin' about poisoned weapons—especially arrows Alan and Carstairs had brought back from South America. And what did Alan say? Eh?"

The vivid memory returned; he could even recall the inflection.

"Yes," Tairlaine replied. "He said, 'Those things aren't poisoned. Arnold tested the whole batch.' "

"Uh-huh. He tested 'em," agreed H.M., sitting back drowsily again, "in just the same way old Ravelle senior tested the furniture of the Widow's Room all that time ago: by removing the poison, and keeping it."

"Keeping it because? . . ."

"Because the plan was beginning to take shape long ago, long before Bender was ever put in the house or entered into the picture as a dummy that was to begin the plot. . . . So, in my calculations, I found that Arnold *could* have the curare; in fact, he was the only one who could have it. But I couldn't fix anything on him, I couldn't have absolute hangin' proof. Next there came along a realization of somethin' I mentioned to you a while ago. It was before we even heard of Guy's murder that I realized why Arnold must be guilty—even when I didn't know how he'd managed the murder of Bender. And it came to me when I thought of the little roll of parchment lyin' on Bender's chest.

"Now, unquestionably the room was locked and impregnable; I don't need to go over all that. Gents, the truth *had* to be that the murder was managed in death-trap form by somebody who wasn't in the room at all. Yet, grantin' that, I still had to beat my brain with the apparently staggerin' fact of the missing notebook. If nobody was in the room, how did the notebook disappear? When the simple truth came to me, I got such a shock that my impulse to kick myself, in the minds of the New Psychologists, would've amounted to a masochistic fixation. Lord love-a-duck, was I an ass?" cried H.M. "There was

Bender lyin' on his back, and the little parchment-roll on his chest. The only way it could have got there was— Well? Carry your minds back to the time the discovery of the murder was made. Got it fixed in your minds? Right. Who was the first person to go to the body and bend over it?"

"Arnold, naturally," said Tairlaine. But he spoke after a long silence, and Masters nodded as he produced a notebook.

"Arnold, naturally," growled H.M. "And what did he do first?"

"He ordered us all to stand back. And we all did," said Sir George, "including yourself."

"And when he bent over the body," H.M. went on, opening his eyes, "could you see him? Could you follow his movements, or, in fact, see anything except his head? You couldn't. And why? Because he was behind that enormous bed that hid everything of Bender except his head, and likewise the brilliant sinner who fooled us all in front of our eyes! If the bed had been smaller—but it wasn't. And why was that little roll of parchment where we found it? Because it was in Bender's inside pocket, where the notebook was. Arnold had only to stick his hand into the pocket, pull out *the notebook and the damning flask,* and shove them into his own pocket. In doin' so, he pulled out the parchment with 'em, and it flopped on Bender's chest exactly where you'd have expected it to be! That's the only sane explanation of how the thing could have landed there; that it fell out of Bender's inner pocket. The trick was worked under our eyes; it was simple and inevitable; and yet it fooled us. You understand now why our friend Arnold was the only person in the whole lot who could possibly have been guilty?"

Masters nodded, tapping his notebook with satisfaction.

"Fine fellow, Dr. Arnold," he remarked. "Just as you say, sir. He gave that in his confession. *With* much pride and pleasure, the chaplain told me. Said our intelligences were . . . well, he made a lot of remarks. But he didn't know anything about the parchment-roll, he said. Claimed he'd never seen it before, didn't think it was important, and simply didn't take the risk of bagging that as well. Exactly what was it, by the way?"

Sir George grunted.

"The inscription? It was a charm against toothache. I gather that Guy must have been pulling Bender's leg with great gusto about the magical studies—didn't he admit that to us, Merrivale? Yes. Guy knew Bender was watching him; never thought Bender could get anything on him; and——"

"Easy now!" roared H.M. "Who's tellin' this? Besides, you're not right. Guy *was* afraid the loony-doctors might get somethin' on him, as you'll see in a minute; but not because of the magical studies. Uh-huh. He did pull Bender's leg about that. Here's the telegram from the expert, by the way; mind if I preserve this as a souvenir, Anstruther?" He fished a crumpled form out of his pocket. "It says, 'LOOK IN THE RED DRAGON AND FIND IT. IT IS LEO THE THIRD'S CHARM AGAINST TOOTHACHE.' And, burn me, to think I actually had the Red Dragon on my mind the night of the murder! Do you remember, when I come in there to the house, I was grousin' about a Latin crossword-puzzle somebody's invented at the Diogenes Club? And one of 'em was a ten-letter word meanin' a collection of magical prayers and charms given by Pope Leo III to Charlemagne in 800? 'Enchiridie'—that's the Italianized Latin of the medieval description we were havin' trouble with, and it means 'Red Dragon.' But I'm not goin' to tangle you up, as I mentioned, with abstruse clews that nobody in ten thousand could be expected to know about. I'm goin' to stick to real ones; to Guy's behavior about that very point; when I go on——"

"But if that's a charm against toothache," interrupted Tairlaine, "and Guy gave it to Bender, then Guy might very well have known about Bender's having an infected gum."

"He did, son," agreed H.M. "Oh, yes. And, when I'd picked Arnold as the murderer, I realized also that Arnold's bein' the murderer was the only thing that would explain Guy's conduct. Think, now! Go back before the murder. Let's assume Guy was spyin' on Bender in exactly the same way Bender was spyin' on Guy. He not only knows about Bender's being tormented with an infected gum, and finally bein' driven to havin' it lanced that very afternoon, but he was probably listenin' at the door of Bender's room when Arnold dropped in on Bender that evening—early. He'd watch Arnold pretty closely, because Arnold was Bender's chief; and he thought that between 'em they were trying to certify him.

"Take that part from the first. If I got it worked out right, Arnold had originally planned the whole blasted scheme rather different from the way it worked out. His cool, plain, straightforward object was to kill Guy in such a way that Alan—the sane man—should swing for it. And, lads, he took an amazin' course. Set out to kill a man and heave the blame on somebody else, and you're doin' the trickiest and most dangerous thing in the whole green field of crime. Because provin' somebody else's guilt beyond question is harder than provin' your own innocence. It's hard enough to fake an alibi for yourself; what you can't do is make absolutely certain somebody else, the man you want to hang, won't have an alibi or a set of clear proofs of his innocence. If he proves his alibi, and you can't prove your own, then you're done for. That double difficulty was what stumped Arnold's cautious mind at the beginning. That double difficulty was what prevented him from killin' Guy and trustin' to luck they'd pick the brother as guilty. Ever read them side-splittin' murder stories in which some innocent person, somebody the real murderer wants hanged, nearly is hanged because at the time of the killing that innocent feller was wanderin' the streets aimlessly for a couple of hours; or was lured away to wander by a fake 'phone call? Now, real life don't work like that. And Arnold, bein' a realist, knew it. He new that it's a very rare day when most innocent people can't produce a pretty good list of witnesses for where they were—especially a thunderin' well-known sportin' clubman like this Lord Mantling, whose personal appearance alone would single him out wherever he went. Under any set of circumstances, even at night, the thing would be too ticklish to gamble on. The only way out of his difficulties, thinks Arnold, is to catch the victim in a death-trap *that would work whether the goat had an alibi or not.*

"And blessed from heaven, a prayer taking form, came news that the room was to be opened. If somebody were to be poisoned in that room, under such circumstances that it seemed a modern murderer had re-set the old death-trap with very modern curare . . . well, that was opportunity. But how the devil could he ever catch *Guy* in a trap like that? He couldn't; Guy knew too much. In fact, how could he catch anybody, since he didn't know where the old trap was and wouldn't have a chance to sneak in and do the business himself? He was blocked—unless the victim, the person to be murdered, gave assistance without knowin' it.

"Do you see why Bender had to die? Bender had to die as a mere matter of camouflage. The police had to believe that, somewhere in that room even if they couldn't find it, was an apparatus that a modern murderer could use to get his victim even though he wasn't there! Once *that* was established, Alan could assemble all Scotland Yard to prove himself an alibi—but, if enough evidence were faked against him as having run the trap, he would still hang. Bender was to die of curare poisoning, and Guy after him. I don't suppose Arnold had any particular animus against Bender. Bender was only a gambit to open the game with; a play for safety, a necessary sacrifice. . . . Am I right, Masters?"

The chief inspector cleared his throat.

"According to this, sir," he answered, flicking over pages in his notebook, "Arnold altered his original plan—hurrum! as you indicated, of course. His first scheme was pretty good. He'd long ago pinched that hypodermic out of Mr. Guy Brixham's room, and he'd got it ready with a shot of curare. Know what he was going to do, sir? He was going to fix it with Mr. Bender to hocus those cards and get himself in the room; as he did. Then, just before he took Miss Judith Brixham out to dinner, he was going to go to Mr. Bender's room and tell his story. He was going to say he'd found Mr. Guy had pinched a lot of curare from Lord Mantling; that there was a secret way into that room, and Mr. Guy meant to have a shot at killing whoever kept the—hum—vigil in it that night. *But,* says our Dr. Arnold, they'll stop that right enough. And, producing his little hypodermic syringe, he intended to show Mr. Bender what he would claim was an *antidote* to curare. As soon as Mr. Bender went in there, let him give himself an injection and he'd be right as rain even if an attempt were made. But let him be sure not to give himself the injection before he goes into the room, or the antidote may wear off . . ."

"And there was curare in the syringe? But the blasted fool!" exploded Sir George. "Suppose Bender did get nervous, as anybody might, and gave himself the injection beforehand? Or, even if he held off from that, suppose he dropped the hypodermic on the floor when he died, and it was found? They'd put it down as suicide! Arnold couldn't be sure—if he was as cautious as you say—that he would be the first at the body; or that somebody wouldn't see the syringe before he stole it away!"

A placid smile crossed Masters' face. He was very bland.

"Sir Henry didn't say Dr. Arnold was a good criminal," he replied. "He only said he was a clever one. There's a world of difference, sir, as you'd understand if you were in my business. Dartmoor is full of the clever ones . . . But, anyhow, Dr. Arnold realized that. He would have backed out of the scheme—even if he hadn't been presented with a better one."

"The infected gum?"

H.M. waved Masters aside. "The infected gum. Right. Arnold heard the day before that Bender was going to have it lanced, and when he was going to have it lanced. Well, then? A dose of curare in a little brandy. Arnold had to prepare his excuse. 'I do not care to have my underlings inefficient,' says Arnold curtly. 'The lancing of an infected gum, and the pain that will come on during the course of the night'—got it, gents? From anybody else but Arnold, that would have sounded crazy and makin' too much of a small thing; but Bender knew Arnold, or thought he did. That was just the sort of trick Arnold would do. 'You had the gum lanced when? Good,' says he. 'The pain will come on later, when the cocaine has worn off. Take this flask. There is a mixture to ease you in it,'—eh, Masters?—'and it will do so if you swill it about the infected region. However, you will not drink any of this until you have gone into the room.

I don't care to have you seen swilling brandy out of a flask before the others'—Arnold's a teetotaler, as I think somebody mentioned—'and in any event the pain will not bother you until late in the evening.' Oh, it was a fool move; as fool a move as most of the things our self-possessed murderer did. But it worked. The only merit of the idea, d'ye see, is that after he'd taken a drink Bender would put the flask back in his pocket. And there it was, harmless-lookin' enough—a thing anybody might carry, and not like a hypo. As the doctor, and timin' himself to get back to the house in time (he was nearly late, you remember, because of that fog; but he and the gal started for home so as to reach it quite early if there'd been no delay); as the doctor, I repeat, he could bargain on bein' first at the body in any case. He could insist on havin' his go at the body and putting his hand naturally under the coat. Since you were lookin' for a *puncturing* mechanism and not a flask . . ."

Masters cleared his throat.

"He says he had a duplicate flask, sir, a harmless one. And he was going to substitute it when the body was taken to another room. But—he had the chance straightaway, to steal the old one under cover of the bed (which he couldn't have anticipated) and he simply took it then."

"But why steal the notebook?" asked Tairlaine.

H.M. snorted. "Because it incriminated *Guy,* that's why. And he couldn't have Guy under suspicion as the murderer. Let's go back to Guy; you'll understand his behavior now. Guy was listening when Arnold gave that loaded flask to Bender; there's no other way to explain it. . . ."

"Have we heard," put in Sir George, "that Arnold saw Bender that night? If we'd known Arnold had an interview with him——"

"You heard, didn't you, that he was expected to drop in on Bender from what Mantling told us?" asked H.M. "Mantling, when he walked in and made Bender jab his neck with a razor, had gone up there expressly to tell Bender not to mention the 'game' to Arnold if Bender saw him that night. Uh-huh. That was another of the things that looked fishy to me. Why should that even occur to Mantling, who didn't know Bender was Arnold's—haa—clerk, unless the two had been together comparin' notes a bit? Anyhow, Guy overheard that little talk. Of course he didn't know the flask had anything wrong with it. But he went down, after Bender had been installed, to watch him; both to make sure he didn't stumble on the jewels, and to make sure Bender didn't find any clew of *Guy's* being the one who had refurbished that room and killed that parrot for——"

"Guy was the one who killed . . . ?" demanded Tairlaine.

H.M. spread out his fingers and inspected them. "Well, Guy had his little sanities too, y'know. A parrot that squawked or a dog that barked in the night might betray a man whose fortune in jewels got itself found prematurely. Besides, Guy was especially worried just then. Hellish worried, gents. Because I think—what's the report on this, Masters?—that Bender had discovered the knife Guy used on the dog, and that's how Arnold got it."

Masters agreed. "That's what he was doing in Mr. Guy's room early that evening, sir, when Mr. Carstairs saw him. He'd spotted the knife in the pocket of that frayed dressing-gown, and he was taking it to Arnold. Dr. Arnold took charge of it, right enough."

"Not much use stressin' why Guy was so interested in Bender's movements in the room, then. But you *will* see why Guy pretended to help the murderer. Guy tumbled to the truth when he saw what happened to Bender just after Bender'd had a swig from that poisoned flask. There was Guy at the window—he saw it, and he knew. Maybe he called to Bender. Anyhow, Bender went down . . . out of Guy's sight. My God, what an opportunity! It must have made Guy dance with joy. The doctor who's trying to put *him* into an asylum has killed his assistant, and Guy has seen it! Blackmail? Gents, he knew they'd never put *him* into an asylum when he knew that! 'Call off your dogs,' he'll say to Arnold; 'don't bother me any more with your tests and suspicions, or——' "

"But wouldn't any accusation like that from Guy be dismissed as more lunacy?" asked Tairlaine.

"No, no, my boy; not if Guy could show the only means by which the murder was done, when the sane police were up a tree. They might think he was a bit wabbly in the head, but he'd have done for Arnold in the sense that suspicion would pile on him in one awful heap. It didn't matter, d'ye see. Arnold had good reason to kill Guy before. Now he had a real reason for doin' it *immediately*. . . . And Guy, at the window, imitated Bender's voice for the very reason Masters suggested before, when he had Guy as the murderer. 'He didn't know how long it would take Bender to die,' that's what Masters said when he thought Guy himself had used the curare; but how much less knowledge would he have *when he didn't even know what poison it was?* Let Bender die, damn him! Let the snooper writhe his tongue out and twist with pain till he gave up; then the Master Snooper was just where Guy wanted him, and Guy was takin' no chances of Bender's being found when there was a chance to rescue him. Didn't you notice Arnold's face when he discovered a dead man had been makin' answers for an hour?

"So we go on to the next crime, and to certain preparations

Arnold made for his last coup. *They* blew the gaff, they were the worst clumsiness, and then was when I spotted the motive for certain. Arnold's scheme was to get Guy alone in that room and use the old hypodermic needle on him. He didn't need to be careful now; we had fixed on a hidden mechanism in that room. But first Arnold had certain preparations to make . . ."

"Well?"

"He had to prepare Isabel for what she was to say the next day. Most of those fellers use hypnosis on a neurotic patient, and he had to give the post-hypnotic suggestions. He couldn't have made her do it, of course, if she hadn't believed in her heart that Mantling was really guilty. I had to test that. You know the old trick, that any good hypnotist can work: 'At exactly ten minutes past three to-morrow, you will ring up a certain person and say as follows, etc.: and also you will have forgotten that this was ever suggested to you.' Arnold was alone with her most of the evening *after* Bender's murder. Now, there are certain things a hypnotic influence can do, and certain things it definitely can't. Under the influence, you can make a person stab somebody with a rubber dagger, because the subconscious mind knows it's only rubber. But you can't make anybody strike with a real dagger. You can make a person, with a post-hypnotic suggestion, go to some friend the day afterwards and say, 'I've just come back from a long trip to Russia, and I've spent some time in prison there'—because the person's inner self might credit that sort of thing as happening to him, as quite possible, and in no way inconsistent with his own character. But you can't make a person say, 'I am willing to swear John Anderson stabbed my brother to death'—unless in his own soul he really believes John Anderson did.

"Isabel believed it. But that cry of hers, 'I must tell you, I can't rest until I do'; that long rigmarole she gave which sounded not like her, but exactly as though it came out of a psychiatrist's bag of tricks; the whole fanciful, too-detailed account with its 'my experiences as a child' and the rest of it; showed that she was the voice, but Arnold was the gramophone needle . . . It ain't necessary to say, is it, that the blood-stained knife, the notebook with the pages torn out, the flask, and the stage-setting bottle of cyanide, were all planted by Arnold in Mantling's room *before* the murder of Guy, and while we were all downstairs? He ordered Isabel to tell something *before it happened*. If later she denies that she said it, we'll take that as only natural; but there were a number of witnesses to prove that she did say it."

"But what about the light in Guy's room, which really did appear?"

"Isabel's one real action. She did get up and look in Guy's room in the middle of the night, without knowing why!—except that there was some sort of horrible, lurkin' memory there; something she'd heard somewhere but couldn't quite place; something that tore her apart, but remained elusive. You'll ask—as I asked you this afternoon—why she spoke of Mantling (who, of course, was never out of his room) as going downstairs with a hypodermic, when Guy was killed with a hammer. And the answer to that is the answer I found for the murderer's actions: it was hypnotic suggestion, given to Isabel by Arnold when Arnold intended to use a hypodermic. But, when he gets to the point, the poor fool plotter saw . . ."

"Saw?"

"That, if he used a hypodermic, we were goin' to think what Masters himself suggested this afternoon: Guy was guilty, and either his death-trap had misfired or he committed suicide. If anything went wrong and Isabel didn't give her evidence, Arnold was finished. Still—he had to risk it. He would have gone through with it, but . . ."

Masters nodded. "Right you are, sir. He struck too hard to stun Mr. Guy with that hammer, and killed him. Then Mr. Guy's jaws froze together, and he couldn't go on——"

"Jaws froze together?" interposed Tairlaine. "What has that to do with the hypodermic?"

"Well, sir, the two crimes; Bender's death and this death—they had to be alike, didn't they? Both men had to die of curare. But they hadn't found a mark on Mr. Bender, so they weren't likely to spot an injection in the other one's mouth. He was going to give that curare through the mouth also; with an injection under the gum. You see, Sir Henry's pointed out that we were to assume some sort of death-trap in that room. Well, when Arnold planned the evidence for Lord Mantling to be apparently seen going downstairs with a hypodermic, we weren't expected to think he was only going to inject it into Mr. Guy's arm or anything of that sort. We were to think he was merely going to *load his death-trap again.* Maybe we should never find out exactly how this mythical (hum!) trap worked, but we had Lord Mantling in as nasty a place as Arnold could devise for one who admittedly didn't administer the dose with his own hand. It was the best Dr. Arnold could do. And, coupled with the other evidence, he thought it'd be enough . . . But, d'ye see, he couldn't pry Mr. Guy's jaws open."

"And so," said Sir George suddenly, "that was why he smashed the jaw with a blow of the hammer, to open it? And he couldn't; so he finished off with a few more smashes . . . or was interrupted by Carstairs coming in . . . Wait, though! How did Arnold get into the house? Carstairs was outside, watching the door all the time."

"He wasn't watchin' the window to the Widow's Room," said H.M. wearily. "Forgotten that it worked very easily when Masters pried it open and got it into good order? Forgotten that it's a ground floor window, that you can reach by walkin' into the cul-de-sac from another street. Oh, Arnold went home right enough. Carstairs' brilliant idea of tracking him must have been as obvious to Arnold as it would have been to any ordinary-witted man. He went home—but he returned. He'd arranged to meet Guy down there. Guy had threatened to split, and was in gay feather. And Guy thought he could take care of himself. He couldn't. But then," said H.M., draining his coffee-cup, "neither could Arnold, y'see."

There was a long silence in the smoke-misted room. Sir George got up and stumped about. Masters, a heavy scowl on his face, seemed uneasy. And at length the little baronet turned.

"There's just one thing," he said, "I don't understand. With all Arnold's care, I don't see why he would risk a long shot and a dangerous trick when his intended bride might have changed her mind at any moment; we saw how she felt about Carstairs. Suppose she did change her mind, and his work would go for nothing? What does Judith think of this, anyway?"

Tairlaine found himself staring again at the little blue-painted cardboard battleships. In a dull way he reflected that if he moved a mine-layer backed by a heavy dreadnought it might blow up H.M.'s harbor defenses. His head ached, and his eyes felt heavy. He remembered an interview not long ago. But he spoke.

"Miss Brixham," he answered, "will stand by her husband."

"Her husband?" barked Sir George. Then he coughed, and they were all silent.

"She and Arnold were secretly married," Tairlaine went on.

"He suggested it. I dare say he can be romantic when he chooses. Personally, I can't. Not yet. She should stick with him; she'd be rather poor stuff if she didn't."

"And afterwards? She'll be a widow, you know."

Tairlaine's hand hesitated over the board. "My whole harbor's in danger," he pointed out. "Yes. That is why the rest of us must be bachelors . . . Your move, H.M. Mine has passed."

THE END

DISCUSSION QUESTIONS

- Were you able to predict any part of the solution to the case?
- After learning the solution, were there any clues you realized you had missed?
- Did any aspects of the plot date the story? If so, which ones?
- Would the story be different if it were set in the present day? If so, how?
- Did the social context of the time play a role in the narrative? If so, how?
- If you were one of the main characters, would you have acted differently at any point in the story?
- Did this novel remind you of any contemporary authors today?
- Did this novel remind you of other titles in the American Mystery Classics series?
- What kind of detective is Sir Henry Merrivale?
- If you've read others of Carr's works, how did this book compare?

MORE

JOHN DICKSON CARR

AVAILABLE FROM

AMERICAN MYSTERY CLASSICS

THE CROOKED HINGE
Introduced by Charles Todd

THE MAD HATTER MYSTERY
Introduced by Otto Penzler

THE PLAGUE COURT MURDERS
Introduced by Michael Dirda

THE EIGHT OF SWORDS
Introduced by Douglas G. Greene

OTTO PENZLER PRESENTS

AMERICAN MYSTERY CLASSICS

All Titles Introduced by Otto Penzler
Unless Otherwise Noted

Charlotte Armstrong, *The Chocolate Cobweb*
Introduced by A. J. Finn
Charlotte Armstrong, *The Unsuspected*

Anthony Boucher, *The Case of the Baker Street Irregulars*
Anthony Boucher, *Rocket to the Morgue*
Introduced by F. Paul Wilson

Fredric Brown, *The Fabulous Clipjoint*
Introduced by Lawrence Block

John Dickson Carr, *The Crooked Hinge*
Introduced by Charles Todd
John Dickson Carr, *The Mad Hatter Mystery*
John Dickson Carr, *The Plague Court Murders*
Introduced by Michael Dirda

Todd Downing, *Vultures in the Sky*
Introduced by James Sallis

Mignon G. Eberhart, *Murder by an Aristocrat*
Introduced by Nancy Pickard

Erle Stanley Gardner, *The Case of the Baited Hook*
Erle Stanley Gardner, *The Case of the Careless Kitten*
Erle Stanley Gardner, *The Case of the Borrowed Brunette*

Frances Noyes Hart, *The Bellamy Trial*
Introduced by Hank Phillippi Ryan

H.F. Heard, *A Taste for Honey*

Dolores Hitchens, *The Cat Saw Murder*
Introduced by Joyce Carol Oates

Dorothy B. Hughes, *Dread Journey*
Introduced by Sarah Weinman
Dorothy B. Hughes, *Ride the Pink Horse*
Introduced by Sara Paretsky
Dorothy B. Hughes, *The So Blue Marble*

W. Bolingbroke Johnson, *The Widening Stain*
Introduced by Nicholas A. Basbanes

Baynard Kendrick, *The Odor of Violets*

Frances and Richard Lockridge, *Death on the Aisle*

John P. Marquand, *Your Turn, Mr. Moto*
Introduced by Lawrence Block

Stuart Palmer, *The Puzzle of the Happy Hooligan*

Otto Penzler, ed., *Golden Age Detective Stories*
Otto Penzler, ed., *Golden Age Locked Room Mysteries*

Ellery Queen, *The American Gun Mystery*
Ellery Queen, *The Chinese Orange Mystery*
Ellery Queen, *The Dutch Shoe Mystery*
Ellery Queen, *The Egyptian Cross Mystery*
Ellery Queen, *The Siamese Twin Mystery*

Patrick Quentin, *A Puzzle for Fools*

Clayton Rawson, *Death from a Top Hat*

Craig Rice, *Eight Faces at Three*
Introduced by Lisa Lutz
Craig Rice, *Home Sweet Homicide*

Mary Roberts Rinehart, *The Album*
Mary Roberts Rinehart, *The Haunted Lady*
Mary Roberts Rinehart, *Miss Pinkerton*
Introduced by Carolyn Hart
Mary Roberts Rinehart, *The Red Lamp*
Mary Roberts Rinehart, *The Wall*

Joel Townsley Rogers, *The Red Right Hand*
Introduced by Joe R. Lansdale

Vincent Starrett, *The Great Hotel Murder*
Introduced by Lyndsay Faye

Cornell Woolrich, *The Bride Wore Black*
Introduced by Eddie Muller
Cornell Woolrich, *Waltz into Darkness*
Introduced by Wallace Stroby